THE BROKEN COMMANDMENT

THE BROKEN COMMANDMENT

VINCENT
McDONNELL

REINHARDT BOOKS
IN ASSOCIATION WITH
VIKING

REINHARDT BOOKS
in association with Viking

Distributed by the Penguin Group
27 Wrights Lane, London W8 5TZ, England
Viking Penguin Inc., 40 West 23rd Street, New York, New York 10010, USA
Penguin Books Australia Ltd, Ringwood, Victoria, Australia
Penguin Books Canada Ltd, 2801 John Street, Markham, Ontario, Canada L3R 1B4
Penguin Books (NZ) Ltd, 182–190 Wairau Road, Auckland 10, New Zealand

Penguin Books Ltd, Registered Offices: Harmondsworth, Middlesex, England

First published 1988

ISBN 1871-06107-5

Made and printed in Great Britain by
Richard Clay Ltd, Bungay, Suffolk
Filmset in Linotron Sabon by
Rowland Phototypesetting Ltd, Bury St Edmunds, Suffolk

A CIP CATALOGUE record
for this book is available from the British Library

Library of Congress Catalog Card No.: 88–61521

For
Joan, with love

‘You shall not kill’

The Jerusalem Bible

Deuteronomy 5:17

I

I have been segregated from the other prisoners for my own protection. Even the rapists and child molesters would spit on me – they who are outcasts themselves. My only human contact is with the warders and the prison chaplain. He still visits me, despite the fact that I have asked him not to. He sits and talks and I listen, and he goes away the better for it.

He has the idea of saving my soul – of persuading me to ask God for forgiveness. 'There is nothing for God to forgive,' I told him, but he like the jury that convicted me was blind, and saw nothing but horror in what I'd done. I knew then that no one would understand but God and there is no need to explain to Him.

My daughters have not been to visit me. The chaplain offered to see them and to persuade them to come, but I said no. After all, this is no place for children.

'You can't live for ever in the past,' he said to me. 'You have to look to the future, Peter.'

But the past is all I have – that series of events that I sometimes see with such clarity that it frightens me. But the persons who peopled them I have replaced with puppets; it is not the real person who cries or bleeds and that is my insurance against insanity. The only one who is not a puppet is myself and I suffer for all of them.

'You must learn to love,' the chaplain said, but I will not love again; more important still, I will not hate either. At my trial and in the papers they spoke of little else but my hatred. Yet it was not hatred that brought me to that courtroom, or brought me here. Had I hated I would be a free man, whatever freedom might mean to one who had lost everything.

But on that Saturday evening in June that seems so long ago now, that evening when I asked my wife Margaret for a divorce, the world was still mine, and I had no thought then that anyone could take it from me. Even Margaret's answer didn't upset me, because I'd known what it would be.

'I'll never give you a divorce,' she said; 'marriage is till death us do part. And what about the children? Don't they matter?' She had a way of using our two daughters as levers, and now when it suited her they were mine. Like our son had been mine when he was dead, but hers while he lived.

'You'll never marry *that* woman,' she said; 'and if you live with her God will punish you both for your adultery.' She had the Catholic's certainty that she alone knew God's intentions, and that she could get Him to do her bidding. She was correct about the punishment but neither of us could have ever guessed the extent of it; or known that it would destroy us and touch everyone we knew.

Our talk could resolve nothing, for what each of us wanted was unacceptable to the other. And, aware of this, we tried to hurt like malicious children. I don't think that Margaret hated me, but I hated her. And potent with the memory of our dead son my hatred hung in the air like the smell of his rotting flesh might; and it probed and hurt like the torturer.

Margaret eventually broke and fled from the house and I listened to the stutter of her Fiat as she drove away. She would go to Cricklewood, I knew, to her parents. 'Let her,' I thought, 'let Sarah and Martin have her.' Because I had no need of her any more.

I left then myself to go to Barbara, she who would take away the hatred. She who had saved me from myself when my son died, and who now wanted to marry me. Who one day would give me another family.

But Margaret was never to get to Cricklewood. She crossed the Finchley Road against a red traffic light and her Fiat 500 was crushed against the central reservation by a speeding van. The policeman who gave me the details when I returned home from Barbara's in the early hours of the morning also told me that it had taken firemen nearly two hours to cut her from the wreck.

When I got to the hospital the surgeons had already amputated her left leg and were fighting a desperate battle to save her right leg and indeed her life. 'Touch and go, Mr Ferson,' they told me. 'We're doing everything we can.'

I wondered if they could see that I didn't care, but I supposed that they would put my coldness down to shock; and I had their pity which I didn't deserve. For while they talked of life I could only think of death and the freedom it would bring. They took me along to a small room where I could wait, and a nurse brought me a cup of tea.

I sat in one of the two battered armchairs and placed my tea on the small wooden table. There was a glass ash-tray on the table containing the half-smoked cigarettes of whoever had waited before me. They had waited for someone to live or to die, here in this tiny room with a cheap print of Van Gogh's *Sunflowers* on the wall. For a moment I felt that I was defiling whatever genuine grief had been experienced within the blue walls, and I looked around furtively as if I was being watched.

It was warm and stuffy and I opened the window and could smell the rain, heavy like the scent of cheap perfume. My reflection stared back from the darkness beyond the window pane and I turned away, not wanting to see the hope in my eyes. I must have retained a touch of humanity because I knew that what I would see would frighten me.

Time trod with heavy boots and I waited in the small room minute by minute, hour by hour. The nurses didn't forget me and they brought me cups of sickly sweet tea. I didn't normally take sugar but I drank the tea that night and was thankful for it. 'No word yet, Mr Ferson,' they told me, 'no word yet.'

Sitting in the room I remembered another hospital and hours of waiting. Then too I had hoped for death, but it was love and not hatred that had fuelled that hope. And no one could understand how I could want my son to die.

I saw him now in my memory, saw his inert body after the operations and heard his cries of pain. I saw his coffin, and the puddle of dirty water that had collected in the tarpaulin which covered and at the same time highlighted his grave. I remembered the coffin being lowered into the hole, and how I was both sad and glad. I had loved him as I had never loved before, nor would love again, and it was love that was both sad and glad. 'God's will,' everyone said, but I damned God, and the ones who saw His hand in my tragedy. Let them have their God; I no longer had need of Him.

Had I now had faith in God I would have asked for death – asked as I had asked for my son to die. My request had been answered then but in God's own time, not mine. And one second is enough time for a man to damn his soul. Four months, the time it took my son to die, was enough time for me to damn my soul endlessly.

The dawn hadn't quite lightened the sky when a doctor came to see me. He was dressed in the green of the operating theatre, yellow rubber boots on his feet. He shook my hand and introduced himself, his own hand still damp from washing away the blood.

'Your wife is in the recovery room,' he said. 'She will be moved into the intensive care unit in a little while. We had to amputate her left leg – we had no choice. Her right leg was also crushed and we've done what we can for the moment . . . the next twenty-four hours are going to be crucial.' He hesitated, searching for less painful words, unaware that nothing could touch me. 'We may still have to amputate,' he added, 'but for the moment we wait. She also suffered internal injuries – there is some damage to the kidneys.'

'Will she live?' I asked.

'Her condition is critical – she lost a lot of blood and has spent many hours in theatre . . . our bodies can only take so much. But it is really too early to say yet.'

She wouldn't die: I knew that now. It would have been too easy – too clean. None of us are entitled to that kind of order in our lives. She would live to mock my hopes of divorce, to do everything in her power to prevent me from going to live with Barbara.

With those thoughts it was impossible to think that I had loved her, that once we had been happy. We had shared so many things in our seventeen years of marriage, had had two daughters and been a family. We had had a son too, and now we had a grave in the cemetery, a reminder that we had also had tragedy – those terrible events from which hatred would grow and cause me to have no compassion for my wife and to wish her dead.

'If you'll excuse me,' the doctor said, and he went back to the world of broken bones and torn flesh . . . and maybe death. But it was a world of recovery and health and life that I saw, and a damnation of all my dreams.

Later a nurse took me along a corridor to a ward at the end. There the nurse handed me over to the ward sister as if I was a lost child, and I followed the sister into a hell that belonged to the living. I felt guilty of my obvious good health and well-being, as if someone else had to pay for it with their sickness: and I wanted to be away from there to a place where there were no reminders of my vulnerability.

Margaret was in the first bed on my left, no screen drawn to hide her. She was the central piece in some crazy abstract sculpture, the culmination of some man's mad vision. There were many things to catch my eye, but I was drawn to the cage that raised the bedclothes from her limbs and to the visible naked stump like a raw joint in the butcher's window.

'I'm sorry, Mr Ferson,' the sister said, 'but with the amputation of a limb it is necessary for us to be able to see the wound. There is always a danger of haemorrhage.'

'It's all right,' I mumbled, shocked by my lack of feeling.

I had to accept that the person on the bed was Margaret because the sister said so, not because I was able to recognize her. She had a white cap on her head, her hair tucked inside it. Her face was obscured by an oxygen mask and only her forehead was visible.

If there had been any pity in me, if I had cared for her only a little, it should have surfaced now. But there was nothing. Except maybe those feelings of ghoulish horror we experience at the scene of a road accident – half pleasure, half fear. My wife could have been an obscure road accident victim, a name in the paper that in a few hours I would have forgotten about.

The sister explained what everything was – the ordered chaos which was necessary for life. The monitors, with life reduced to a bouncing green dot and a bleep. The drains and the oxygen and the drip, the plastic transfusion bag of blood, not the tomato red of television thrillers but the dark brown of melted boot polish. One by one they were pointed out – each and every one my enemy, an obstacle to my hopes.

'She is fighting,' the sister said, 'she wants to live.' She looked at me from behind her gold-rimmed spectacles, the horrors she encountered here unable to destroy her concern. It wasn't a mask, for the eyes can never lie. 'Is there anything you want to know?' she asked.

'No . . . nothing, thanks.'

'The next twenty-four hours are going to be critical,' she said, repeating what the doctor had said. 'If there are no complications there will be a good chance of saving her leg.'

But if not. What good a body without legs and a lifetime in which to regret? One moment to be numbered among God's chosen few, an inheritor of the earth, and the next moment to see it all wiped away.

The sister gave me a few moments by the bedside, and the little Chinese nurse who had hovered nearby smiled reassuringly at me. It was as if to say, I will do my best: I will return her to you one day. She was giving me a balm but I had no pain and I took what didn't belong to me.

The sister took me back to her office and there she listed the rules and regulations. 'It's for the patient's well-being,' she said to me. 'After all, we want your wife to get well as soon as possible.'

'Of course,' I said, 'I understand,' but my hypocrisy didn't shame me. I want my wife to get well, I implied, but in the deep recesses of my mind I imagined life with her dead. Freedom, that illusory dream, would be mine. No need for the trauma that leaving my daughters would entail; no need to wait for the divorce that could never be. Barbara and I would be able to marry, and she would be a good mother to my daughters and to our own children when they were born.

I went out of the hospital with the dream clutched to me, out into the promise of sunshine in a still damp world; out to where there were no reminders of suffering. I had had no sleep but the dream sustained me. To be free after seventeen years. Free of a relationship which now existed only on paper and which Margaret was adamant would be broken only by death. She had imagined some time in the distant future when old age would make death inevitable. Her religion told her that she could be called any time, but it is always someone else who is called, never ourselves.

Before I met Barbara I had never thought of marrying

again; in fact I had never imagined any future in which Margaret did not have a place. Then an affair which had begun in tragedy, which had been something to keep me sane in the midst of my son's final weeks – those weeks of his dying that I will never forget – that affair took on a new significance.

'I want to marry you,' Barbara said. 'I've given too many years to my business and I can't take it to bed.' We'd laughed at that but we knew only too well that it wasn't at all funny. She had given thirty-five years to other things – the making of money, the accumulation of material things – a luxury flat, a car, expensive holidays, the expensive habits that one acquires. Now she wanted marriage, love, children, a home. But there was a time limit. In this world there is no forever. The child-bearing years were scarce now; every day that passed was a threat. 'I want you, Peter,' she said. 'If you can't get a divorce we will live together. You tell your wife that.'

I'd told her all right, and she had mocked me and had stormed out of the house. Now she might never return. But worse still was the possibility that she would return, not the woman who blitzkrieged Sainsbury's on a Friday evening barking 'excuse me' at the more leisurely shoppers, but a cripple who would use all her strength to cling. Demands would be made of me, demands which could be fulfilled only by love, and not by duty or a sense of guilt.

The prospect frightened me because I so much wanted to be free. The children were my only consideration, but they wouldn't be children for ever. One day they would both go, and Margaret and I would find ourselves alone. Two hostile strangers sharing the remainder of our lives, Margaret's deformity reminding us of our inadequacy.

The suffering might teach her the compassion which she hadn't shown to our son, the compassion I had begged from her, and which she had refused. It might be her turn to beg now, but you can't wring pity from a stone, just as you can't chip away the hatred from a man's heart.

It was what I thought that morning as I left the hospital, unaware that everything is possible. Unaware that the events of that summer were to tear the hatred from my heart, bit by bit, like one might pluck the feathers from a live chicken. And that in the autumn when the leaves lay wet in the gutter and life retreated from the threat of winter, love was to flare for a moment within me and I was to give everything – even my very self.

2

'You're late,' Barbara accused as she opened the door of her flat to me.

'Sorry,' I said, and stepped past her into the hall. 'I was held up at the hospital.'

'She hasn't died?'

I shook my head, the weight of the day heavy about my shoulders. I'd seen my daughter Clare cry, and had been humbled by her tears. But they stirred little compassion within me, only made me more aware of how far removed from a human being I'd become. My other daughter Nuala just stared blankly and silently accused me. She knew I didn't care. My mother-in-law Sarah had cried too, but her tears humbled no one. Her husband Martin went out into his garden and a little later I watched him cut the grass, not with the electric mower he'd bought the summer before but with the old hand-drawn mower that had caused his back trouble, and which he had sworn he would never use again. He cried while he cut the grass that didn't need cutting – he cried more than any one of us but he never shed a tear.

He shamed me, that tall old man with the grey hair and the shabby suit, and I cursed him for it. I'd always thought him a fool but today he'd shown me what it was to have dignity, what it means to be sad and alone. He actually showed me the future but I wasn't aware of it. All I knew was that I had to get away from whatever ghost had taken over Martin's eyes. Later I discovered that it wasn't a ghost at all but nothing – simply nothing that had watched me.

I had to get away from them all – from my daughters

because I had nothing to give them; from Sarah with her accusations and blame; from Martin and his tearless crying. I wanted peace now, and comfort, not Barbara's accusation of being late.

She closed the door now and turned to face me. The hall was gloomy and for a moment I imagined that there were dim passages and brutal secrets behind the dark oak panelling. I held out my hands to Barbara and hesitantly she came towards me, her face becoming clearer as my eyes adjusted to the gloom. I put my arms about her and pulled her close. She was dead for a moment – I could have been embracing a corpse – and then she put her arms about my neck and I let the darkness and the comfort engulf me.

We live for moments, and when they come we want to hold and savour them. But the first strawberry can be eaten but once, no matter how sweet it may be. Now I wanted to hold on to my moment, but as I tried to do so it vanished like a flurry of snow-flakes falling on a wet pavement.

Barbara pushed me from her and we stood at arm's length. Her face was a mask, painted, unreadable features, the original face hidden by her years in business, by the lies and the deceits. But the eyes hinted of uncertainty, and I knew she didn't feel sure of me any more.

'You're quiet,' she said. 'It can't have been that bad.' I could sense her uncertainty, that she felt that pity, if nothing else, might draw me back to Margaret. I think she realized that pity might be stronger than the so-called love I professed for her.

'I was thinking about us,' I said. 'We may not need that divorce after all.'

'But you said on the phone that the doctors were optimistic.' Was there a hint of hope in the voice? Or was my hearing playing tricks with me?

'That was hours ago. I'll tell you everything – over a drink.'

She watched me for a moment and I could have sworn that the eyes were no longer uncertain. Then abruptly she turned and walked away. I followed her, the hem of her sensible skirt clutching at her calves. She opened the door of the lounge at the end of the hall, and the light inside rushed out as if it was claustrophobic and clung to us. It followed us inside, glad of our company.

I sat on the chrome and leather couch under the window, and Barbara brought me a whisky. I patted the couch invitingly, but she appeared not to notice. She sat instead in one of the two chrome and leather armchairs which matched the couch, turning the chair so that she sat facing me. 'So?' she said.

'There have been complications with her leg – problems with circulation apparently. She had to have an emergency operation this afternoon.'

'Will they have to amputate?'

'Not immediately. Unless there's a deterioration in her condition they won't do anything until tomorrow. Then depending on my decision they will try more surgery or amputate.'

'Your decision?' She had a way of turning her head slightly when puzzled.

'They can't be certain that surgery will be successful. What it will do is weaken Margaret even more. If they then have to amputate . . . well, she might not survive such a course of action. So do they amputate now? Life without legs, or the probability of death . . . They've left the decision with me for the moment.'

'And have you decided?'

'No.' I helped myself to the whisky but its warmth in my stomach was like an inflammation. I looked at Barbara but there would be no help from her, just as there had been no help from the doctor when he spoke to me earlier that evening. I had wanted to tell him that only yesterday I'd hated my wife, that I'd actually wished her dead. That the decision he was asking me to make was impossible even had I loved her. Except that if the decision was based on love I might console myself with that. Based on what was already a dying hatred, combined with my own desires, there could be no consolation.

Had someone asked me yesterday if I wanted a say in whether my wife should live or die I would have said yes, and been glad. Now I would give anything to have the decision taken from me.

'You'll have to decide,' Barbara said.

'What would you do?' I asked.

'I'd prefer to die. I couldn't live without legs.'

'But if you had to make the decision for someone else?'

'I can't help you, Peter. She's your wife. But you know what my decision would be.'

I did know, and because I did I thought that I knew her. But what can we know about someone when we don't even know ourselves? There were depths to Barbara that I couldn't have dreamed of, but all that I was to know later – too late to be of use to any of us.

She couldn't help me, but then no one could. Only love could have helped, as it did a year ago when it was my son's life and death I had to consider. In the end what I wanted then meant nothing and I was powerless to help him. From my helplessness hatred flourished, until it began to die this morning in the ward of a Hampstead hospital.

No one could understand a year ago how I could profess to love my son and yet want him to die. Some could understand my wish to have him aborted when we discovered that he would have spina bifida. But once he was born his life became sacred – that life of operations and pain and futility. The doctors gave him but months to live, and that with the best medical care. Without the care he would have died quickly – died with the dignity that every death is entitled to.

Hatred breeds a desire for revenge, and twenty-four hours ago I might have wished that my wife should be crippled in an accident. I could imagine my pleasure and gloating. Now I would want none of it. Yet a say in her survival was thrust into my hands, mine to do with as I wished. To say amputate or to say do not, and to know then that every passing moment might be one nearer her death and my freedom. And yet I knew that whatever the decision I would one day regret it. Not for the day, but for every second and minute and hour of my life.

'You could always let the doctors decide themselves,' Barbara said now. 'After all, Pilate washed his hands.'

I ignored her sarcasm. 'That was after he made the decision.'

'She should have died.' She stopped a moment to stare at me. 'It's true what they say. Once a Catholic, always a Catholic.'

'It has nothing to do with it,' I said, going on the defensive. 'And I don't claim to be a Catholic any more.'

'You never forget the threat of the fires,' she said, her sarcasm hurting me, but again I ignored it. Real lovers try to hurt each other, I told myself, wanting desperately to believe it. Barbara might ridicule the idea of hell but it existed all right. During my son's short life I had felt the fires, and indeed she was the one who had saved me. I didn't know then that I had been saved for another hell. I didn't know until I found myself in it.

'You knew what you wanted for your son,' she went on, 'so what's the difference now?'

'I loved him,' I said, still capable of suffering.

'Maybe it was only a pretence,' she said. 'You knew that Margaret would not allow him to die no matter what you wanted. Had it been my son I would have killed him myself.'

I had loved him, but had the doctors said, 'Here, take him – do with him what you want,' would I have put my fingers around his throat and kept them there until he died? I wanted him to be aborted when we were told he would be handicapped, but Margaret would not agree. When he was born I couldn't say whose pain was worse – mine or his – but it was enough that I wanted an end to it. Yet Margaret had insisted on keeping him alive, had eked out our mutual suffering until there was no more left.

Barbara wouldn't have allowed it. When she spoke of killing him she was merely stating fact. That much I did know about her. 'We make such charity of helping people to live,' she'd once said, 'and yet we are shocked at the idea of helping someone to die.' I was shocked myself and had asked where such views had come from, but she wouldn't be drawn.

Yet it was a woman with such views who had saved me from myself last Christmas. I had known her for five years on a business basis – her employment agency supplied the company I worked for with office staff. I'd had to cancel an appointment with her because my son's condition had deteriorated and I was wanted at the hospital. When we met later I apologized, and in answer to her questions I blurted out the whole story. I'd expected silence, or encouragement to believe that everything would be OK, or else words of reproach for my attitude. Instead Barbara agreed with me, and I felt what the leper must feel when he finds one of his kind, overwhelmed at the thought that he is no longer alone.

Frightened of being alone I clung to Barbara, finding to my surprise that she wanted to cling too. It was later that she told me about her previous lover – a man five years her junior, who had recently thrown her aside for a girl not yet twenty. It had brought Barbara's thirty-five years into perspective – made her realize that forever only belonged to the young.

We found comfort together for our individual hells, and when my son died it was Barbara I turned to. She understood the grief I'd felt at his death even though I had asked for it. She understood my feelings on seeing his empty incubator and the no-entry sign on the door of that room along from the Baby Care Unit. The room had waited four months for him, and now that it had him I hated it and I had never felt so empty in my life.

Barbara took my emptiness and filled it with herself. She put her arms around me, and comforted me while Christmas rolled by leaving no one safe from its hysteria. Then the new year came, bringing with it a semblance of sanity and a realization that life only stopped for the mad or the dead and that I had to decide now if either was preferable to living.

But living implied more than mere existence. I wanted no more part in Margaret's life, and when she asked me if I was going to return to our bed – the bed I'd vacated when she refused to have an abortion – I said 'no', and stayed alone in my single bed in the tiny attic room. There my hatred and desire for revenge kept me warm during the cold winter nights. And there was also the comfort of knowing I had Barbara. Then one day she told me she wanted to marry me, and I found myself telling her that I loved her and at the same time wondering if she could see the lie on my face.

I looked across at her now, her oval face caught in the light from the window, a face that held her age well. It would never tend to fleshiness, but the expression would harden if life did not give her what she thought to be her due. A round face would have softened the expression but the eyes would betray her – hard eyes, the blue of cold-knotted hands.

'The truth always hurts, Peter,' she said.

'Truth?' I echoed.

'About ourselves. We all have an ideal for ourselves – the

brave, the honest, the compassionate . . . We never see the coward or the fool.'

'We can't all be cold bastards,' I said. 'We have to live with ourselves you know. Most times it's easier to live with the fool.'

'Which is why you'll tell them to amputate.'

Her mocking voice angered me and I tried some of the whisky, but there was no courage there. 'I can tell them to amputate,' I said, 'amputate and be damned.'

'Damned is right,' she said. 'Do you know – can you imagine what life is going to be like without legs? Do you, Peter? Do you hate her that much?'

I had no defence against her words and I found myself in a spotlight of silence. I didn't look at Barbara, but instead looked around the room which reflected her as surely as a mirror. The severe white walls with the abstract prints – mathematical shapes in sharp colours, the chrome frames that would always be cold to the touch. Her chrome and leather furniture – her chrome and glass coffee table. The polished wooden floor hard beneath my feet, the sheepskin rug before the walled-up fireplace. The recess to the left of the fireplace housed the television and the black, slim-line music centre, and from a shelf above a creeping fig trailed its green tendrils. With the other house plants, they were the only live things in that dead room.

I couldn't avoid Barbara for ever and eventually I was drawn back to her. Our eyes locked across the few feet of empty space that separated us – close enough to touch, yet as far away as if we were at opposite poles. The embrace at the front door was of another time entirely. It was as if I had imagined it.

'She'll ruin your life, Peter,' she said, a mother explaining something to a child. 'Is that what you want?'

'She can't touch me.'

'She's like God – she reaches everywhere.'

'Not any more,' I said.

'Are you still going to leave her as we planned?'

'Of course,' I said. I had another try at the whisky, confident that I was on safe ground. 'Let her call me what she likes,' I thought, 'she still needs me.' The whisky was potent now and it warmed me.

'So you're going to leave her at the end of the month like we planned? Like you told her yesterday?'

It had been easy then. Margaret had a way of taunting like a child might taunt a puppy to see him show his teeth. Like the puppy, I'd wanted to get back at the antagonist, and it had given me pleasure to tell Margaret that I would leave. She might not agree to the divorce I wanted, but all she was preventing me from having was a piece of paper. I could say now that nothing had changed, and yet I knew that the accident had made a difference. I couldn't leave now – at least not yet.

Barbara saw my hesitation and the contempt it generated on her face hurt me. 'One woman,' she said, 'crippled . . . confined to a hospital bed and she still frightens you.'

'It's not that.'

'So what is it, Peter? Maybe you only want a bit on the side. Someone to ease the ache in your loins. Is that it? A whore who does it for nothing?'

The evening was closing in, and the light had hidden itself in some secret corner and had pushed the dusk out towards us. It suddenly seemed to have become colder in the room and goose pimples made my bare lower arms tingle. I felt isolated and wanted to be somewhere else, away from Barbara's desire and ability to hurt me. It could have been Margaret sitting there before me, wanting to make our love – even if it wasn't the real love of romantic fiction – curdle before my eyes. 'Do you want to destroy everything?' I asked.

'We have to shape our lives,' she said.

'You can't always change the world.'

'No one can change the world,' she said, 'we just make the best we can of it. Your problem is that you see the failure before you try.'

'Maybe I should go along to the hospital and kill her,' I said brutally. 'Is that what you want? It's you that's frightened of her . . . you're frightened and jealous of a cripple.'

She laughed, a cruel laugh that I should have heeded. 'You flatter yourself,' she said. 'I could never be jealous. There isn't anyone I value that much.'

'Maybe I should go,' I said, half in jest.

'I think you should go,' she said, and her words made the room colder.

I looked across at her, her face frighteningly bereft of expression. As with Margaret, it was now difficult to imagine that I had ever made love with Barbara, that we had laughed and been happy. I had come to her this evening for comfort – I'd wanted her to put her arms about me as she had done at Christmas and to make the world all right. 'You think that every woman is different,' Margaret had once said. 'Well they are different, but what you'll find out for yourself one day is that they are all the same too.' I'd laughed then but I didn't feel like laughing now.

I gulped down the mouthful of whisky in the bottom of my glass – barren comfort when there were other possibilities. I wanted to be angry with Barbara but there was no anger left within me. I felt tired – the lack of sleep, the hanging about at the hospital, the tension and now finally this – had drained my strength. Wearily I got to my feet. 'Thanks for the drink,' I said.

She didn't speak, crouched motionless below me. Her white silk blouse was loose and billowy, and left a small piece of white shoulder exposed. For an agitated moment I wanted to touch the flesh, to stroke it endlessly with my fingers. One stilled moment and then my pride nudged me and it was gone.

I walked to the door and turned to look at Barbara but she seemed oblivious of my presence. 'Goodnight,' I said, leaving her to the gloomy room. I knew it wasn't an end to everything – we'd had our conflicts before. But one day there might be an end, and I would find myself alone. Yet that need never happen if only . . . If only, though, was a million things and any one of them could destroy us. Lonely, and with an old damned feeling that once only Margaret could induce, I closed the door of the flat behind me.

The evening was chilly and I put on the jacket I had left in the car. It offered warmth against the chill but no protection against the doubts that assailed me. I'd had a feeling for some months that I was getting my last chance for happiness; if I let it slip now there might be no other.

Yesterday life had seemed simple. I'd known Margaret would refuse me a divorce; I'd asked only for Barbara's sake. She was the one who would have liked marriage; for myself official pieces of paper didn't matter any more. Last night Barbara and I had laughed at Margaret's promise to destroy our chance of happiness. A fit and able woman as we thought then – what hope did she have? But now, crippled and helpless, she could destroy everything. Just as she was destroying the only weapon I had in my fight against her – my hatred.

I tried to push the thoughts away but they wouldn't go. And I knew that Barbara was right. Helpless or not, Margaret still had the power to reach out and touch me; maybe more so now than ever before.

And yet tomorrow I had to make a decision that might mean life or death to her – or freedom or enslavement to myself. Tomorrow I had to be God – I who was hardly worthy to be a man.

3

The sleepless Saturday night, and the tension, and the two whiskies I'd had before going to bed, took their toll the next morning. In the bathroom they made the harsh white suite and the white tiles hurt my eyes even before I switched on the light. The bathroom mocked my weakness because I'd allowed Margaret to have her own way. I'd wanted a pale yellow suite with beige and lemon tiles in pleasing patterns. But the house belonged to Margaret; it was her reflection that one saw.

I filled the sink with cold water and immersed my head, but the shock brought only a moment's relief. It couldn't take the sandpaper feeling from my mouth, nor ease the hand that was trying to crush my brains against the side of my skull. I finished my ablutions and helped myself to a couple of aspirins from the medicine cabinet.

I dressed and went downstairs, past the green floral wallpaper that was scuffed and faded. Margaret had wanted me to re-decorate the house, but my heart wasn't in it. 'Get a decorator,' I'd said, knowing that she wouldn't. She would never pay out money for anything she felt we could do ourselves. It was by doing it ourselves that we'd managed to acquire a detached house, but we'd paid the price of our marriage for it. I'd often thought that we might have been happy had we settled for a semi we could have easily afforded. But maybe we were doomed anyway, like the lemmings who throw themselves into the sea.

'No one said goodnight to me last night,' Clare accused when I entered the kitchen. 'I stayed awake for ages and ages . . .' Her brown eyes watched me – my eyes, the ones that stared back at me from the shaving mirror. But while hers radiated the innocence of an eight-year-old child, mine reflected the cynicism of a thirty-eight-year-old man. This morning they had retreated deep into my skull as if trying to escape the light.

'I'm sorry,' I said, 'but you can have two kisses to make up for it.'

She offered me her cheek, cocking her head to one side. I moved round the table and kissed the unblemished flesh, making a sucking sound with my lips so that she couldn't claim that the kisses weren't real. But she would never know my feelings for her; that I loved her more than anyone else on earth; that I had a terrible fear that something horrible would happen to her. One day her body would lie broken and bleeding like the body of the little boy I'd once seen lying on Tottenham High Road before a passer-by had removed his own jacket and covered the body with it. I would feel like the car driver, who had been doubled up, retching emptily in the gutter, and repeating over and over again between the bouts of retching – 'I never saw him . . . I never saw him . . .'

'There you are,' I said, 'two priceless kisses.'

'What's priceless kisses, daddy?'

'It means you can't buy them, silly.' Nuala had her mother's impatience, unable to tolerate weakness or ignorance in anyone. She mocked Clare and myself; mocked our kisses and our make-belief that the world was all right, and everyone was happy. Nuala never conjured up the image of a battered and broken doll, and at thirteen had no need of me any more.

'She called me silly,' Clare said. 'Tell her to apologize . . . tell her, daddy.'

'She didn't mean it,' I said.

'She did . . . she did. She has to apologize.'

Her shrill voice hurt my head as surely as if somcone had

tapped on my skull with the knurled end of a walking stick. 'Enough,' I said, 'enough . . .' – my voice rising. 'Apologize' was Margaret's favourite word. 'The children will apologize . . . you will apologize' – everyone to apologize but herself. It seemed as if she could reach into the room from her hospital bed, reach and touch and turn to dust.

I'd always wanted to be a better father to the girls, but work took up most of my time. And then there was the barrier Margaret had made between myself and the children. She would hold each and every misdemeanour and parade them for me when I came in from work. She would make the girls apologize, and then they would be punished. It was always daddy's punishment, never her own. It was a small victory over me, but in her possessive desire to have all the girls' affection for herself, any victory was welcome.

Yesterday, when I thought Margaret would die, I saw it as the chance to have the girls' affection for myself. It would make up for the loss of my son – he who had been conceived to save our marriage. In other circumstances it might have been funny – adults placing so much responsibility on a baby. It might have been funny if it wasn't for the memory of his living and his dying.

Clare said nothing more about an apology, but watched me with a child's uncertainty. I wanted to reassure her but there were no words to express my love. I turned away and made myself a coffee – black and sugarless. Sarah was in the garden hanging out a few items of washing. She probably hadn't slept much, and would have been up before dawn, busy about the house, trying to distract her mind from the present and the future. Maybe from the past too, because it's the past which has the most capability of hurting us.

She came in from the garden, having about her that certain smell that people who spend long periods scrubbing clean skin acquire. She held the view that cleanliness is next to godliness, and would prescribe soap and water as the two best tools to use in fighting the devil. 'I rang the hospital,' she said. 'They want to see us this morning.'

'How is she?' I asked.

'She had a comfortable night.'

'Good,' I said, but the word meant nothing. But Sarah's use of the word 'us' did mean something. She had no say any more in the life of her daughter, but she couldn't accept it. She wanted to be involved just as I would want to be involved if it was Clare who was ill. Never mind if she was thirty-five and had children of her own. But some time in the future I would have no say. There was no thought then that one day we might have no love for each other.

'I want to go to the hospital,' Nuala now said.

'Can I come too?' Clare put in. 'Please, daddy.'

'No . . . not yet. Maybe tomorrow, but only if the doctors say so.'

We'd told them that Margaret had had an accident, and that she was very ill. We had not mentioned the amputation, or said anything about death. Nuala might have coped, but Clare would not have understood.

'I want to come,' Nuala insisted.

'No,' I said, weary of having always to fight. I wanted to lie down in a soft darkness, to let sleep creep up on me, to be aware of drifting off into nothingness. But Nuala's mocking eyes made me aware of reality, and for a moment it could have been Margaret who was sitting at the end of the table. Margaret with the short, dark hair and the prim mouth and the arid breasts.

I had to make a conscious effort not to lash out at my daughter, and the guilt welled up within me. There was but a child sitting at the table. She didn't have Margaret's hardness nor her contempt. This was no world for children, where even a parent could vent his meanness, callous as the torturer.

'We'll see tomorrow,' I said, 'and I won't have any more arguments. Now I have to phone my office, and you two had better get ready for school.'

I spoke to my service director, and told him what had happened, and he muttered the usual things we all say in a time of tragedy. I was aware that they meant little, yet I found myself thanking him, carrying on the conventions that enable us to live with each other.

'There are problems at Feltham Service,' he said. 'I want them sorted out.'

'I'll go over tomorrow,' I said.

'Good. Now this figure you've given me for faulty new videos: it just isn't good enough.'

'I'm working on it at the moment,' I said.

'Well, I want to see a downward trend. And while we're on the subject of faulty stock . . .' He listed about everything – colour sets, ex-rental sets, scrap sets . . . It was as if I had never mentioned Margaret. He wasn't to know that I didn't care about her, but maybe like himself he thought no one gave a damn about anyone.

'I'll see to it all,' I said, wanting to tell him to go to hell, and I hung up cursing him and his bloody company. Once it had been my company but not any more. Maybe it wasn't his company either. We could all carry pretence as far as we wanted; even to blinding ourselves.

We should have been born with a control panel which could select our function at any time. One could become the service executive at the flick of a switch. But evolution hadn't seen it that way, and we had to be everything at once. I needed to be able to think clearly, to erase the effects of last night's whisky, to make decisions. But problem piled on problem, each wanting the same moment of my time.

To the director Feltham was a problem to be sorted out. But it was more than that to me. Apart from the fact that I was the one who did the dirty work, the Feltham manager was an old friend. Our friendship had endured for twenty years, just as my marriage had endured for seventeen.

In the measure of time, where even a lifetime is but a flicker, was it possible I had been in love with my wife such a short time ago? Suddenly I felt alone, not wanting to accept that it had all gone. Could I ever have been young and free and in love? Freedom . . . not nothing left to lose, but everything to lose, and no thought that I could ever lose it. Now I had a premonition about the future, when everything would be lost, even that which I still had.

I went back to the kitchen, where the girls were ready for school. Clare kissed me goodbye, still in need of love. Nuala looked on with cynicism, and I knew that I had lost her. She was Margaret's daughter – she always had been. Clare on the other hand was partly mine. Margaret and I had shared her as Solomon might have suggested, unaware that to share was not to love. We should have given, not taken away for ourselves. Solomon after all had been right.

I was left alone with Sarah, the last person I would want to be shipwrecked with. She wasn't the mother-in-law of the proverbial jokes; that type of person implied humour, a trait Sarah was sadly lacking in. She was centuries too late; she should have been born in the puritan era of Oliver Cromwell, he who had savaged both her people and her country.

'Did Martin go home last night?' I asked.

'He didn't want to stay,' she said. 'He takes things badly. I told him to go along to his allotment today. It would help to take his mind off things.'

'It would help,' I said, visualizing him digging over the ground he'd already dug, burying his pain in the soil. 'Did they mention a time at the hospital?'

'About ten . . . when the doctors are on their rounds. They will want to amputate . . . ?'

'They virtually said so last night.'

'You can't let them do it.'

'I may not have any choice,' I said.

'You can't know,' she said. 'You must leave things to God.'

'You want her to die?' I was brutal, ashamed the moment I'd spoken. What could I gain by hurting her? Age deserved respect even if the person herself did not.

'She can't live without legs,' she said, as if it was scientific fact. 'She would never be able to accept it.'

'If they don't amputate she might die,' I explained patiently. 'I don't want her death on my conscience.'

'It's all on your conscience,' she said. 'If you hadn't driven her out of the house on Saturday she would be fine today. But you don't have a conscience. Any man with a conscience would not want a defenceless baby to die. You're not fit to make a decision for anyone.'

'So you make it,' I said, 'you make the decision. Leave her to God like she left the baby.' I hesitated for a moment and then walked out of the room. Sarah could only see what she wanted to see; she couldn't understand the love I'd had for my son.

I went into my study, the only part of the house in which I belonged. The antique desk restored for me by my company's polishing department, the leather swivel chair, the parquet floor, the maroon curtains at the window that overlooked the garden – they were mine. Margaret had had no say in here. It didn't matter to me that the desk was too big for the room, and that you couldn't open the door fully. It suited me and it seemed only as if the desk was protecting my privacy.

I sat in my chair in my room, with my signed Lowry print on the wall. I liked it better than the oil paintings which hung in the hall and in the sitting-room. The blue mountains and skies and rivers weren't my scenes, unlike the Lowry with its terraced streets and chimney stacks and smoke pointing the direction of the wind. I was at home in the city, among the houses and the people and the traffic and the noise. Margaret thought cities to be the invention of the devil: dens of vice and corruption. But it's people who corrupt, not places.

I took the analysis sheets for Feltham Service from my briefcase, but a practised glance only confirmed what I'd known for weeks. The figures told a worsening story, and in a company where figures counted more than anything else, it looked bad for John.

My head didn't hurt so much but felt as if it was filled with lead. Yet I managed to absorb as much of the figures as was necessary. At nine thirty I went back to the kitchen and waited for Sarah to get ready. We made the journey to the hospital in silence, Sarah not bothering to plead any more.

The doctors were on their rounds and we were asked to sit in the waiting-room. We sat with the others who were waiting, united by our predicaments, yet strangers resenting each other's presence. In tragedy we want to be alone.

We had waited half an hour when a nurse came and called my name. I got to my feet, but Sarah made no move, and when I asked her if she was going to come with me, she shook her head. I knew then that the decision was mine alone, and that the blame would also be mine. I went with the nurse to a small office where the surgeon from the previous morning and two other men were waiting. A sister hovered in the background, a folder in her hands. The surgeon introduced the other two men and we shook hands.

'Your wife has had a comfortable night,' the surgeon said, 'but I'm afraid there have been more complications with her leg. She will require surgery this morning.'

It was what I'd expected, but having expected it made it no easier. 'What are the chances of surgery being a success?' I asked.

'The problem is pretty severe,' the surgeon said. 'There is virtually no circulation.'

'And the consequences of that?'

'Gangrene I'm afraid . . . we would have no choice then.'

'And are we close to that?'

'All cases are different, Mr Ferson.' It was the smaller of the other two men who spoke now, an older man, clearly the senior of the three. 'To answer your first question – the chances of surgery being successful are poor. It will involve a long operation. Immediately afterwards we may have to amputate . . . not a course of action I would want to take. There are other considerations too . . . we have to take into account the damage to the kidneys. The very large blood transfusions haven't helped either . . . It has all been a very great strain on the body.' He trailed off and they were silent and they waited.

They were patient men and they were used to waiting, and they waited for me. I tried to find something from the past – a few moments from a time when Margaret and I had been happy. But it's only the bad times we remember, and only then because they remind us that tomorrow there may be more to face.

'It might be best to amputate,' I said, never having felt so uncertain in my life.

'I think it's the correct decision,' the surgeon said.

'Can I see her?' I asked.

'Certainly. Now if you would sign the consent form . . . the sister will deal with it. If you would excuse us, Mr Ferson.'

They left and I signed the form, taking care not to read what I was signing. I tried not to think about it, but the images it conjured up were of freak shows and people pointing, and the open stares of children and pity. I went back to the waiting-room and sat beside Sarah. I said nothing, but she knew and started to cry. It generated no sympathy for her – only resentment. It was a reminder for the ones who really grieved and loved, and too much of a reminder for those of us who did neither.

'There was no choice,' I whispered to her, 'they have to amputate.'

'No.' She didn't get hysterical, and the crying, like the iceberg, was almost all beneath the surface and I knew it to be genuine. Somewhere within her she still retained a drop of the milk of human kindness. We all have it but surely mine was hidden too deep ever to be found again. After my son's death it was as if I had wanted no one else to have it.

'It's your fault,' she said, 'all your fault. God will punish you.'

I wanted to ask why He had punished her; why He allowed His chosen few to suffer; but she would have no answer. Except that which might have shown me up for the damned, and I didn't need anyone to show me that.

'It'll be a few hours,' I said. 'We can go home if you want. Or we could go and have a cup of tea . . .' She didn't reply, and I knew she wanted to sit with her grief – to nurture and indulge it like a child with a grazed knee. I knew I couldn't wait there for two hours, and I decided that I would go to Feltham now. 'I have work to do,' I said to Sarah. 'I'll be back in a few hours if you want to wait.'

I left her, and instead of going in to see Margaret I went straight to the car park and got my car. I drove up Haverstock Hill and went through Hampstead Village.

There were roadworks by Jack Straw's Castle, and the traffic edged its way along by the pond. I watched a little girl of about three feeding the ducks, laughing joyfully, unhindered as yet by any convention. Yet life would beat the laughter out of her and nothing would ever be funny in the same way again. Seeing her, it was almost impossible to imagine that my own two daughters had been that young once.

It was a time for being a child; when home simply meant love and security, and parents were people you could trust. My childhood had been happy; there were no suppressed memories of ugliness and fear. And I had wanted my own children to be happy. I'd wanted to give them everything, unaware that there is only one thing you can give a child – and that simply is their childhood. You can give them everything and yet steal away the most precious gift.

We had a lot to answer for, Margaret and I – one of us no less to blame than the other. I wasn't thinking of a judgement day when God would check off our sins, but rather the judgement of every day. Like the laughter of a little girl; or a boy and his dad fishing; or a baby at the breast, the oldest comfort of all. The girls had been denied even that because Margaret thought it an animal trait, unaware that we are animals before we are anything else.

I made my way down to the North Circular Road and turned left. I put my foot down and stayed in the outside lane. At the Chiswick roundabout I took the exit before the one for the M4 motorway and Heathrow airport. Some miles further on I turned on to Hounslow Road, and a few minutes later I was pulling into the service department car park. I tried to make the switch from human being to service executive, but it wasn't easy. Margaret and Barbara and Sarah and the girls all formed a kaleidoscope in my mind. My personal problems mingled with the problems of work, now one coming into focus, now the other, now all mixed together like an abstract painting that could have hung in the Tate.

I didn't go through reception but tried the goods entrance further along. To my horror the door pushed open and I just walked in. Before me were a series of racks laden with televisions and video recorders, the anti-theft cages unlocked. The deserted stores was on my left, the door open. In the video repair room Cliff Richard sang about a devil woman.

Anger flared within me, and I shuddered to consider the consequences had I been the service director. It boded ill for John, and I could only hope that he had a few positive things on his side. I went up the centre of the workshop to the manager's office. John was seated behind his desk, amid total disorder. He was embarrassed to see me and got to his feet awkwardly. We shook hands, his palm cold and clammy like that of someone who is dead.

'Sit down,' he said. 'Can I get you a coffee?'

'If it's no trouble.' I sat on the chair on my side of the desk, having had to put a bundle of papers on the floor first. John rang through on the internal phone and spoke to someone.

'Don't argue, Julie,' he shouted, 'just do it.' He slammed down the receiver and began to straighten out some papers on his desk.

'So what's the problem then?' I asked.

He managed to hold my gaze for a moment, then looked down at his desk as if mesmerized by the disorder; unsure how he'd got into such a state, or, worse still, unsure how to get out of it. 'I've got staff problems,' he said. 'My assistant manager . . . two of my engineers and one of the office girls are on holiday. I've one engineer off sick and one on jury service. There's no storeman – the company can't afford to employ one – and in case you've forgotten, you stopped all overtime four weeks ago. How can I run a service like that? How many times have I asked for help? And what do I get? Nothing.'

'The door wasn't locked when I came in,' I said.

'I can't be everywhere.'

'It's not good enough, John. Had I been one of the directors you wouldn't have a job now.'

'I might not have a job anyway,' he said bitterly. 'You haven't come here to wish me the time of day.'

'There have been too many complaints,' I said. 'Even the shops have been moaning. One day soon now they'll run crying to the sales director and then what?' I let the threat hang and waited for his response. Just then the girl arrived with my coffee and banged it down on the desk before me.

'There's a customer in reception,' she said.

'Thanks . . . ah . . . Julie,' John said. 'If you'll excuse me, Mr Ferson.'

I tasted the coffee but it was lukewarm and I couldn't manage it. I decided to have a wander round the workshop, to see things for myself. But I wasn't prepared for the chaos. There were televisions and videos everywhere, stacked on each other without protection. One of the repair jigs had been stripped bare and now stood like a gaunt skeleton, panels strewn around it.

I chatted to some of the engineers, but they were sullen and uninterested, and badly lacking in morale. Barry, one of our better engineers, told me that he was leaving. 'I couldn't work here any more,' he said.

I realized that there was little I could do here, and I went back to the office. John didn't make it difficult, and I had his resignation in a few minutes, wiping out our friendship in the process. 'I'm sorry, John,' I said, 'I feel a right bastard.'

'It's not you, Mr Ferson,' he said. 'It's this bloody company. We've got two-way radios, computers, paging systems . . . and the worst service in the business.'

Mr Ferson he called me, and I knew then that he didn't see me as human. He would shun me from now on as if I'd got the black death. I'd sacked men before – some had gone without the benefit of resignation – but it had never really hurt me until now. In fact it hurt me more now than agreeing to the operation had hurt me this morning. Had I stopped to consider this fact, had I given it a moment's thought, it might have changed the future. It might have shown me that it wasn't just the sacking that had destroyed our friendship, but the fact that I was beyond friendship. I was no longer the man John remembered. But that wasn't surprising because I wasn't the man I remembered either.

I spent some time on the telephone informing the service director, arranging for a relief manager and two engineers to help out, the help John had desperately needed. Had I only given it to him weeks ago . . . But crying was for children.

'BK employment agency rang,' my secretary Carol informed me. 'They didn't leave a message.'

No message, but there was no need for one. It simply meant that Barbara wanted to see me tonight. With that piece of good news to savour, I rang the hospital. They told me that the operation had been a success and that everything was fine. Two strange words to describe a tragedy. But then I'd just spoken to the director about solving a problem which in other words meant that I had destroyed another man's career.

I wanted to get away; there was nothing more to do here. John came to the door and we shook hands. 'How's Margaret and the family?' he asked. Normally it would have been one of the first things he would have inquired about, and indeed I would inquire about a man's family myself. But I hadn't even considered it, and it was another pointer towards my damnation, but I was too blind to see.

'They're fine,' I lied, not wanting his sympathy, or indeed his curse if he felt that way inclined. I left him at the door, and I actually felt sorry for him. I didn't know then that I should have kept my sorrow – that soon I would need it all for myself.

4

I didn't want to return to the hospital, but I had no choice. It is not easy to say to hell with everything, for we are all prisoners of one kind or another. The sister told me that Sarah had gone home, and that Margaret was comfortable. 'The leg has been amputated,' the sister said, but the clinical word couldn't hide the reality. Sharp knives cutting flesh and buzzing saws cutting through bone; electric saws now, no need for the surgeon's assistant to sweat. And then the furnaces where tiny flames spurted from burning fat. Human flesh reduced to ashes until phoenix-like it would rise on the last day, bone and sinew and nerve and muscle, all joined together again in the image of God. But of what comfort would that be to Margaret when the terror came?

'You can go in,' the sister said. 'Your wife has a visitor at the moment . . . a priest. I didn't want to let him in but he said he'd driven up from Dorset.'

'Father Mason,' I said. 'He's a family friend.'

She nodded. 'Well, if you'll excuse me, Mr Ferson.'

Father Mason was standing by the bedside staring out towards Hampstead, his hands clasped behind his back. He turned as I approached and took a step towards me. We shook hands and the strength of his grip belied his frail physique.

'Ah . . . Peter,' he said, the words clipped as if by scissors. 'This is a sad thing.' He held my hand tightly and I could feel the tension in his body. 'I was away yesterday and didn't get word until this morning.'

'It's good of you to come,' I said.

'I offered my mass for her this morning,' he said. 'With God's help she'll be well enough soon. All we can do is pray very hard – you too, Peter.' He released my hand and looked at me closely, his eyes filled with that intense belief that always amazed me. 'You know what they say, don't you? That God listens more attentively to the lost sheep.' He smiled and clapped me on the shoulder. 'Take no notice of me; we've known each other a long time, eh . . .'

'I suppose we have,' I said. I took no offence at his words, for he wouldn't have known how to give any, and because he was the only real priest I'd ever known. He had been in Korea in the fifties until his health had deserted him and he had had to return to England. He'd wanted to return to Korea when he recovered, but the church authorities wouldn't allow him. 'I damned them,' he'd once told me in the early days of our friendship, when he was stationed in London and would drop in uninvited at any time. He would have a mug of sweet tea in the kitchen of our flat, and eat half a dozen cream-centred biscuits. Later, after Nuala was born, he would sit her on his knee and put tiny bits of cream in her mouth, waving Margaret's protests aside.

Sometimes Father Mason and I would go along to my local and we would have a few halves of bitter. 'Told the bishop he was a damn fool,' he would say to me, perched on a barstool, the barmaid a few feet away, elbows on the bar and her large breasts sagging forward under their own weight. 'I told him that God wouldn't see it any other way. They made allowances of course – Korea and all that – but you can't damn a bishop.'

He'd been correct in his assumption, and one day they'd packed him off to Dorset. They supposed that he couldn't do much harm down there, and it was also a way of breaking his spirit. No authority likes to be questioned, and all rebellion has to be crushed.

They hadn't broken him, but his shoulders sagged a little

as if the weight of their authority had pushed him forward; and his hair was greyer and thinner than it had been when he'd officiated at our wedding.

He walked over to the bed and I followed him, and we stared down at the face of the woman we had both loved – that Father Mason, I assumed, still loved. She looked peaceful, and for a moment there might never have been an accident – I might not have told them to amputate.

'She's asleep,' the nurse who was in attendance said.

'Has she been conscious?' I asked.

'Oh yes . . . though she's not quite sure what's happened to her. But she knows her name . . . and the children's names – Nuala and Clare.' The nurse repeated them, pleased to have remembered.

'They're our daughters,' I said, 'Nuala and Clare.' But no mention of my name. Muddled or not, she was aware of the one name she shouldn't mention.

Father Mason stared at Margaret's face for a moment, then reached down with his hand and touched the forehead, tracing the sign of the cross with his fingertips. The face became agitated, as if the sea had washed over it, and then it was calm again. I watched without emotion and got two chairs from under the window and we sat on them by the bedside, among the equipment.

'How are the girls?' Father Mason asked. 'I suppose they have taken this badly?'

'Children are always hurt,' I said. 'We haven't allowed them to visit yet.'

'They're so impressionable,' he said. 'Usually they're closer to the mother and take things more to heart when she's ill. Give them a few days, though, and they will never believe anything happened. Margaret will be up and about by then with God's help. She's a determined woman and once on her feet there'll be no stopping her.'

I stared at him and I realized that he didn't know. When

Sarah rang she mustn't have left any details. Except that Margaret had had an accident and was in hospital. He didn't know that even with God's help Margaret would never be up and about again.

'No one's spoken to you about her?' I asked.

'No. I called at the house but there was no one there. Sarah had left the name of the hospital so I thought you might be here.' He looked at me closely, but I couldn't be certain of what he saw in my eyes. 'What's wrong, Peter?' he asked. 'There is something wrong.'

I told him, realizing that I was using him. I wanted to hurt him, because through him I could hurt myself. I told him in the way that the ghouls might relate the details of an accident they'd witnessed; all about the blood and the entrails and the bits of body lying on the road. There were no entrails in my story, but I more than made up for it.

We call ourselves human beings, and think ourselves above the animal. But the animal if he only had the sense would deny us. The animal, it is said, can sense evil, and had there been an animal in the ward it would have slunk away from me. That afternoon I would have denied the existence of God, but not of the devil. He was there beside me and I was his willing servant. But I didn't see him because I wasn't looking for my own reflection.

The old priest had anointed the dead in Korea, or rather the bits of the bodies that had been human beings before the bombings. No man should be asked to do that, but someone has to. Someone has to scrape up the bits of flesh and someone has to anoint them. Now I had transported Father Mason back to those days, only this time the body was of someone he loved.

'I didn't know,' he said, and I waited for him to turn to God, but even the priest was aware that God could do nothing. Miracles were for other peoples and times and places. Not for the ward of a Hampstead hospital on a sunny afternoon.

'So it requires a bit more than masses and prayers,' I said.

'We must be thankful for life,' he said; 'and you must not doubt the power of prayer. God works in strange ways and we cannot always see the reason or purpose. But there is a reason . . . there always is.' He stared at me as if daring that I should contradict him, but I'd already had my say and was beginning to regret.

'Margaret might not see His purpose,' I said.

'It's going to be difficult,' he said, 'and so soon after the baby. That was a terrible blow for her.'

'It wasn't a blow,' I said, 'but just an opportunity for her to play the martyr. She might not find it so easy now when her own life is the spoils.'

'You'll have to be strong for her,' he said. 'It won't be easy because you will have to be strong for yourself too.'

'It's too late for that,' I said. 'It's all over between us. I was going to leave her before this happened.'

He was hurt again, the bullets I was firing going deep into his flesh. 'I knew things were a bit shaky between you,' he said, 'but I didn't know about this . . .' He shifted his weight on the chair, and shook his head to himself, finding for a second time in the space of some minutes that God again could do nothing. 'You have to think of the children,' he added. 'You can only consider yourselves when you've considered them.'

'You should be telling this to Margaret,' I said bitterly.

'I'll tell her,' he said. 'It takes two to make a marriage as well as to break it.'

'I'm glad you agree. Maybe she's only reaping what she's sown. Though she wouldn't accept that of course. She only takes the bits that suit her. Like we should love our enemies and lie down and allow them to trample all over us.'

I wanted him to fight back – to damn me as he had

damned that bishop so long ago. In the pain he might inflict I could find some solace. I could hide behind it and use it to justify what I'd done. He was God's representative, and God had done all this to me. It seemed right that His representative should suffer, like one complains to the shop assistant about the shoddy goods. But Father Mason had nothing with which to fight, and he remained silent.

'I must go,' I said when I couldn't bear the silence any longer, and he came with me, a barrier between us now that had never been there before. It was entirely of my making; Father Mason had done nothing to form it. We said our farewells in the car park and shook hands because we were civilized.

'We've known each other a long time now, Peter,' he said to me, 'so I'm talking to you as a friend, not as a priest.' He rubbed his cheek with his hand, knowing what he had to say but unable to find the words. He had been more at home in the cold ward than out here in the sunshine. He should have gone back to Korea, where he could have preached to the ones who had never heard of God. He had nothing to offer someone like me who had lost faith in God a long time ago.

'Don't do anything foolish,' he said to me. 'Margaret needs you now more than she's ever needed you before.' I opened my mouth to speak, but he hurried on. 'I know all the arguments . . . I know what you're going to say . . . But we have to forgive and forget; we can't live with hatred and bitterness.'

'Maybe God should forgive and forget too,' I said. I hesitated a moment. 'Are you coming back to the house?' I asked.

'I can't,' he said, 'I've got to get back to Dorset this evening.' He too hesitated, but there was nothing more to say.

I knew that I'd hurt him, and as I pulled away he stood by his old Morris 1000 to watch me. I'd hurt him for the decision I'd made this morning – for what I'd done at Feltham, and for the fact that the only chance I'd got for a new life for myself might be evaporating at this very minute into thin air.

Yet it wasn't me who'd hurt him, but the man who had taken over and now controlled me. The man who sometimes frightened me with his hatred and his anger. Who sometimes wanted to hurt like a child might want to hurt, and at other times wanted to be loved like a child might want to be loved. The thoughts jumbled up in my mind as I drove home and they were still jumbled up when I got there.

Sarah was in the kitchen cooking dinner and the girls were in the sitting-room watching television. I told them that I'd just seen their mother and that she had had an operation on her leg and that the doctors said that she was doing fine; and that maybe soon they could visit her. I lied to them, as we all lie to children and then wonder why they no longer trust us.

Sarah had cried her fill and there was a redness around her eyes to remind me. I thought that she might have some words of reproach for me, but her tears must have washed them all away. She was out of place in that big clinical kitchen. The white tiles covering every inch of available wall space up to five feet from the floor weren't hers. And she hated the brown quarry tiles on the floor – a danger to children and cold discomfort to bare feet winter or summer. It was Margaret's kitchen – a place for cooking in. There was no room within its walls for living.

I laid the pine table we kept in the kitchen – the dining-room was only used on occasions. It was something to take my mind off the picture I had of Margaret in a wheelchair in this room, a rug covering the empty space where her legs should have been.

Clare chattered about school while we ate, excited because she was going on an outing to the zoo. 'I want to see the giraffes,' she said. 'They're so funny.' She giggled at the image her child's mind conjured up, and I desperately wanted to share it with her. But my image of spindly legs and a long neck most likely wouldn't be her image anyway. Clare still had the ability to weave the child's fantasy around that ungainly creature.

But Nuala had lost the magic. Watching her sitting across from me, it was difficult to imagine that she might ever had had it. She caught my eyes and held my gaze across the few feet of space between us, the blankness in her expression almost frightening. It was too much for me and I looked away.

'I saw Father Mason at the hospital,' I said to Sarah, 'but he couldn't come back with me. He had to go back to Dorset today.'

'I knew he'd call,' she said.

'Mom was anointed?' Nuala stared at me with a child's expression now. 'You just said that she was OK.'

'He didn't anoint her,' I said. 'He just called to visit.' It was the truth, but I felt that I was lying because Margaret had been anointed.

'Oh.' She believed me only because Sarah hadn't contradicted what I said. But it wasn't Nuala's fault. It was Margaret who had taught her not to trust me.

She had allowed the girls to feel her stomach when the baby kicked, and had told them that I wanted to destroy it, gritting her teeth because she thought that anything to do with reproduction was dirty. They had seen their brother through the glass in the Baby Care Unit, and were told that I didn't want him to have his operations, their child's minds equating the baby's suffering with me. They had attended his funeral and had seen the tiny white box lowered into the wet earth, Margaret and Sarah crying, myself as cold as the December day, raw as the wind that mercilessly punished exposed flesh. It didn't end there though – my affair with Barbara added new fuel. Margaret told them about my new woman; how I loved her and not them; how they wouldn't have a father any more.

To my surprise it had been Nuala who had been the more affected. It was a teenager's reaction. She had just found out about life and love, not the closeness and security that love can bring, but the biological aspect of it, the cold explicit facts of sex. Nearly all children are shocked when they realize that their parents still make love. For Nuala it was a double shock because I made love with another woman. I had the added horror of mortal sin.

Nuala had never mentioned the possibility of my leaving her, but Clare on the other hand had clung, putting her arms about my neck one night, giving me the impression that she would never let go. She only had to speak and I would do her bidding, but she never said a word. She was the weak link in my determination to make a new life for myself, the only hope Margaret had of holding on to me if she only realized it. We could have been a family sharing joys and sorrows alike, but we were human before we were anything else – we had the capability of losing everything.

After dinner Sarah and I went to the hospital and silently sat by Margaret's bedside. She was still in a world of drugs and pain, and she drifted towards us a few times. Though Sarah spoke to her, I'm sure that Margaret was not aware of our presence. Her face was pale and might have been lost in the whiteness of the pillow if it wasn't for the short dark hair that outlined it, and the eyebrows like two black feathers that had come out from the pillow's stuffing.

Sarah had brought a picture of 'The Sacred Heart', and she placed it on the bedside locker among the medical paraphernalia. It was a cheap, plastic-framed picture, garish and almost vulgar; it had no place among the drips and the machinery and the suffering. There was no need for a reminder of torn flesh and pierced hearts and blood in here.

I didn't comment on the picture; nor on the flowers and

digestive biscuits and Lucozade which Sarah had also brought. It was her guarantee that Margaret had a future, that she would live. That one day she would eat the biscuits and drink the Lucozade, and on another day would come home.

We stayed until the bell rang and a couple of minutes beyond, playing out a role to the end. We hovered a moment by the bedside among the tubes and the wires. Sarah had her Holy Water and she traced the cross on Margaret's forehead with a wet finger. Later they would send her to Lourdes to bathe in the miraculous waters.

The idea angered me and I wanted to shout 'Leave her alone.' Let Sarah find her own way to the kingdom of Heaven, and not through the suffering of others. It was like black marketeers making money on the misfortunes of people who had no defence against them. But I realized that Margaret would want the ritual as a mother in time of famine might need the loaf of bread. It said something to me about faith but what it said was later to be proved wrong. I didn't know then that God was to take Margaret's faith and give it to me, and then to tempt me as the devil tempted Christ when he offered Him the world. But my reward was to lose the world, not gain it.

I didn't kiss the face or touch it with my fingertips because I couldn't pretend. We left Margaret to the nurse who had hovered in the background during our visit. She hadn't wanted to intrude into our tragedy, but she was unaware that the only compassion we had was for ourselves.

We went out into the cool evening and I was glad to be away from any reminders of my vulnerability. There was a lot of traffic and people about, proof that the world still went on, that none of us is indispensable.

I took Sarah back to the house and stopped outside on the road. 'Aren't you coming in?' she said. 'You know the girls need you.'

'That's strange,' I said. 'They've never needed me before.' I watched her in the rear-view mirror, her body sunk into the seat, a bulging sack of potatoes that a farmer had wrapped some clothes round, then stuck a head on top to frighten away the crows. He had pushed the head down until the ear lobes touched what would have been the shoulders, and the chin hung over the edge as if it had been added as an afterthought.

'Your place is at home,' she said, 'with your family.'

'I don't have a family,' I said, the bitterness in my voice surprising me.

'You have children . . . and a wife . . . They need you.'

'Margaret never needed anyone.'

'She needs you now,' she said. 'You're all she's got.'

Seventeen years was a long time to wait for someone to realize the truth. But now I only wanted to mock her foolishness, for I was the very one Margaret did not have. Sarah and Martin would not live for ever, and children have their own lives. I was the one Margaret needed; a slave to the crippled – a wheelchair pusher; the one who would lift her in and out of the bath, wearing gloves and with eyes averted of course. She wouldn't want me to feel tempted, not for my benefit but for her own. God after all would forgive me because I didn't know any better.

'I've got to go,' I said.

'No good'll come of it,' she said. 'You'll damn both your souls.'

'If only we all worried about our own souls,' I said, 'and didn't worry about others. If I'm not damned for this I'll be damned for something else.'

'You'll regret it,' she said, 'but only when it's too late.' She made to say something else, thought better of it, and began the struggle to get out of the car.

I left her on the pavement solid in her tweed suit and severe hat, her handbag clasped before her. She had an aura of permanency, and I knew that no one would take the world from her. What I didn't know was that one day she would help to take the world from me.

5

Barbara must have watched me arrive, for she had the door open, and she put her arms about my neck the moment I was in the hall. She pressed her small breasts against me, bringing my passion out from where the day had hidden it. 'I rang you,' she said, 'but you weren't at work.'

'I got your message,' I said, trying to kiss and talk at the same time.

'Am I forgiven?' she asked. She knew the answer to the question, but like the child who knows the ending to the fairy story, and yet still wants to hear again how the princess was rescued by the dashing prince, she wanted the reassurance of my forgiveness.

'You're forgiven,' I said, aware of the reason why there had to be forgiveness. It might be forgotten now, but it would raise its ugly head again.

'I'm glad,' she said, nestling close to me. 'I was rotten to you last night.'

'At least we won't be able to fight about that again,' I said.

'Did they have to amputate?'

'There wasn't any choice. So our fight was for nothing.'

'No,' she said, pulling away from me, 'it wasn't for nothing. It showed us what can happen . . . There will be other decisions just like that one. We have to learn not to fight over them.'

'Well, as long as there are no decisions tonight,' I said, aware that there was always tomorrow. We'd fight until there was nothing left to fight about, and when that happened it would be over between us. Standing there with the intimacy of our embrace still warm about me, it was still possible to imagine a time when we would be strangers. And yet strangers wasn't the right description. For to be strangers implied the possibility of getting to know each other – of being friends. But for Barbara and myself all that would be in the past, the memory of it all too real.

'Tonight is peace night,' she said, 'and you're taking me to dinner.'

'I am?'

'Soon as I get my shawl; I've booked a table.'

'What if I hadn't come?'

She smiled, and there was an assurance and certainty in her eyes that she would always get what she wanted.

On the way to the restaurant I went over the day's events, finding it difficult to imagine that it had been such a short time ago since I had agreed to the amputation. I told her about John and how I had allowed self-preservation and the good of the company to destroy our friendship.

'You can't blame yourself,' she said. 'It's a tough world.' She reached out her hand and touched my cheek with her fingertips, the skin pleasant against my own. But I could also feel her long fingernails, and I knew what they could do to my flesh. She smiled at me, and it would have been easy to pretend that this was the real woman. But as in cheap, three-dimensional pictures, where the movement of the eyes brings another view of the object into vision, so it was now with Barbara. I kept seeing the other side of her character: the side she hid behind the smile and the hint of make-up and the small teeth that flashed like a toothpaste advertisement. It was the cold businesswoman, who could bring to bear in her private life the same ruthlessness she applied in her business one.

Barbara wanted children, wanted a family before the change of life sucked her dry and left her with nothing more permanent than her name above a small office in Islington, and the comfortable life-style that her business had allowed her. At thirty-five she had already felt the approach of the menopause and had tasted fear – for the first time in her life, I supposed, forgetting all those years when I hadn't known her; enough time for an army of fears to march through her, leaving terror in their wake like the terror that remains when you wake from a nightmare, not certain if the echo of the scream you can still hear is real or imagined.

Barbara's fear was my enemy. It was the fear that would cast me from her; it was the fear that had sent me away last night and the fear that telephoned me today because it is easier to be frightened and with someone than to be frightened and alone. I could pretend that it was love that telephoned, but I would be fooling only myself. It was the fear that would decide my future, the fear that I had to overcome. The love after all was on my side.

At the restaurant we were led to our favourite table, and for a while I just savoured the privilege of having money and success, and a beautiful woman and the attention of the waiters. We had kebabs for starters, and then chicken and mushrooms and potato and rice and nan, and two glasses of cold lager. We sat and ate and chatted about the food, and about Barbara's plans to go to the US on holiday in August. 'I haven't been on holiday in two years,' she said, 'so I think that after my battle to survive the recession I deserve four weeks.'

We didn't talk about our problems but they were there with us, as real as the tables and the chairs and the lighted candles, and the lager like glasses of liquid sunbeams.

The restaurant was full up, but like all good restaurants it didn't appear crowded. There were groups, loud and jolly, and couples like ourselves, quiet and reflective, maybe hiding their own hells. Or just sharing their joy, for I knew that life brought that too.

We had coffee to finish, the cream covering the bitter sweet liquid. It was like life in a way, life bounded by conventions. We lived a pretence, even with ourselves, and underneath the veneer the doubts bubbled. In wild-life films we saw nature in the raw – the 'kill or be killed' law of the jungle. We professed our horror, but only because it came close to ourselves, to the animal that lurked within us. We knew what we wanted, but we had trained our animal and had burnt his feet with hot-plates like they trained the dancing bears of old.

'So she will live after all,' Barbara said now. A candle flame danced in each eye, giving an appearance of jollity, but I wasn't fooled. There was always the possibility that the bear might forget.

'I never really doubted that she would,' I said.

'So what happens to you and me now?'

'We'll get ourselves sorted out. We'll be happy yet.'

'Do you really believe that?'

'I have to believe it,' I said. 'When I stop believing it I die.' It wasn't strictly true, for my doubts were stronger than my beliefs. 'I want to live with you,' I said. 'One day I will do so. But I have another life too; whether I like the idea or not it exists. I have to think of my daughters, and though I don't love my wife I have to consider her too. Pity isn't a lot to give but it's all I've got for her. At the moment it's tying me to her more tightly than love ever could. I can't walk out on her now . . . But when she recovers – well, then, you and I will start our own life. My Catholic conscience, as you call it, will be clear. Now how's that?'

'A long speech . . . if you mean it.'

'Why wouldn't I?'

'Maybe you don't love me.' She had her elbows on the table and her body hunched forward, and she watched me. Had I not known her I might have thought her vulnerable, and I would have been pleased that she needed my love so badly. But I did know her, or I thought I did and so I didn't try to fool her.

'I don't love my wife,' I said, 'and there is no other woman in my life. I've been alone for too long. If I lose you now I know that I will not find someone else. You're my last hope.'

'You make me seem like some rescue service,' she laughed.

I reached across and squeezed her hand. 'You are a rescue service,' I said. 'Come on, we'll go home.' I beckoned the waiter and gave him my credit card. He returned with the slip which I signed. I gave him a one pound tip and he beamed all over his dark, sad face. He led the way to the door and held it open for us.

'Goodnight, Mrs Ferson,' he said. 'Goodnight, Mr Ferson.'

I saw Barbara flinch, and the irony hit me like the slap of a wet wind on a street corner. I found myself leaving my good feelings of a moment before behind me in the restaurant, and the waiter closed the door, cutting them off from me. I took Barbara's arm and felt her shiver, and I led her to the car. 'He saw the name on the credit card,' I said, 'and he just put two and two together. In fact he took us for man and wife. Don't you see . . . in a way you are my wife – more than Margaret ever was.'

'No,' she said. 'No . . .' She said something else when she was in the car, but I'd closed the door and it was lost.

I got in beside her and started the engine. 'It'll soon warm up,' I said, reaching across and squeezing her hand. But it was no longer the hand I'd squeezed in the restaurant. 'Don't let it upset you,' I added. 'He was only trying to be nice.'

She turned to look at me and for a moment I thought she was going to cry. And then it was just a reflection of the street lamp in her eyes, the light playing tricks in the gloom. 'Mrs Ferson,' she said half to herself. 'If we can fool others how much easier it is to fool ourselves. I'll never be Mrs Ferson; there will only be the one.'

'Nonsense,' I said. 'One day we will laugh about this.'

'We'll laugh all right,' she said. 'Now would you please take me home, Peter.'

I stopped for a red traffic light further on and an old Anglia pulled in beside us, the car held together by road grime. There was a young man driving with a passenger beside him who should have been at home doing her school work. She had her arms about his neck and was nibbling his ear-lobe as if he was a gingerbread man. They sensed me watching and they turned to look. He said something, obviously of great wit, for they both laughed. Then the lights changed and he sped away before me, the car laying down a smoke screen.

I envied them and I was old enough to be their father. They had the freshness of youth, their whole lives before them, no strings yet to tie them down. Tonight they would make love, no risk of pregnancy because the girl would be on the pill, no promises because he wouldn't know how to make them and she wouldn't know how to ask. They might even have another laugh at the middle-aged couple they saw in the flash car, beyond it of course, sex but a memory.

It saddened me, and I felt a melancholy creep over me like the heavy sweet smell of incense in my youth. Like the quietness in the church, then the tinkle of the bell and the restrained murmur of the congregation. There had been something missing, though, like watching a magician and knowing how the trick is done. But all around me they didn't know, and they lifted up their eyes to the saviour. And the bread was white in the priest's hands, and I bowed my head with all the rest, but only so that they might not see my doubts. Just as I wanted to hide my face now so that Barbara wouldn't see my uncertainty.

We arrived at her flat and I pulled into the slip road. The

four parking spaces were occupied, Barbara's Metro occupying one of them. 'You'll have to park on the main road,' she said.

'I didn't think you'd want me to come in,' I said.

There must have been something in my voice, because she turned to look at me. 'I want you for myself,' she said, 'but I know I shall never have you. I want to hate your wife because she comes between us. I want to hate your daughters too, but because you love them I want to love them. They're a part of you, something neither Margaret or myself can ever be. If I was a Catholic I would have been taught how to pray. I would go down on my knees every day and pray to God to let me have you. I would pray that He would take Margaret because she prevents me from having you. And if that didn't work and I got the chance I would wring her neck like you'd kill a chicken. I wouldn't care if there were a thousand hells and I should burn in them all for ever.'

I said nothing – I had no words. I watched a bus go down the hill, the heads and shoulders of people highlighted in the windows. The laburnum by the exit to the slip road was in flower, and the street lamp gave the flowers a cotton-wool appearance and a shade of orangey yellow. They were like tiny glowing lanterns, unreal – too good to be true. It was as if they had a latent power to do harm to me as Barbara had the power to hurt me.

'I've shocked you,' she said. 'But that's the Catholicism in you. It's like the grain in the wood; you can no more get rid of it than you can cut the grain out of the timber.'

'It might not be a bad thing to have,' I said, 'in view of what you've been saying.'

'I should send you home,' she said, 'but I've been too lonely these last few days. Come on – park the car before I change my mind.'

I wanted to tell her to go to hell, but the need passed and I did what she asked. In the flat she made coffee and we sat in the kitchen to drink it, a kitchen which was smaller than the one at home but just as impersonal. The only warm part of this flat was the hall, which Barbara had never touched, leaving the oak panelling as it was. And there was warmth in the big double bed with its sheets and pillow-slips and continental quilt from Harrods, part of the warmth being in the aura of the name itself. It conjured up money and security, as if one might actually outlast their superb goods.

But the room itself was cold, with its arctic-white embossed paper and polished wooden floor and white wardrobes and dressing table and bedside cabinets. There was a teamaker and radio alarm clock combination which never failed to give me the impression of being the control panel for some horrible instrument of torture.

The room was always tidy. There were never any underclothes or tights or shoes lying about. The dressing table was always neat and ordered, never any tops off bottles or wisps of hair in the comb or brush. It wasn't that I liked untidiness, but even something amiss – a ball of cotton-wool stained with mascara, a discarded tissue, a tea stain by the teamaker – would have been an indication that a human being used the room.

We used it later, if used is the word. It was fulfilling animal desires I felt rather than making love. There was passion and pleasure, and the long long moments of suspension and Barbara's moans, and then what is part of our own dying.

Making love is a strange phenomenon. Beforehand it is passion and excitement and tension – the craving need of the body for release; and afterwards the relaxation and the peace. But tonight there was no peace – the first time that this had happened. We both sensed it as we lay in the darkness, but we didn't speak about it.

Barbara didn't offer any protest when I eased myself out of the bed. I dressed in the dark, finding my clothes by feel alone. 'I'll call tomorrow night,' I said to her, leaning on the bed to kiss her. 'You don't have any objections?'

'Should I have?'

'I don't know.'

'You call,' she said, 'if you want.'

I left her then, neither of us speaking about love. I knew she would get up when I'd gone and tidy her clothes, which she'd thrown on the floor when she'd undressed. She would lay out her outfit for tomorrow, have a bath, make a cup of coffee. She would wander around the empty flat, which I had the feeling now would always be empty.

It was to be our home when I left my wife, at least until the children came along. Then we would buy a bungalow with a large garden and have swings and see-saws and slides and a pond with fish and lilies in it. And the pond would drown the children and the swings and slides would stand forlorn, and rot and rust and be a reminder of our damnation.

Always before I had regretted leaving Barbara, had only got out of the bed with the greatest reluctance. I would make coffee, and we would drink it in bed, the glow from the teamaker softening somewhat that harsh room. We would talk and plan and promise. But tonight I wanted none of it, and I was glad that I had a single bed and that I could be alone. For I couldn't be certain that when I was asleep and my guard was down my guilt would not be visible for everyone to see.

6

I went to my office the next morning glad to get back to routine, to have problems to deal with which demanded nothing of myself. I didn't visit the hospital in the afternoon but I spoke to the sister on the phone.

'Your wife is comfortable,' she said. 'Her parents are visiting at the moment, but I'm afraid that the patient is asleep.'

But I couldn't escape the evening visit, and I had to sit with Sarah and Martin and endure an hour of almost total silence. Earlier that evening Margaret had had surgery to remove a blood clot, and she was once again in the world which she had inhabited for the past few days.

Sitting there the place depressed me, its bright paintwork and polished floor and its view of the Heath from the window seeming to mock the sick, lined in a row along the length of the ward. I had never been really ill in my life, and illness in any form appalled me. Illness makes some people want to devote their lives to helping the sick; but I just want to be where there are no reminders of suffering.

Later that evening I visited Barbara and drank more whisky than was good for me, but the depression remained. It seemed to rub off on Barbara, and the thought that we were of little comfort to each other at the very time we needed to be only depressed me even more. And I came away after a little while glad to be alone.

The whisky waited all night for me, and the next morning I discovered that I had merely swapped one hell for another. But this hell by comparison was bearable, and by the time I reached my office a couple of aspirins had eased it. And even if they hadn't, there were enough problems on my desk to take my mind off the severest of hangovers.

It was mid-morning when the sister from the hospital rang me and told me that my wife was conscious and wanted to see me.

'Are you certain?' I asked, my surprise making me forget myself for a moment.

'Certain of what, Mr Ferson?' She had an Irish brogue that caressed like a warm wind previously softened by gentle rain.

'You . . . you say she wants to see me?'

'Dying to see you, she is. Wants to know if you will be in to see her. I told her that I would ring you and that you would be coming in to see her straight away.'

'I'm afraid I can't come,' I said. 'I've got a meeting . . .'

'I think you should come,' she said.

'It's not possible . . .'

'I think you should make it possible,' she said, and her brogue now reminded me of granite and frost and stinging rain. 'We can only make her physically better, Mr Ferson . . . it's her family who can help her the most if you follow me. She will only have blame for us.'

But she wouldn't blame them; the blame would be mine alone. She would know that I didn't care, and I wondered if she would realize that at first I had wished that she should die. What would she see in my agreeing to the amputation but a wish to hurt and defile her; a wish for revenge because of the baby – because of the way she had treated me.

'I can come now,' I said to the sister, 'but you'll have to allow me in before visiting.'

'It would be breaking the rules,' she said, 'but the once won't kill us.' She'd softened the brogue a little and the rain was gentle again.

I informed my secretary that I would be away for a few

hours, and I left my work problems behind me on the desk. In the car apprehension began to gnaw at me, and my thoughts began to dip and fly like a child's kite. 'She wants to see you,' the sister had said. 'Dying to see you. . .' I might have laughed at the absurdity of her words if it wasn't for the tension within me.

I stopped at a florist's and bought two dozen red roses. My mind still on the confrontation to come, I came back out on to the pavement. There was a newsagent's next door to the florist's and the wheelchair must have emerged from there. Or else it was coming along the pavement and in my preoccupation with my thoughts I hadn't noticed it at first. But now it was before me as if it had materialized from the air.

I was used to wheelchairs – one sees them regularly on the London streets – but this was the first time I had really noticed one. It wasn't just any chair – it was our chair, the 'our' written in letters ten feet high. I stared at the woman in the chair and I suppose she mistook me for one of those people who make life difficult for the disabled by staring at them. But it wasn't the woman I actually saw but Margaret.

Up to now my images of Margaret as a cripple were unreal . . . like colour must be unreal to a blind man. But now the image became too real; it was harsh and stark in the sunshine. Suddenly I became aware that I had stopped on the pavement and was blocking the wheelchair's progress. I mumbled an apology and stepped past, not looking back. But I was aware of eyes watching me.

I continued my journey, my thoughts on what awaited me. Blame and accusation, I imagined, and a desire on Margaret's part to hurt me. But I couldn't weaken my resolve, otherwise the wheelchair would become mine, a growth on my life like a cancer that could never be cut out. I would have only whisky to turn to then, and I knew too well the price that that balm demanded.

At the hospital I met the sister, small and plump and red-faced, with twinkling blue eyes that defied me to think that she could ever say a harsh word to anyone. 'Come in,' she said. 'Who cares that you'll get me the sack.' She led the way across to the bed where Margaret seemed asleep. 'Mrs Ferson,' she said, 'I've got a visitor for you.'

Margaret opened her eyes and stared at us, not certain if we were real or not. 'Your husband, Mrs Ferson,' the sister went on, 'come all the way to see you. Brought you flowers too, he has. Here, let me have them,' she said to me, 'and I'll put them in water.'

Margaret smiled, a crinkling around the mouth that only the eyes saved from being a grimace. The feeling of the smile was in the eyes for a moment, and then there was only the pain and the fear. I smiled at her, a practised reaction, and somewhere inside of me I felt my useless pity.

'Peter,' she said quite clearly, and she reached out her hand to me. My hesitation was momentary and I stepped forward and took her hand. It was soft and pliable – as if someone had moulded plasticine around the skeleton of a wrist and fingers. An old skeleton, because the bones felt brittle and seemed as if they would snap like twigs. So I held the hand lightly, but she gripped with a strength that surprised me.

Tears welled up in her eyes and ran into the creases on her face – deep furrows of some African tribal ritual. Crying was a trick she had utilized in the past, at a time when she still wanted me for herself as distinct from now when she wanted no one else to have me. It hadn't worked all those years ago and she had dispensed with it, using it only in times of grief for the relief I supposed it brought her.

This crying was no trick and it touched my pity; and for a moment I felt human. I took my handkerchief from my pocket with my free hand and held out the white square of linen to her. Her left arm had a drip attached and was immobilized. But she made no move to take the handkerchief in her right hand, which still gripped my fingers tightly.

The tears flowed, running round by her ear and wetting the pillow. I bent down close to her face and, avoiding her eyes, wiped the wetness from her skin. It was the first charitable act I'd done for her in ages; indeed, the first charitable act I'd done for anyone. It was a moment to repent, but instead I began to bluster to cover up my weakness. 'It's all right,' I said, 'there's no need to cry . . . everything is fine.'

'Peter,' she said again, the grip on my hand getting tighter, if that was possible. 'I'm frightened, Peter . . . what's happened to me?'

'It's OK,' I said, 'you'll be fine . . . really fine.' I looked for help from the sister, but she had gone to get a vase for the flowers. 'There's no need to worry,' I went on, feeling inadequate. 'You'll be out of here in no time.'

'Will I?' she asked.

'Of course you will,' I encouraged, aware that I was betraying her cruelly. It wasn't a deliberate betrayal, because I couldn't have told her the truth – told her that she would be out all right, but out to what? To the world of the invalid . . . to the wheelchair . . . to dependence on others. To the world of fear which she now sensed, and the world of bitterness which it would become. How could I tell her that she would never walk again? That the earth no longer belonged to her?

'Sit beside me,' she said.

'I'll get a chair.' I tried to move away but she wouldn't release my hand.

'Sit on the bed,' she said, 'here beside me.' For a moment our eyes were locked and then she started to cry again. 'I'm sorry,' she said, 'I'm sorry . . .' The crying came from deep within her and I could feel her churning up inside. Again it touched my pity, but apart from that I felt cold and alien as if I had no emotions.

I sat on the bed and stared out of the window at the Heath and the trees and the people, wanting to be out there with them. Away from the crying that travelled up my arm to register on me as if I was a machine for measuring the torment in another person's soul. I still had the handkerchief in my hand, crumpled up and gripped tightly as if it were my lost emotions I had in my fist and I was frightened of releasing them. So I sat beside her and held her hand, but she was as much a stranger to me as the woman I'd seen earlier in the wheelchair.

'Would you dry my face?' she asked.

I nodded, and I dabbed away the tears. 'You can put the handkerchief away now,' she said. 'I won't need it any more.'

'I can't stay long,' I said. 'I have a meeting this afternoon.'

'I'm glad you came,' she said. 'I've been so frightened. They . . . they wouldn't tell me anything but I know something terrible is wrong . . . I can feel it.'

'You've just had a bad accident, that's all,' I said.

'You wouldn't lie to me?' She pulled me around to face her and I could see her fear.

'No,' I said. 'I wouldn't lie to you.' It was the worst form of deceit – like promising the future to the dying – but there was no other way. To tell her the truth required kindness and understanding, and both were sadly lacking in me. I averted my eyes in case she should see the lies in them, and at the same time I didn't want to see the trust in hers.

'I'm sorry,' she said. 'I haven't been nice to you for a long time; but I'll make it up to you, Peter . . . I'll make it up to you for the baby. I promise.' She squeezed my fingers to tell me how much she would make it up to me but I felt nothing. For years she had made my life a misery – she'd driven me to hate her – and now it was all to be wiped away like a fingerprint on glass. A few kind words and I was to forgive everything. But I wasn't God: I had no mercy left in me. She had squeezed it out of me like she might squeeze out the last bit of toothpaste from the tube.

'You don't believe me,' she said, but there was no accusation in her voice.

'You're frightened,' I said. 'It's only natural that you should be.'

'But you have to believe me . . .' She was squeezing my hand but she was the one who wanted the reassurance. 'I thought I was going to die, Peter. When I came to myself there seemed to be only darkness . . . no heaven or hell – only the darkness.'

'You were shocked,' I said, 'that's all.'

'No, it wasn't shock. It . . . it was God showing me my life. It was Limbo, the place we go to where . . . where there isn't anything. It was because I had wronged you . . . I was frightened of the darkness – I knew I would never see anyone I knew ever again. I remember praying to God to give me life . . . to give me another chance. Not for myself but for you. I want to give you back everything you ever had.'

Silence sometimes is the most damning of all admissions. It was all I had to offer her now . . . my silence. It felt uncomfortable, like a hair shirt might feel, and I wished for something to break the force field that seemed to envelop us. It was time stretched out and strained and sharp like a frost-edged wind, and I wanted to draw my arms close to my body and huddle from it.

'I don't hate you,' she said. 'You do believe that, don't you?'

I nodded, my eyes examining the pattern of the green bedcover, a raised pattern that might have been Egyptian hieroglyphics – an ominous warning at the entrance to some tomb. It could have been a warning to me of the consequences of not forgiving and forgetting, but had a warning been written on the bedcover in letters of blood I should have paid it no heed.

'I don't think I love you either,' she said, and her admission should have told me that everything else she had said was true. But I couldn't accept that the worm could turn and in turning become human. By the time I did realize the fact the human had become a worm again and the cycle was complete. 'But I will love you,' she insisted. 'I will learn to love you again.'

She wouldn't learn to love me because you can't learn to love. And you can't teach someone to love either. I should have told her this but I remained silent, and she built her hopes for the future on such perilous ground as that.

'Peter,' she suddenly said, and her voice compelled me to look at her. 'Will you do something for me?'

'What?' I asked, wary of promises that could entwine and tangle like ivy, and suck me dry like that parasitic plant might suck the sap from the tree.

'You need to ask first?'

'I have to know, that's all,' I said, irked. 'I can't read your mind.'

'It doesn't matter now . . . it wasn't important.'

'If you say so.'

'It is important,' she said, and there was fear in her voice, as if the world was about to be taken from her. 'I want you to kiss me . . . to make everything all right.'

I wasn't prepared, and my thoughts were like frantic bluebottles trapped behind a closed window. My senses became heightened and I could pick out quite clearly the noises around me: voices and the sound of an air-conditioning fan, and quick footsteps in the corridor, and the hiss of compressed air and a chorus of bleeps like the song of some electronic bird. I could see that the windows needed cleaning and that there was a ragged edge of white paint around the glass. And I could smell the hospital, not only the smell of disinfectant and surgical spirit, but the overpowering smell of sickness and suffering.

I had to be in some sort of trance – some outside power had control of me. Otherwise I would never have bent down close to that face and kissed it. It wasn't really a kiss; no more than the touch of my lips against her forehead, but I still averted my eyes from hers in case she should see the Judas in me. I wanted to think that I wasn't betraying her; she had asked and I merely complied. But she had asked me if she would be OK and I had lied. The kiss was an enforcing of that deceit.

It is easy to look back and say what should have been. After all, the pain that blinded me then had eased. The memory of my son does not have the capability of hurting me any more. But that day it had its potency and its need of reparation. Yet I kissed her as if none of that existed, as if I'd never had a reason to hate her.

But at times we are driven to do strange things, even to kiss the one we do not love. Even if the kiss should be no different from touching your lips against a window-pane wet from condensation, and having no more sense of feeling than that of cold and dampness. Margaret had killed my feelings for her, and now, coming to realize that she needed me, she wanted to revive them. She wanted to love me and to make me happy, but on her terms, not mine.

I think she was aware of the fact that we might have no future together no matter what – or was aware as anyone could be in her condition. At least, that's what I read into her silence, and to the fact that she released my hand.

'I have to go,' I said, mouthing my words at a piece of white pillow slip, avoiding her eyes.

'How are the girls?' she asked, the first time she'd allowed anyone else to be included in our conversation.

'They're fine. They haven't been in to see you yet. Sarah and I thought it best to wait until you were a bit better.'

'Will you bring them tonight? I want to see them.'

'If you want.'

'And Martin . . . is he taking it badly?'

'Not now,' I said, 'that you are going to be OK.'

'He would be hurt,' she said. 'He would be hurt more than anyone.'

'He'll get over it,' I said, aware that there was only so much digging he could do, and that he couldn't go on mowing the lawn for ever. But he would never get over it; none of us ever would.

'I'm glad you came,' she said.

'I only had the half hour,' I said. 'I must go.' I got to my feet. 'I'll bring the girls this evening, then.'

'Do,' she said, and her eyes asked for other things I could never give her.

I turned away from her and walked out before she could make any more demands of me. I left her to the ward and the sun streaming through the window, and the world beyond the glass that she would never again possess. On my way out I noticed the roses lying discarded on the sister's desk. She had obviously been called away to deal with something more important than flowers.

Outside the hospital I had a chance to assimilate my thoughts. I'd tried to imagine beforehand what our meeting would be like, but I could only picture Margaret as I had known her. That Margaret would not forget or ask forgiveness. So I had pictured it as a meeting of blame and accusation, not of reconciliation and a wish to be human again. But it was too late for that, like rain after a long drought; all our love was long since shrivelled and dead. We could no more be man and wife again than the desert could bloom or the earth stop spinning.

I knew that I could never hate her again; hatred, like love, could die. It wasn't because my son didn't matter any more, but because the score was now settled. In view of the pain that would soon be hers, I no longer had the power to hurt her.

I saw her reaction to me as a direct result of the accident and the fright she had received, and I knew it would not last. She would become the cold woman again, and have extra reason for her coldness. Though I might pity her, I knew that I could never love her, and I could not base a relationship on pity.

I would help Margaret as much as I could, help her to make a new life for herself without me. Beyond that I couldn't go. Or at least, so I thought. I didn't know that in a few months I would be stripped bare to my vulnerable humanity, and that that in the end would demand everything of me.

7

It rained that evening. I came home to find Clare waiting for me in the hall, hopping from one foot to the other. 'Gran says I can go to the hospital,' she said. 'You're going to take me, aren't you, daddy?'

'I'll take you,' I said, not caring now that the summer had gone.

Her face lit up and she turned and ran into the kitchen and I heard her voice glad as Christmas. I stood still for a moment surrounded by Margaret's influence – her wall-paper and her paintings and her telephone seat and her grandfather clock and her parquet floor beneath my feet – and despite it all I was happy for a moment.

We left after dinner and went first to Cricklewood to collect Martin. 'It's great news,' he said, when we told him that Margaret was conscious, 'great news indeed.'

Clare chattered on the way from Cricklewood, but at the hospital she fell silent. In the lift she put her hand in mine and I knew that she was both frightened and excited at the same time. Her simple gesture made me human, made me realize that someone loved me and trusted me. That some-one depended on me and could turn to me for solace. I held the tiny hand tightly and could only think what a fool I was.

I had spent so much time searching – for success and money and happiness . . . and for love. And all that time I had had it but was too blind to see. And because I was blind I'd lost out on the simple things – like the pleasure a man feels when his little daughter puts her hand in his because she needs him. It is unselfish love, for the child asks only for love in return. I wanted to pick her up and hold her in my arms like I used to when she was a baby; but instead I just tightened my grip on her hand and tried to obliterate from my mind the thought that one day soon I planned to leave her.

Someone had brushed Margaret's hair, and maybe they had put a little make-up on her cheeks because her face was no longer lost against the white of the pillow. We let the girls go first and they kissed her, Clare suddenly shy and retreating to my side. Martin shook his daughter's hand, as shy as Clare, but he had no one to retreat to. Sarah was not to be outdone by anyone, and she bent over the bed and began to cry.

'Why is gran crying?' Clare asked in a frightened whisper.

'She's just happy,' I said, 'people sometimes cry when they're happy.' But Sarah wasn't crying because she was happy but because of the fact that there were no legs beneath the bedcover. She cried a little, then straightened up and moved away and began to dry her eyes.

I had a clear view of Margaret now; she looked at me and smiled and I could only think how strong my pity was, and how the thought of an innocent child like Clare being deceived could move mountains. The pity overwhelmed me like a tidal wave, and for the first time since my son's death I felt near to tears. Tears that would be of little use to anyone but myself. But convention was there again, and grown men don't cry; and yet without the relief that the tears would bring I was helpless for the moment.

'Aren't you going to kiss mummy?' Clare asked me, releasing me from my stupor of pity and isolating me at the same time. All the attention was mine now, and it was easier to walk over to the bed and bend down to touch Margaret's forehead with my lips than to stand in the gaze of so many eyes.

It was Margaret's opportunity; she grabbed my hand and

for the second time that day I was a meter for measuring her desperation. There was no escape, and I had to remain hunched over the bed as if I was suffering from stomach cramp. It was Clare again who saved me: as if my show of affection had reassured her she approached the bed again, her shyness gone and her child's eyes on the basket of fruit which Sarah must have brought in that afternoon and which stood on the bedside locker beside my roses.

'I'm going to the zoo,' Clare said. 'We're going on a coach. I'm going to sit upstairs where all the people look funny.'

'There's no upstairs on a coach,' Nuala said. 'Everyone knows that.'

'Yes there is,' Clare insisted. 'We always sit upstairs when we go to gran's.'

'That's a bus,' Nuala scoffed. 'You won't be going to the zoo on a bus.'

'Won't we, daddy?' Clare turned to me, her face pleading.

'I don't suppose so,' I said. 'Anyway, when you're bigger you can travel on the top deck of a bus all by yourself. When you know the way you'll be able to visit your gran's on your own.'

'I know the way now,' she said, 'I know all the stops and all the buses. But I can't reach the bell yet; Nuala always rings the bell.'

'Someone will be ringing a bell here in a minute,' I said. 'There's supposed to be only two visitors at a time. I think Martin and myself had better wait in the day-room.'

'It doesn't matter,' Margaret said, trying to grip my hand tighter.

'We'd better stick to the rules,' I said. 'We'll let Sarah and the girls spend a while with you. I'm sure they've got a lot to tell you.' I took my hand from hers and turned to Martin. 'We'll wait outside,' I said, and he came with me without protest.

We sat in the day-room with half a dozen other people and watched television – a quiz for families. Maybe it just so happened that it was one of those evenings when they had genuine close families on; I don't know, to be honest, never having seen the programme before. But I could feel their warmth as if it was emanating from the screen, and it made me feel terribly lonely.

Life was but a grain of sand – the time it took an oak tree to flex itself or a building to begin to mellow. And yet we marked a hundred years with honours. For most of us a hundred years was nowhere near attainable, and yet we squandered what we were given as if there was an endless supply of tomorrows and somehow we would have enough time at the end to redress all the wrongs. We act as if there is a second chance, when we know only too well that there is only the one opportunity given.

Was there but the one chance for happiness and a man made what he could of it? Did it mean that if I did not take what I had then what I reached for would turn to dust? Along the corridor was my family; I knew my place was with them, especially now when they needed someone strong. I could walk along there and take what was mine, take what my wife had to offer and give what little I had of myself. It was all there before me for a moment; I had only to reach out and take. But pride and memory and a blind hope for the future prevented me.

'Margaret looks well enough,' Martin said, 'considering what she's been through.'

'She's a determined woman,' I said. 'She'll outlive us all.'

'It's the truth that'll kill her,' he said, 'if there's no one there to pick her up.'

'She'll be all right,' I said. 'She's survived before.'

'She managed to cope when the baby died,' he said, 'but she won't be able to cope now. I . . . I suppose you won't be staying with her?'

'No,' I said, 'I won't be staying.'

'Ah . . .' he said, 'it must be sad for a man to be always searching . . .'

There was nothing I could say to him except that I needed to search, that I needed the dreams and the hopes; even if, like the dream I'd had for a son, they should become nightmares. That was the problem with dreams – they only had the ability to hurt when you wanted them to come true.

I'd wanted a son to make up for the fact that I had lost out on my relationship with my own father. He was dead before I realized that I had loved him, and that we could have been friends. In my youth I'd gone to football matches with John, whom I'd as good as sacked the other day, and his 'old man', as he affectionately called his father. My 'old man' could have come with us but I'd never asked him to; we hadn't been close enough for that.

But I would take my son, and later when he got older he would take me. We would go to the Arsenal, or to Spurs if that was where his loyalty lay. We would sit high up in the stand and shout and wave. I would tell him about Greaves and Law and Best and 1966 and the World Cup. And how his father, a grown man, had almost cried at full time, and how later I celebrated with John; and who cared now whether Hurst's shot had crossed the line or not – we had won, hadn't we?

I shook my head to myself, overwhelmed now by sadness as earlier I had been overwhelmed by pity. There was nothing to say to Martin and he had nothing to say either, and we sat now without talking.

After a while the girls came back to us and I realized that they were as precious to me as any son. And yet I didn't know them. I didn't know their likes or dislikes – their hopes or fears. If I had had a dozen sons would I have failed them too?

'Mom wants you to go in now,' Nuala said to me.

'You go,' I said to Martin. 'I'll come in later.'

'Sarah . . .' he said, the misery of a lifetime in the one word.

'You go,' I urged. 'Margaret's your daughter too.'

'If you're sure,' he said. He got to his feet, his grey suit baggy and shiny from too much washing and ironing, his face taking on the appearance of the suit as if from habit. But about him he still retained his dignity, like a beggar may still have dignity as he stoops in the gutter to pick up the thrown coin.

'I'm going to come and visit mom every evening,' Clare said.

'Are you now?'

'And at the weekends. I can come two times at the weekend.'

'Be quiet,' Nuala said. 'I want to watch the television.'

'She doesn't care,' Clare whispered, loud enough for Nuala to hear.

'And you do,' Nuala said scathingly. 'Daddy's pet!'

'Stop it,' Clare shouted. 'You stop her, daddy.'

'You both stop it or you won't come here again,' I said, and the threat in my voice must have been real, because they both retreated into silence.

But the incident had drawn attention to us, and a nasty pleasure seemed to invade the room. The pleasure was on the face of the old woman across from me, sitting there in her pink, floral dressing-gown, frayed at the edges and threadbare from age and use. It was the same pleasure that you feel on seeing a traffic warden begin to issue tickets just as you drive off from the yellow lines yourself. The woman stared at me in synchronism with five other pairs of eyes . . . waiting. But I outstared them all, and one by one they went back to watching television and I had a hollow victory over them.

To my surprise it was Sarah who came and asked me to go

in to Margaret. I had no more excuses except for the truth, which is that I didn't want to because my pity frightened me. It could force me to do things I would not want to do, to ask Margaret to forgive me and to promise never to give her reason to have to forgive me again.

Martin was sitting by the bedside but he and Margaret were silent. Father and daughter, but they were strangers. Like Nuala and myself, like one day Clare and myself would be. That evening I only thought that we would be strangers.

Hampstead was grey and miserable in the rain and I walked over to the window and looked out. I could see cars on the road below and someone waiting by the pedestrian crossing, a black umbrella held above the head. A man came down from Hampstead on a bicycle, heading towards Kentish Town. He stopped to let the pedestrian cross, and in a moment both were gone from my view. Two individuals standing out from the crowd. I was seeing them as God is supposed to see us, as He would see and judge and one day punish me.

I came back to the bedside and sat on the chair next to Martin. Margaret reached out her hand to me and I gave her my own to hold. 'How are you?' I asked.

'I'm tired,' she said. 'I feel very weak.'

'Do you have any pain?'

'In my back,' she said, 'and in my legs; sometimes my legs hurt terribly.'

'It's supposed to be a good sign,' I said. 'You must be getting better.'

Martin shifted his weight on the chair beside me and for a moment I thought he was going to damn me, but he was beyond damning anyone, and aware of the fact and maybe shamed by it he got to his feet mumbling about waiting in the day-room. He put the chair away and I tried to get up myself.

'Stay, Peter,' Margaret said, 'please stay.'

Martin mumbled his goodbyes and left, but he was the one who should have stayed. 'Poor dad,' Margaret said. 'He's had an unhappy life. My mother is not an easy woman to live with.' She stopped a moment. 'I'm like her, Peter, am I not?'

'I wouldn't know.'

'You do . . . and you're right. She was criticizing you this evening.'

'It doesn't matter.'

'It matters to me.' She pulled my hand and my head swung round towards her as if it was attached to my arm with a string. She held my gaze for a moment, and then I looked away. 'She said that you were still seeing that . . . that woman . . . Are you, Peter? I have to know.'

I didn't answer and she began to cry. The teardrops, as if weighted with salt, balanced for a moment on the eyelids and then tumbled over and ran across her cheeks. For a moment I saw her as the girl I had once loved, the girl I had danced with and cuddled in the cinema and respected. The girl I had married and had been happy with at first, and who had given me a beautiful baby daughter. The baby who used to grab my thumb and put it in her mouth, while the mother fussed and wondered how she could sterilize a thumb.

All those years ago I would have put my arms about her and held her tight and made the world all right. But then and now were light years apart. If we'd had a thousand lifetimes we still wouldn't have had enough time to put it all right. It was what I thought, unaware that in the end it was to take but a moment.

'You don't love me any more,' she said, a statement that asked for no reply. 'I . . . I don't think you'll ever love me again. Maybe that's to be my punishment. But I'll try to make it up to you. When I'm well . . . when I'm out of here we'll go away together. We'll go to Majorca like we did for our honeymoon. You used to chase me on the beach and when you caught me you used to bury me in the sand. You remember, don't you, Peter?'

I remembered like I remembered so many other things, but you can't push a wheelchair over sand was all I could think of . . . you can't push a wheelchair over sand. And you can't make me happy – not ever again. Someone else makes me happy now and I will go with her to Majorca, and we will run on the sand.

We are all children: we never really grow up. As children we played our games of pretence, hanging on to them as we got older and eventually taking them with us into adulthood, there to enact them again, sometimes with the ability to make them come true. Some succeed, with the Rolls-Royces and the yachts as evidence of their success. For most of us, though, the game is only a game after all, but we never come to accept it for that. We go through life with the eyes of the child and the wants of the adult, aware that we can never reconcile the two. There are a few people unaware of this fact – the lucky ones who never grow up. But for most of us it is the thing that damns our happiness, that prevents us from enjoying what we have.

It was what made me dream of freedom from Margaret and a new life with Barbara. If the dream did not exist I could have put my arms about Margaret's shoulders and comforted her. I could have told her that we would go to Majorca, but I didn't.

The bell rang for an end to visiting and I got to my feet and put the chair away. 'I have to go,' I said. 'We'll come and see you tomorrow.' Her eyes were pleading for so many things at once, but there was no one to give anything to her. 'Goodbye,' I said, and I left her to her demons, aware that they were only the outriders. She had yet to face the demon of knowing that she was a cripple.

On my way out the sister called me into her office and informed me that the doctors would tell Margaret tomorrow that her legs had been amputated; they wanted me on hand to comfort her. And I wondered if there would ever be an end to the irony.

Martin came home with us because I assumed that Sarah didn't want him to acquire the habit of being alone. But even with us he was alone and he drew out my own loneliness; we were Siamese twins joined by our wanting. I came into the house with him but he immediately went out into the garden. The girls went off to watch television and Sarah retreated to the kitchen to make tea.

I'd had enough of lies and pretence for one day, and tonight I didn't want to see Barbara. Tonight I wanted no more demands made of me. So I went into my study and rang Barbara and told her that something had cropped up, not sure of what the something should be if she asked. But she didn't ask.

'It's just as well,' she said, 'because I have to go to Milton Keynes tomorrow to see my lawyer. I'm catching an early train so I'm hoping to get to bed by ten.'

'I see,' I said, suddenly feeling disappointed. 'You're not risking the drive?'

'You know me and motorways,' she laughed. 'When those juggernauts come up behind me I panic. I'm just terrified of them. I think I'll stick to the train.'

'Get a London lawyer,' I said.

'Oh, I couldn't dream of getting rid of Ray. He's been with me since I started my business. He's really an old friend. When he moved out of London I just had to stay with him.'

'If you say so.'

'How's Margaret?' she asked.

'She wants to make up . . . wants me to love her again.'

'She'll strangle you,' she said bitterly. 'She'll never let you go.'

'She can't touch me any more. I've told you that already.'

'So you have . . . Look, phone me tomorrow; I'll be back by two.'

'I'll phone,' I said, and hung up. I saw Martin in the garden and I went out to him. It was still raining, but lightly now, and the rain had released the smell of the earth and it contrasted with the heady perfume of the roses. Looking at Martin I felt useless and insignificant. I knew nothing about gardening, never having grown a vegetable or a flower in my life. And yet even one potato was worth all the work I ever did for my company. Service Executive they called me, but of service to whom?

I produced nothing that was essential to man and in any logical revolution I would be disposed of, a taker and not a giver. Martin the fool, with his knowledge of soils and fertilizers and carrot-fly, was the real man – the man who had existed since the beginning of time and was able to produce food for his own table. I was just the parasite who took from his store and gave him nothing in return.

It seemed important now that I should know him – this stranger who was a better man than I could hope to be, who had never betrayed or hurt anyone. 'How about a drink?' I asked. 'I'm going along to my local for a pint.'

'I . . . I won't bother,' he said, '. . . thanks.'

'Well, if you do change your mind I'll be in the public bar.'

'You are going to the pub . . . ? To the "Cricketers", I mean?'

'Yes,' I said, and to put him at ease I added: 'It's the only decent pub around here.' But my effort didn't help, and the embarrassment reddened his sallow face.

Deceit is a terrible thing. Even Martin didn't trust me. He'd thought I'd only asked him out of decency, that in fact I was going to Barbara and had used the pub as an excuse. But in that he was wrong about me. For I had no decency, and I would have worried about no one's feelings. It wasn't decency that asked Martin but my own selfishness. I had been alone for too long.

Sarah offered no protest. While I was in the pub with Martin I couldn't be with Barbara. To allow Martin a few halves of bitter was a small price to pay for that.

So we went and we had best bitter, no need in me now for the balm of whisky. The last occasion I had had a drink with Martin was when Clare was born. Eight wasted years, and not one second from them could I have again.

There was a darts match in progress; a player dropped out to make a phone call and I was persuaded to take his place. I didn't have the eye or the steady hand or whatever it is that one requires, and my partner and I lost the game. We got ribbed about it, and Martin had a laugh, and we were men for a little while and even I felt human. Martin called the next round and I let him, not wanting to undermine him as a man. He had his pride – whatever little Sarah had left him.

We were quiet then as men sometimes are, content to sit and watch and listen. I think we both intended to have only the two drinks, but we were reluctant to break up the evening and I ordered another round. The beer and the atmosphere and the joke Terry the barman told us about the horse who played cricket – I think it was all of it combined that made Martin maudlin.

'It's a long time since I had a drink with anyone,' he said. 'I'd almost forgotten what it's like.'

'A man needs a drink,' I said. 'He needs another man's company.'

'Well, it's too late now,' he said, staring at his glass of bitter as if mesmerized.

'It's never too late,' I said. 'You have to be optimistic.'

'I suppose,' he said, but I knew that he would never be optimistic. What I didn't know is that he was right not to be. Optimism after all has the ability to hurt, and it is better to have no hope. It was a lesson I was to learn later, but I paid more for the knowledge than Martin ever paid. But maybe that was because I had so much more to lose.

'So they tell Margaret the truth tomorrow,' he said.

I nodded. 'Well, she has to be told some time.'

'Poor woman,' he said. 'When she spoke tonight about her legs it almost broke my heart.' He shook his head helplessly and then leaned over his glass of beer and began to cry.

'We'll go,' I said, embarrassed not by Martin's tears but my own lack of them. He came with me and we left our unfinished glasses on the table. Terry waved us goodnight and the dart players turned to look at us, glad I supposed that the pain was not theirs. They would talk about us now and about our tragedy, and they would pity us.

'I'm sorry,' Martin said when we were outside. 'It's not Margaret I'm crying for but myself.'

'Don't worry,' I said. 'It sometimes helps to cry.'

The rain had gone and the night felt crisp – more like October than June. We walked back to the house in silence, and when we got there I would never have known that Martin had cried.

'It helps to cry,' I'd said, not really aware that night of the truth of my words. For tears are the only things that might help me now. But I have no tears, only the block of ice within me that they have become.

8

I waited alone in the day-room while the doctor told Margaret that she would never walk again. I waited like the condemned man waits for the last dawn and the steps of the executioner. The summer was with us again and outside the earth was drying out in the sun; but I felt cold, the sun unable to touch the block of ice within me.

The doctor came and told me I could go in. 'She needs comforting,' he said. 'You can be of more help to her now than we can. You're the only one who can give her what she needs.' He talked like a priest, and I supposed that they both had similar roles.

I went in to Margaret but I had nothing to give her. I sat on the edge of the bed and she turned away from me. There were no tears or hysterics, and I could only think that the doctor was wrong. There wasn't anything that anyone could give her. Only God could give her anything now, and I thought again that she should have died. But this time I wished it for herself and not for me.

'You knew,' she said, and I was amazed that there could be so much accusation in two words. She turned back towards me, her face small and frightened like that of an animal caught in a trap, an animal who knows that there is no escape, and is patiently waiting for the inevitable. 'You knew,' she said. 'When you were here yesterday and I offered you everything, you knew. You knew I had nothing to give you. Didn't you?' she added, stung for a moment when I didn't respond, and my only response then was to nod.

'You signed for them to take my legs,' she said. 'How could you sign?'

'You would have died if . . .'

'Died! Died! Do you love me . . . ? You have to tell me if you love me. Do you?' She waited but I had no answer. 'And you worry that I should die!' She didn't know what emotion to assume, and she tried them all in a moment – anger and fear and pain all marched across her face, but the trap stayed sprung. 'I loved the baby too,' she said. 'Don't you understand that? You hate me because of the baby . . . the baby I had for you. I did it all for you and you hate me for it.'

'I don't hate you,' I said.

'Maybe not any more . . . you've got your revenge now. You don't have any more reason to hate, do you?' I thought she would cry, but not a trace of a tear appeared in the eyes. 'I want to hate you,' she went on. 'I want to hate you for what you've done to me.'

'You hate me,' I said, 'if you want.'

'It would be too easy to hate you,' she said. 'It's what you would want. I won't hate you but I won't ever let you go. Never . . .'

I thought that she had played all her cards, but she had one left. 'I love you,' she said, as if it was her final trump, unaware that to me it was faceless. She reached out and took my hand, thinking that it would move me, but it only pushed me farther away. 'Tell me you love me,' she said, '. . . even a little. Just that you care for me . . .' She was desperate for anything – she would have settled for a scrap. 'Tell me that you will care for me again,' she insisted. 'Please give me that . . .'

I took my hand away and stared out of the window, the Heath retreating back into the trees that separated it from the sky. The sun played tricks with light and shade, and I could almost sense the gloom and silence in among the trees. Not the absolute silence of nightmare, but the latent silence of a haunted house from whose dark corners might come suddenly a bedlam of ghosts and demons.

There were people out on the Heath – Lowry figures who had escaped from my industrial landscape. I envied them their apparent freedom – apparent because none of us is free; though at times we have to pretend that we are because we cannot live with reality for ever. We have to pretend that life is the idyll of the television commercials; that there are never hangovers from the booze; that the sleek, fast cars do not kill; that the little child with the golden breakfast cereal will not be assaulted and murdered, unable to understand the lust and then the pain. We have to pretend that love can never die, or hatred then sprout in the vacuum that remains. We have to pretend, for without the pretence there is only madness . . . or God. But I could pretend nothing now. It was truth that was needed, not pretence.

Margaret seemed to accept the inevitable, and I thought that we would never be close again. I feel the guilt now that I felt that morning, the guilt that urged me to put my arms about her and to love her even in pretence. Her encounter with the possibility of death was also an encounter with loneliness, a vision of the future. She had seen the inevitable loneliness and was trying to hold on to something to make the future bearable. But I had nothing for her.

'Do you . . . do you love her?' she asked now, breaking into my thoughts.

'I want to be happy,' I said ambiguously, 'that's all.'

'We were happy once . . . you and I were happy. We *were* happy,' she insisted. 'At least admit to that.'

'We were happy,' I said.

'You made me happy, Peter . . . you can make me happy again.'

I didn't answer this time, but I looked at the picture of 'The Sacred Heart' which still stood on the locker. He was God and the picture was a symbol of His suffering. He had become a man and had sweated blood. He had been nailed to a cross and had died in agony. He had known what it was to suffer; He had despaired for a moment, asking that His pain be taken away. 'She loves You,' I thought, 'she loves You and not me. You take her pain . . . You make her happy.'

It is God Who gives pain . . . it is God Who gives us loneliness. When He gave Adam a mate, far from taking away his loneliness He actually gave loneliness to him. 'Love me,' the picture pleaded, as Margaret pleaded, but I had no love for either of them. We were locked it seemed in different time capsules . . . powerless to help each other. 'Pray,' Father Mason had said the other day, but he couldn't tell me how. It wasn't that I didn't know any prayers. In fact they had been engraved on my soul as a child and I had never forgotten them. I'd forgotten 'Gray's Elegy' and Shakespeare's sonnets, but I could still recite the 'Our Father'. Though only like someone who knows the words of a song and cannot sing.

'What do you want from me, Peter?' she asked now. 'What can I give you?'

'Nothing,' I said. 'I don't want anything.'

'You couldn't love a cripple,' she said.

'It has nothing to do with it . . . I . . . I just don't love anyone any more, that's all.'

Yesterday I had kept the truth from her and now today she was having to take it all at once. I felt sorry and helpless, but the truth had to be spoken. What was there to be gained by lying and pretending, by offering hope where there was none?

I looked down at her, small and beaten, and for a moment my resolve weakened. It was a face I had once loved and once hated . . . the small mouth and the small eyes no longer sharp and burning. The nose with dents either side of the bridge, as if someone had pinched the wet mould with a thumb and forefinger while the clay was still wet. I used to rib her about it when we were first married, and one night she had cried and I had put my arms about her and had comforted her. Now when she had so much more reason for crying I had no comfort for her.

There was nothing I could do here, so I said goodbye and came away. Outside it was difficult to imagine that anyone suffered, that pain and hatred and loneliness could exist in the sunshine. While my son was alive I'd wanted no one happy. I'd wanted the world in mourning, everyone dressed in black and poker-faced, the flags at half-mast. Now I wanted to see people happy, to be assured that there still could be some joy in the world. For while the joy existed I could hope for a share of it.

I came away from my past with all ties broken, I thought. My happiness and my future were waiting for me, guiding me towards them like a lighthouse beacon might guide a sailor. But it was the smuggler's fire of old I saw, the fire that lured the unsuspecting ship on to the rocks, there to lie helpless and be savaged.

When I got home from work that evening I found that Sarah had sent the girls next door and that she and Martin were waiting for me in the kitchen. It was always a cold room, even in the summer, but this evening it had the chill of a tomb. I had never felt at home in the house, but now I felt distinctly alien, and I thought the house more Sarah's than mine.

'We went to the hospital,' Sarah said. 'You should be ashamed of yourself . . . treating a sick woman like that.'

'She just cried,' Martin said, the only one who had tasted the salty tears. I thought for a moment he was going to cry himself, as he had done last night.

'Of course she cried,' Sarah echoed, 'to be treated like that.' She had a carving knife in one hand and a fork in the other, and she brandished them now like some medieval warrior. A small joint of lamb was on the table before her, but she seemed unaware of its existence. It was me she wanted to carve, to skewer me with the fork and plunge the knife into my heart.

'I told her the truth,' I said. 'You want me to tell her lies?'

'You call it truth,' she said angrily. 'You treat a sick woman like that and you call it truth.'

'She has to know some time,' I said.

'You should have waited,' Martin said.

'Waited for what?' Sarah turned to where he stood with his back to the sink unit, his head and shoulders framed by the window. 'To go away from his wife . . . to go off with a whore . . . is that it?'

'She's no whore,' I said.

'No! So what is she? What would you call her?'

'My wife one day,' I said, wanting to hurt her.

'You already have a wife,' she said, 'and you have two daughters to consider. Or have you given no thought to them?'

'I'm not divorcing them,' I said.

'You can't get a divorce . . . Margaret needs you.'

'She should have thought of that before, but she didn't care for anyone but herself. Suddenly now she needs me – you all do.'

'Margaret needs you,' Martin said. 'We don't matter.'

'I never wanted her to marry you,' Sarah said, as if Martin hadn't spoken. 'I always knew it was a mistake.'

'Your so-called mistake was mine,' I said angrily, 'but I'm about to put it right. You should be pleased with the divorce. You'll be getting rid of me, won't you?' I talked about divorce, but at present I had no hope of getting one. I had no grounds for divorce, but Sarah didn't understand the law and it gave me the power to hurt her.

'God doesn't recognize divorce,' she said. 'You'll burn in hell for it.'

I laughed, the soundtrack of some horror movie. 'I'll have company,' I said. 'Whatever else, I'll have company.'

It was as if I'd touched something within her, maybe reminded her of her own sins, that she too could burn and that the fires had no favourites, for she fell silent. Margaret's wall clock, an imitation copper frying-pan, ticked with a ponderous regularity, every beat one second nearer the flames. It was out of place in that kitchen, as much out of place as I was. We were Margaret's possessions, nothing more. Except that she possessed me no longer.

I stared at my in-laws, man and wife, husband and lover; but what were they but words? The two people before me had been young once, had been children, had loved and married. They must have made love, at least the one time, but where had the love gone?

'You have to think of the future,' Martin said.

'I've thought of my future,' I told him.

'But not your wife's.' Sarah emphasized the point with the knife. 'Don't you realize that Margaret hasn't got a future? The only future she's got is ours . . . yours, mine . . . the girls' . . . there isn't any other.'

I didn't grasp then what she meant, but I did see it all later, too late for any of us except maybe for Margaret. In a way she was the only winner. But that evening I saw a different future to Sarah's, a future of bitterness for Margaret, full of others' good deeds and sympathy, useless as light to the blind. I saw her in her wheelchair, knitting . . . not chunky jumpers which might have kept out the cold, but the little woollen skirts that people use to cover the spare toilet roll in the bathroom . . . little brightly coloured unnecessary things which old ladies sell at fund-raising events for charity.

I saw Margaret's life being as useless as the toilet roll cover, yet no one was willing to admit to it. She would regard herself as doing good work for charity, unaware that another word for charity is love. That's how I saw it, but I was wrong.

'So you haven't given a thought to anything,' Sarah said. 'Don't you know that Margaret cannot live in this house as it is now? It needs to be altered . . . things have got to be done.' She'd obviously realized that her earlier attitude was getting her nowhere and had decided to change tack.

'You could always buy a bungalow,' Martin said, wanting to add something himself.

'A bungalow,' Sarah said scathingly, wanting to vent her anger on someone, Martin the only one she could hurt. 'Why would she want to leave her home?'

He said nothing, but began to chew his bottom lip. I knew it wasn't a sign of anger but merely a nervous reaction. Martin was a dead man already; she had broken him long ago, and he'd learned not to question or argue. Now I saw him as a reflection of what I could become myself in thirty years. If I kept quiet, if I accepted, I would become Martin's double, and Margaret and Sarah would trample me into the ground. It would happen if I let it, if I weakened my resolve. Suddenly I realized why Barbara had shunned me on Sunday night. It wasn't because of her fear that she sent me away, but because of the smell of my defeat. It was the same aroma that Martin carried around with him, that I myself despised him for. It was a revelation, and I knew then that they had the power to destroy me. But I would never allow them to.

'It's only been a few days since the accident,' I said, 'but if it makes you happy I'll make some inquiries tomorrow. Now I'd better get the girls or the dinner will be ruined.'

Clare was my saviour, and during dinner there was no more talk of divorce or house conversions. She chattered about her visit to the zoo, the only one among us who wasn't putting on an act. Even at thirteen, Nuala had learned to put on a mask for the world. But she and Clare didn't even know the truth.

I looked from one to the other and theirs was the only pain I cared about. I wanted to protect them and yet I planned to leave them. But would I? Was the certainty I felt when talking to Sarah just for my own benefit? To say to myself I can do it and to actually end up believing it? But there was no future for me here, whatever future I might find elsewhere.

What had Barbara said on the phone that afternoon? 'You have to reach out for what you want and if it's out of reach you have to step forward. It's how the child learns, Peter. Even the baby knows that one day it has got to let go.'

Put like that it seemed simple: I could go tonight. That was how some people saw life. It was how Barbara saw it. Reach out and take, and if you have to trample on someone do it well. Don't just step on them, but grind them into the ground. 'No one gets in my way,' she'd said. 'If I want something badly enough I'll get it. Sometimes I think I could commit murder to get what I want. You would never murder anyone, Peter. You've never needed anything badly enough for that.'

I'd laughed at what she'd said, but the joke wasn't at all funny; and I had the uneasiness of the man who is watching an inferior juggler and who is frightened that at any moment the china plates are going to crash to the ground.

We finished dinner and went to the hospital, and this time I sat in the day-room and no one insisted that I go into the ward. Martin sat with me but we didn't talk. The girls came out after a while and then Martin went in.

'Mom was crying,' Clare said. 'She was crying all the time. And gran was crying too.'

'It's OK,' I said to her. 'It's OK.' And I wished that it was all OK and that she didn't have to be bewildered.

I went into the ward when the bell rang for an end to visiting, and during the goodbyes I was able to be anonymous. I noticed that the drip had been removed and also some of the other monitoring equipment, a sign that Margaret was getting better. 'I won't be in tomorrow afternoon,' I said to her, 'work's a bit hectic at the moment.' But she said nothing, only stared at me with empty eyes that had cried too much.

We went silently and no one spoke until we were in the car. 'I want to go home,' Sarah said. 'If you could take us to Cricklewood.'

When we got there it was Sarah again who spoke. 'Don't go leaving the girls on their own,' she said, and I saw straight away the reason why she had wanted to go home.

'I won't leave them,' I said. 'Barbara can come over. She's very good with children and they may as well get to know her.' I watched the barb go home and could only think that my own pettiness was worse than Sarah's. But I couldn't let her win. One victory and everything might be hers.

She was lost for words, like a politician confronted with the truth. But like the politician the loss was momentary. The pettiness was hers again, and she wanted to hurt. 'Maybe we should ask the children,' she said. 'Do you want another mother?' she demanded of Clare, the venom in her voice suddenly directed at the little girl.

'I don't want another mummy,' Clare said, her voice full with a fear of the unknown.

'It's OK,' I said, 'you don't have to have a new mom. Your gran is just being angry and spiteful.'

'Why, daddy?' she asked.

'Because she's happiest like that,' I said. 'But you take no notice. No one is going to make you do anything. We'll go home now and I'll cook your supper and read you a story if you want.'

Sarah hesitated for a moment, thinking I supposed of something to say, but she didn't say anything and began to struggle to get out of the car. Martin tried to help her but she brushed him off. She made it eventually and leaned in at the door to say goodnight to the girls. But she didn't have anything to say to me.

We drove home in silence and had cheese on toast in the kitchen, the girls watching the little black and white television. I cleared away when we'd finished and waited until the programme was over. When the ads came on I switched off the set. 'I want to talk to you,' I said, '. . . about your mother,' and they stared at me for a moment and then went back to staring at the blank television screen.

I hadn't wanted it to be like this, and for a moment I was tempted to put the television on again and forget the whole thing. But if I left it Sarah would eventually tell them, and from her viewpoint, not mine. So quietly I told them and I hurt more than they did. It wasn't easy but I managed, and whatever happened now at least they couldn't be told again.

Nuala cried more from disbelief than hurt – she cried and I was unable to help her. Clare cried too, but only because Nuala cried, and my eight-year-old daughter climbed down from her chair and came to me and I took her comfort and gave her my own inferior comfort in return.

They cried and they tried to understand, but do any of us really understand? I said nothing, for there was nothing to say. What's the use of words when it's miracles that are needed?

You can't beat youth into submission, just as you can't cry for ever. It was Clare who stopped crying first. She pulled away from me and went over to the television. 'Can I watch again, daddy?' she asked. I just nodded, and as the sound filled the room I got up and left them to the world of fantasy.

I went into my study and rang Barbara, and it felt good to hear her voice. It seemed impossible that it was only twenty-four hours since I hadn't wanted to see her. 'Maybe you could come over,' I said, when I'd explained to her why I couldn't call. 'Just for an hour or so. We could have a cup of coffee.'

'It wouldn't be a good idea,' she said. 'The children . . . well, you know what I mean.'

'They'll be in bed.'

'No,' she said. 'I couldn't come. You're . . . not going to be angry?'

'Just disappointed,' I said. 'It'll be two nights in succession I won't see you.'

'Last night was your fault too.'

'So tonight you're having revenge?'

'You're a fool,' she said. 'I have no need of revenge.'

'I seem to play the fool a lot,' I said.

'You are angry.' She sounded as if it was the first time I'd ever been angry. 'Well don't take your anger out on me,' she went on. 'And what was that something that cropped up last night? I don't seem to remember you telling me.'

'Don't you? Well, it wasn't much. I had to practise being the fool, that's all.'

'Go to hell,' she said, and hung up on me.

'Goodbye,' I said to the dead line. I got the dialling tone and dialled her number. But before it could ring I replaced the receiver. I leaned back in my chair and stared out of the window at the gathering darkness – the apple trees in the garden like soft pencil outlines on grey paper. 'Our garden,' Margaret had said when we bought the house. 'Just imagine it, Peter. We'll have a patio and tables and chairs, and in the summer we can have breakfast out there. And we'll never get rid of the trees . . . never.' We hadn't got rid of the trees, and the patio existed, but we had got rid of our marriage.

I went back to the kitchen and when the programme was over I sent the girls to bed. Nuala went reluctantly but she didn't say anything. Clare went quietly and I read her the promised story and kissed her goodnight.

'We won't have another mommy?' she said, still uncertain.

'Of course not. You have a mommy already.'

'I'll still like mommy,' she said seriously, 'even if she has no legs.'

'I know,' I said, aware that she was the only one who really cared.

'Goodnight, daddy,' she said, and I turned off the bedside light and left her.

I stopped by Nuala's closed door, but all was silent and I made my way downstairs. I felt restless, like an animal that senses an approaching thunderstorm. I went out into the garden and I could smell sleeping flowers and earth and mown grass, and the merest hint of smoke as if someone a long way off had a fire outdoors, maybe a barbecue or just burning rubbish.

It was difficult to believe that I was in London, that the city was spread out all round me. If I listened intently I could hear traffic like the hum of some giant machine deep underground. And I felt that peculiar loneliness that one sometimes feels in a crowd, that total isolation that only the presence of others can instil.

I went back into the house and made myself a coffee and watched the news. It was the usual litany of man's coldness and cruelty and inhumanity to his fellows, an exact parallel to our own private lives. There was no sense to it all, and I went to bed in my comfortless room hoping that dreams would not disturb my few hours of peace. As it was they left me alone, but they must have known that soon all my nights would belong to them and they could wait.

9

I made inquiries about building firms and eventually found one that specialized in work for the disabled. I spoke to the owner, Mr Harris, and he promised to call that evening. When I expressed surprise at his promptness, he told me that he gave this type of work priority.

He arrived promptly at six thirty, a veritable giant of a man who I felt certain could have demolished buildings with his bare hands. I took him into the lounge, where he managed to fit himself into one of the two large armchairs.

'Would you like a drink?' I asked.

'If you've got a beer, thanks.'

I got him a beer and he drank half of it down in one go. 'I do all sorts of conversion work,' he said, 'but I specialize in converting houses for the disabled. I've been doing it ten years – since my daughter broke her back in a riding accident. I adapted the house for her and learned from my mistakes. Having the house done gave her a certain amount of independence, though her husband was wonderful. She'd never have made it but for him. Well, you know what women are like – beauty and all that. Another man would have run off. But he loved her, Mr Ferson, and he stuck by her. Love is the only thing that can help in a situation like that.' He stopped for a moment. 'Still, you're a sensible man. Age gives us something, you know. You won't be running off with the girl next door, now will you?'

'No,' I said, 'I won't.'

'There you are . . . you could say that your wife is cured already. When she sees the house she'll only wish she had had it done years ago. It'll make life even easier than it was before. Look, I'll show you the brochures I've brought.'

I was reeling under his barrage, trying to catch my scattered thoughts and drag them back to me one by one. But I had but a moment's respite, and then he was off on the brochures as if we had only minutes to spare. He showed me the adapted kitchens and bathrooms, the electric lift on the stairs, the hoist over the bed, the ramps giving access to the front and back doors, and many other helpful aids and ideas.

'It seems like what we need,' I said. 'If you could let me have an estimate?'

'I'll call tomorrow,' he said, 'and go over the house. And don't worry,' he added at the front door. 'Remember what I told you. It's people who can really help, not converted bathrooms or that . . .'

I'd told him nothing of my private life, but it was as if he was talking directly to me. 'Love,' he'd said, but how could I tell him that love was dead? If I had told him about my son, what could he have said then? What could he have offered me that might have rekindled the love? Or would he have instinctively known that my love was beyond redemption? That I wouldn't love anyone ever again, not even myself? That what I felt for Clare wasn't love at all, but something inbuilt in the parent, the instinct to protect its young that every animal possesses?

I told Barbara about the builder later that evening. 'So you see,' I said, 'it's beginning to take shape. A few more months and we'll be together.'

'You believe that?' she said.

'Don't you?'

'I only believe in what I've got.'

'Well you've got me, haven't you?'

'We never have another human being,' she said. 'You

can't capture someone's mind. They only ever give a little, and we hold on to what we can.'

'So what do you want to hold on to?' I asked jokingly.

'You've never given anything,' she said. 'You'll never give anything.'

She made me angry and I wanted to get back at her, but I knew that I would only hurt myself. I stared at her and realized for the first time that she would never give herself to anyone, not fully give, anyway. We could have been identical twins, but camouflaged on the surface so that you wouldn't know unless you looked really close. But anyone who was like us could tell, as if we had some sign to guide them like the Freemason's handshake. Barbara knew me because she knew herself; but I could never know her because to myself I was a stranger, and unless I got to know the stranger I would never know anyone.

'And you say you love me,' I accused.

'I need you,' she said. 'I want to share my life with you. It's more certain than any love could be. The problem with love is that when it dies there's nothing left.'

'It doesn't sound too promising, now does it?'

'There are no guarantees,' she said, 'not even with love.'

It wasn't promising at all, but later when we made love there was no need for guarantees or promises, and it was possible for me to pretend that there was no need for any. It was enough to sustain me for a while, but once out of the flat there was the need for reassurance again. It wasn't enough to know that I would leave Margaret; I wanted to be certain that when I left there would be something waiting for me.

The weekend was typical of a British summer and it was sunny between the showers. Mr Harris called on Saturday morning, and as Sarah had returned I let her deal with what she thought was required. Everything was eventually covered, and even Sarah was satisfied.

We went to the hospital twice that day, and there were

other visitors too. The Morgans from next door, some women Margaret knew at the church, a couple of women whose children went to the same school as the girls. I was secretly thankful to them all and I let them have the limelight. I sat for most of the time in the day-room, telling the afternoon visitors that I would have all the evening to myself, and the evening ones that I had had all the afternoon. For the moments I was with Margaret I just joined in the small talk, the false reassurances that everything would be all right, the thanks to God that she was alive, and how we should be thankful that she wasn't much worse.

Margaret was quiet, obsessively so, but I'm certain that all who saw her put it down to the accident. I felt, though, that she was withdrawing from us all, even from the girls. And I knew too that the blame was mine and mine alone.

Clare was the only one who put her thoughts into words. 'Mommy doesn't like me any more,' she said. 'Why doesn't she like me, daddy?'

'She likes you,' I said. 'She's just upset to be in hospital.'

'If she doesn't like me,' she said, 'I won't like her, I'll like you instead, daddy.'

'You do,' I said, wondering if all the love I would ever have would be second-hand; the love that others had rejected and that was then given to me because you've got to give it to someone. Would I always be picking up people from the rejection of others? And feeling the inferiority and the insecurity of my position?

After visiting the hospital on Sunday afternoon I took Sarah and the girls to Cricklewood. I returned home myself, ostensibly to catch up on some paperwork connected with my job, but in reality because the house at Cricklewood always depressed me. I had actually decided on sorting out some papers when the door bell disturbed me. I answered the door to find that my visitor was Father Boland, a priest from our local church.

'I . . . I heard about Margaret,' he said, 'and I thought I'd call.'

I took him into the sitting-room and he sat in one of the armchairs and stretched out his legs, black trousers immaculately pressed, black leather shoes distorting the room's reflection. And I wondered how long his housekeeper had laboured to get a shine like that.

'So how is Margaret?' he asked.

'She's fine,' I said, taking the chair opposite him.

'And the girls?'

'They're fine.'

'Ah . . .' He was lost for a moment. 'I saw Sarah,' he said eventually. 'She told me about the . . . ah . . . accident. She . . . ah . . . happened to mention that you were going to leave . . . were going to get a divorce.'

'I am,' I said, 'when Margaret comes home.'

It shook him. I think he had thought that Sarah was exaggerating, and that I was going to laugh at the absurdity of the idea that I might actually consider leaving my wife. But he must have faced life in the confessional if he hadn't faced it in reality, and he quickly recovered, getting his shepherd's mask back on his face. He was a man as I was, but he wasn't going to confront me as a man. It was the priest who was going to talk to me, that other man who lived within him.

'You realize that the church doesn't recognize divorce?' he said.

'I know,' I said, 'but I don't recognize the church.'

'But Margaret recognizes the church.'

'Will your God punish her for my sins?'

'He's your God too,' he said, 'and He will punish you. It's your soul which is in danger.'

'I'll take care of my own soul,' I said.

'It's a man's duty to take care of his soul,' he said, 'but I have to think of my flock.' He had his hands together, but now he opened them out as if to embrace the world, those hands that had never embraced anyone. His face I supposed was meant to have a look of piety – of caring – but it resembled that of a businessman who's had too many good lunches on his expense account.

I thought of Father Mason in Korea, going out into the villages after the bombing. To help the victims of the carnage and sometimes the victims of torture and rape and murder and of sick unfeeling violence. To anoint the bloody foreheads and the severed limbs and arms and not know whom they belonged to.

What did the man before me know about his flock? What did he know about the hell of London? The hell of life as some people had to live it? The down and outs in the gutters, the drug addicts in the toilets at Piccadilly underground, young men and women willing to sell their bodies for a fix, seeking something in life that just wasn't there. Maybe looking for this man's God, but he had never ventured out to bring God to anyone.

What did he know about the lonely and frightened people in his own parish? The old lady who had been mugged and was now too frightened to go out, who spent her nights on the couch, too frightened to go to sleep because her dreams were as bad as reality. What did he know about the pregnant girl who had no one to turn to for help? And who eventually found her way to the abortion clinic.

Did he think that life consisted of what he saw in the detached houses of his parish? Of sipping glasses of port in comfortable drawing-rooms, the colour television and video recorder in the corner. Two cars in the garage and talk about the wonderful three weeks in the Bahamas, and how one didn't know whether it was a good idea to buy a share in a villa on the Costa Brava or wherever.

He talked to me about his flock, but what did he know about life? Did he ever hunger or thirst? Did he know what it was to marry a false reality? Did he know what it was like to watch your son die? Or to see one of your children ill? Or to be trapped in a maze to which there was but one exit? And that blocked by barbed wire which you knew would tear your flesh.

'I have my own life to live,' I said to him now, 'and no one can live it for me.'

'And the children?' he said. 'What about the children?'

'The children belong to Margaret,' I said. I knew it wasn't strictly true, for Clare still was mine, but he wasn't to know.

'You're a bitter man,' he said. 'I feel sorry for you.'

We stared at each other across the fireplace, two human beings separated by a mystery I was certain neither of us understood. Only one of us could be right – the other had to be wrong. When I thought about it like that it was frightening; to be wrong didn't bear thinking about. It's the moment we all face from time to time, the moment when there are no atheists, only those who doubt.

I stared at the priest and I could only hope that his God might have some pity for him. His life had been as dry and barren as a withered tree. He had vowed to be celibate, to let his seed spill wantonly in the dark night, troubled by what dreams only he and God knew. The church would care for him in his old age, and would bury him when he died. He would become one of the faithful departed and his body would return to the earth, and weeds and grass would grow out of his barren loins.

'I can't change your mind?' he said. 'I can't get you to forgive and forget?'

'There's nothing to forgive or forget.'

'We all have something to forgive,' he said. 'It's one of the prices of life.'

'Your price, not mine.'

'No,' he said, 'it's not my price but God's.'

'It's too dear a price,' I said.

'We can only try,' he said, resigned to the fact that he had lost. But the truth was that he had been resigned before he started. He had fulfilled his duty and could do no more. In a moment he could return to his own life, forget about Margaret and the children, and the fact that he thought I was damning my soul. He had tried – he had done his best. He might even use it as material for a sermon, to tell his flock how much he cared for them. But his great failing was that he wasn't a man, and not being a man he couldn't be a priest. Even Christ had been a man, because He knew that He had to be a man before He could be God.

Father Boland got up to go; he stood a good three inches above me and carried two stone more than I did, but his clothes hung on him as they hung on the hangers in his wardrobe, and his little piece of white collar could do nothing for him. 'I'll pray for you all,' he said, echoing Father Mason's words, but it was difficult to imagine that they both served the same God.

'Do,' I said, not having anything else to say, and not wanting to reject the one thing he had to offer. At the door we shook hands and the priest went back to the only world he knew or understood. The world of the quiet church and the candles and the incense and the privacy of the confessional with forgiveness and mercy, and an empty promise not to sin again.

I lived in the real world, a world of abortion and violence, of materialism, of hunger and hatred, and of failed marriages and cripples and hurt children and loneliness. A world where man had the capability of destroying all of mankind. What had Father Boland to offer in the face of that? What was the use of prayer when the bomb was on its way? It was eat, drink and be merry – more relevant today than ever before.

I had but one life, and the only guarantee that I had was that at this very moment I was alive. That I could take what was being offered now. There was no guarantee that it wouldn't be taken from me tomorrow. After all, it had been taken from me before. Taken by the God and the people Father Boland claimed to serve. I had no need of his God any more, or indeed of his people. I was free of all of them.

10

Mr Harris sent me his estimate, and with Sarah's approval I gave him the go-ahead. Early one morning he came with his builders, men in overalls faded from years of work but clean and fresh as newly laundered sheets. They brought chaos in bags and boxes and tins; and there were ladders and dust-sheets and the smell of plaster and paint, and the sweet aroma of sawn timber.

'They're good men, Mr Ferson,' the giant said. 'They'll do a good job, and if you ever have reason for complaint just let me know.'

But I never had reason to distrust them or cause for complaint. They left something of themselves behind in the house besides the warm smell of beer, discarded lunch wrappers saying 'Mother's Pride', and copies of *The Sun* open at the racing pages and marked with blunt pencils and dry fingerprints. They were men whose skill was almost insolent in its use, their cheery, weathered faces belying any sense of awareness of their own ability.

Looking back now, that was one of the happier times of my life. I worked by day and went to the hospital in the evening with Sarah and the girls, and sometimes Martin or a friend or a neighbour would come too. Afterwards the time was my own and I spent it with Barbara.

She was a great tennis fan, and we watched the Wimbledon highlights each evening cuddled up in bed under the duck-down quilt. When the tennis was over Barbara usually made coffee and I watched the cricket. She laughed at me and the cricketers, and we drank the coffee and ate cream crackers and later felt the crumbs scratch our naked flesh.

Our life was like part of a dream, and we could never be sure that we wouldn't wake one time and see it all disappear into the darkened corners of the room. We forgot our rows and our differences, our doubts and promises, and were simply happy. But it was really a sad happiness. I think we were both aware of the future, not aware of what exactly would happen but that something horrible inevitably would. We could foresee our doom and yet we never spoke of it or admitted to it.

I can't say whether we loved each other or whether we might have grown to love each other. It was enough that there was something holding us together, and we were satisfied with that and didn't look for more. It was what I thought, and I assumed that Barbara thought the same. Later I was to discover that she was frightened of the future, frightened of the time when I would leave her, and she was laying up her own guarantees. By the time I discovered this it was too late to change a single thing or have back even one moment of the happiness that was most certainly ours.

One day Margaret was moved out of intensive care and into a small private room paid for by our insurance. Another day and she was sitting in a chair by the bedside. We all praised her, and when she got a wheelchair we urged her to go along to the day-room and meet the other patients. But she stayed in the small room with the radio she never listened to and the television she never watched. It was a long day to be alone, and when her visitors came there was no one among us who loved her enough to be able to help her. While her body got better her mind withdrew into the dark recesses that frighten us.

I thought she had given up the fight to have me back, but one evening she asked me to come alone the next day. 'I want to talk to you,' she said.

'What about?' I asked, but all she wanted was my promise and in the midst of the visitors I could but give it to her.

'I want to go home,' she said to me the next evening. She sat in the wheelchair by the window, maybe reminding herself of the world she had once possessed and which she could now only observe. She had dressed, especially for me I supposed, and the simple blue cotton dress complimented her. She wore a cardigan over the dress, and the inevitable blanket trailed to the floor. She looked as vulnerable as a child, and the sight drew out my pity.

'Of course you want to go home,' I agreed, 'but it won't be too long now. You'll just have to be a little patient.'

'But it won't be a home,' she said. 'Don't you see?'

'It was never really a home,' I said. I spoke matter-of-factly because the truth didn't matter to me any more. I stared at her and she had to turn away to avoid my eyes. The light caught her hair, dark and heavy, recently washed and conditioned, and having the vigour that comes only from prolonged brushing. For a long time now I'd learned not to notice her, but suddenly seeing the richness and sheen of her hair I was touched, touched for a fleeting moment because I thought she had done the brushing specially for me. But it was a flicker that ignited within me, a flicker from the past from a time when I knew how to love.

She turned back to me and I thought I detected in her eyes the beginning of an awareness that all was lost. 'I want to make things better,' she said, 'but I can't if you won't let me.'

'It's too late.' I shrugged my shoulders dismissively, killing her hope with one careless gesture. 'You had seventeen years to make it better.'

'Sometimes we have to learn . . . like children.'

'The child is frightened of the dark,' I said, 'as you are frightened. But it's not something to base a marriage on.'

'I am frightened,' she said. 'You're the only one I've got.' She was trawling in the depths for something, laying bare her soul. Had I been a caring human being I would have seen it, seen her heart torn open like the picture of the heart on the locker. But I was blinkered by the past and my determination not to relive it. She was promising that it would be different, but she had promised to love me once before and she'd promised then before her God.

To Margaret our marriage had been a piece of paper and from the paper came everything else. But in reality the opposite was true. The secret was to give, because without the giving there could not be anything. Margaret never gave and she taught me not to give either. Our marriage had lasted like so many others last, only for the sake of the children.

Margaret wanted me to gamble with the only hope I now had, but the past was stacked against me like loaded dice. If I was a winner then I won everything. But a loser . . . What I didn't know was that the dice had already been thrown and I had lost. Ignorant of this, I told Margaret that it was too late, that we had lost everything and had no future together. And she stared out of the window as if seeing her future being enacted on some imaginary stage out on the Heath.

'If you leave,' she said quietly, 'I'll die.'

I could have cursed her quietness and acceptance. I wanted her to fight to give my actions justification. Not that I couldn't find enough justification in the past, but I wanted it here in the present too. I wanted her to scream and rant and rage. I wanted the nurses to come running to see what I had to endure, and to sympathize with me. But Margaret knew me better than I knew myself. She thought that if she could generate enough guilt within me, I would return like the lost sheep. What she didn't know was how deep was the chasm between us, so deep in fact that even the guilt could not cross it.

'I asked Father Mason to call this evening,' she said. 'I wanted to tell you at the beginning . . . but I couldn't. But there's still time . . . you can go now and he'll never know.' She stopped to turn and look at me. 'I just hoped that you might listen to him. I . . . I knew that you wouldn't listen to me.' Her voice warned me that she was near to tears, and she blinked rapidly as if to dam them. 'I'm frightened, Peter . . . don't you understand?'

'I understand,' I said.

'You're going to wait?'

'There's no reason why I shouldn't.'

She didn't answer, but turned again to stare out on Hampstead. She looked small and lost in the chair, like the pictures of Victorian children we see in large high-street stores, and which people buy and hang on their walls, sentimental images from a time that had as many false ideals as we have today.

Father Mason arrived and shook hands with both of us and he got himself a chair. 'Making good progress,' he said. 'You'll soon be home. Willpower is a wonderful thing. It'll be just like old times. Remember when I used to call and we would sit on the "padio" as Nuala called it. She would have been about three then, I suppose. Time, eh . . . what do we do with it?'

He wanted no answer but I could have told him none the less, told him how we squandered it as if there was no end. Time was the only thing we were given in this life, a chunk of time like one might cut the heel from a loaf. And all we do is waste it and allow it to go stale. I could have told him many things but in the end I stayed silent.

'Well then,' he said, 'what can I do for you good people?' He looked from one to the other of us . . . waiting.

'Nothing,' Margaret said. 'Nothing . . . now.'

'Peter?'

'Margaret wants you to renew our marriage vows,' I said. 'To witness our promises to make life as miserable as possible for everyone, but especially for ourselves.' The bitterness in my voice surprised me and it shocked the priest into silence, but he quickly recovered.

'Once in Korea,' he said, 'I had to administer the last rites to a villager who had been tortured and left as an example to others. He was dying and in great pain, but he still had his wits about him. I comforted him and damned his torturers. I was a priest – God's servant on earth – and all I could do was curse the sinners. But I had a man's soul to consider. "You must not hate them," I said to him, "you must try to forgive them." You know what he said to me? He told me that he felt sorry for them because they had once been children like his own children, and how could they have become monsters? He was going to meet God and it wouldn't be right to have hatred in his heart. That Korean man humbled me. We buried him that day and we prayed for him but it was ourselves who needed the prayers. We put a little wooden cross on his grave but he deserved a marble monument, because he had the one thing that few of us attain . . . forgiveness.' He trailed off and gave me a moment to think. 'It took me a long time to forgive his torturers, but eventually I did forgive them. That Korean man in his dying taught me how to forgive. It's not easy but it makes us better people . . . afterwards we can live with each other again. If we can't live with ourselves we can't live with each other.'

I didn't really understand him then, but I do now. But even had I understood, it wouldn't have made any difference. My mind was made up and there was no breaking of my resolve.

'You've been married too long, Peter,' he said, 'to start searching for something new. We're creatures of habit, and although our habits may not always be best, sometimes they can save us.'

'I've got my own life to live,' I said, able to look him in the eye. 'Only for a while I'd forgotten about it.'

'Well, start to remember it now,' he said. 'Discover its values.'

'It has no values,' I said, 'only a price. I've paid enough as it is.'

'You can't buy happiness,' he said.

'It can't be bought,' I said, 'but it can be stolen from you. I've accepted for long enough. And for what?'

'A woman without legs is no good to anyone,' Margaret suddenly said. 'Peter is right . . . I have nothing to give him any more.'

'No,' I said, shaking my head, 'it's not that you have nothing to give me. It's just that I don't . . . well, I don't love you any more . . . I couldn't love you again. We don't have a marriage . . . we haven't had one for a very long time.'

They were only words, but I could hear them tear Margaret's flesh as they went home, and, worse still, I heard them tear her mind too. 'I'm sorry,' I said, more words uttered only for my own benefit. But Margaret began to cry, not the sobbing of a woman but the frightened sobbing of a child. I stood up, powerless to help but desperately needing to do something. But Father Mason stayed me with his hand. 'I'd go,' he said, his voice cold like water on a winter's morning, and having the same recoiling effect on me. 'There's nothing you can do here.'

I opened my mouth to say something – a protest, a word of contrition, but I saw there was little point. I was sorry, but for the wrong reasons, and it was love and hope and peace that Margaret wanted, not my sorrow. From somewhere within her she had dredged up enough courage and hope for this meeting. She had brushed her hair and put on a blue dress, not for my benefit as I had thought, but for encouragement for herself. She had known that the odds were stacked against her, but desperation pushed her forward. She was the gambler putting the last coin in the slot machine, he who has just lost a fortune at the tables. But the tumblers had fallen into place and there was no payment.

At the door I glanced back. Father Mason was beside Margaret, his arms about her shoulders. I knew then that it was all over, that we had grown too far apart ever to be one again. But Margaret would be better off without me. It was Barbara who needed to watch out.

I waited for Father Mason at the entrance to the hospital, and he came down about twenty minutes later. 'They've given her a sedative,' he said to me. 'It might bring her some peace.'

'It's what we all need,' I said.

'You're a bastard, Peter,' he said, shocking me. 'May God forgive you for making me call you that.'

It was a moment I do not care to remember even now. There was something obscene about it, among the plastic orange chairs and the aquarium in the waiting area.

'He has more to forgive than me,' I said.

'I hope He can forgive you,' he said, 'because I cannot.'

'You just told a parable about forgiveness,' I said, stupid with my own superiority.

'They tortured a stranger. You torture your own. Like the Korean, I find it difficult to think that you were ever a child.'

We stood for a moment in silence, and then parted to go our own ways to judgement – salvation or damnation. As with Father Boland, only one of us could be right. And I had no confidence that the right was on my side.

On my way home I stopped at a dingy working man's pub in Kentish Town, where there were about half a dozen Irish labourers in the public bar. They were big men wearing trousers and jackets which had once been Sunday best. They were strangers in a strange community, in a city notorious for not caring, and they seemed to take comfort from the closeness of each other. But I had no comfort, and on my entrance they were no longer the strangers. But they paid me little heed, aware I think that I had none of their humanity.

There was a pay-phone in the corner at the end of the bar, and I do not know how many times I took coins from my pocket with the intention of phoning Barbara. But as the alcohol took hold of me I lost interest.

The whisky dulled my mind, and the happenings of the evening didn't seem so important any more. The truth, after all, had to be spoken some time. That's what I told myself, and in the end I was willing to believe it. But that was only because not to believe didn't bear thinking about.

I stayed in the pub until closing time, and by then was very drunk and in no fit state to drive. But I didn't care at that moment, and I reached home without incident. The devil, they say, takes care of his own and maybe he took care of me that night. But soon neither the devil or anyone else would care for me again.

11

A friend took Sarah and the girls to the hospital the next evening, which meant I didn't have to go. I didn't have to sit in that cramped room, with no excuse now to escape to the day-room. So I stayed at home, claiming I'd had Margaret all to myself the previous evening. When they had gone I sat in the garden with a whisky, but despite the drink I still felt that the world was no longer mine.

It was a warm evening, and from a few gardens away I could hear the rat-tat-tat of a petrol-driven lawnmower, and further away the noise of the traffic. There was a slight breeze, and now and then the apple tree seemed to whisper to it. The grass needed cutting, and once I would have got the lawnmower out and enjoyed the physical task; but this evening I couldn't face anything but the whisky.

When they got back from the hospital I went into the kitchen to meet them. 'How's Margaret?' I asked, still pretending I was human.

Clare looked at me, her face puzzled, but she didn't say anything. Sarah was removing her cardigan and breathing like a winded wrestler, and so she couldn't say anything. It was Nuala who answered, her voice cold as the breeze from the garden, but only something evil would whisper with it now. 'You should know how she is,' she said, 'after yesterday evening.'

'What about yesterday evening?'

'You made her hate herself,' Sarah said, 'treating her like that in front of the priest.' She had removed the cardigan by now and was twisting it in her hands, squeezing the life out of it as if it somehow was alive.

'She wants to die,' Nuala said. 'She doesn't want to live any more.'

'Mommy was crying,' Clare said, 'all the time we were there. She cried and cried.'

'She said she was going to die,' Nuala added, re-emphasizing her earlier words, 'that . . . that she'll kill herself.'

'There's little fear of that,' I said, laughing at the absurdity.

'You can laugh?' Sarah said. 'You can drink whisky and laugh?'

I looked at the empty glass in my hand and carefully placed it on the table. They watched and they waited – maybe for some sign of my certain inhumanity. 'But what did they expect from me?' I thought. 'Crazed anger or violence or a litany of curses?'

'I can't help Margaret,' I said. 'She's beyond anyone's help.'

'You can help her,' Sarah said.

'So what about her God – can't He help her?'

'God can't help her now,' Sarah said, 'only you can.'

'When my son was dying I asked you both for help. God could do nothing then either. I wanted an end to suffering but you refused. Prayers and masses and holy water seemed of more importance. Get your holy water now and your masses and your holy pictures.'

'Mommy broke the picture,' Clare said. 'She broke the picture of the heart. She threw it on the floor and the nurse came and picked it up, and then we had to wait outside in the corridor. But mom stopped crying then.'

'Don't worry,' I said. 'She won't cry any more.'

'She won't cry any more,' Nuala mimicked. 'As if you would care.'

'You be quiet,' I warned.

'I won't be quiet. We all know what you've done to mom.'

'Shut up,' I shouted. 'How dare you speak to me like that! Now go to your room and stay there.'

'I don't care if I have to or not,' she said contemptuously, hesitating for as long as she dared.

Clare began to cry, not looking at me but staring at the floor. I wanted to help her, but there seemed to be no decent feelings within me. It was as if they had been wrung out of me like water from a wet cloth. And these were the moments I had wanted, the moments when I could be a father to my daughters.

'You must think yourself a great man,' Sarah said, 'hurting the very ones who cannot fight back.'

'A good cry won't do her any harm.'

'And you call yourself a father.'

'We're not born fathers,' I said, 'and I haven't had much practice. Margaret saw to that. Like she saw to so many other things. But she won't be seeing again, now will she?' I waited for her argument, but she had none left. She opened up the bundle in her hands, surprised to see that it was a cardigan. She stared at it for a moment and then turned and went out of the room. 'Are you all right, love?' I asked Clare, going down on my haunches beside her.

She lifted her head to look at me, fear and tears in her eyes. I wanted to put my arms about her, but it was to take comfort for myself, not to give any. 'You can watch television,' I said, 'if you want. Or shall I put something nice on the video?'

She shook her head and turned away from me and I knew that there was no comfort to be had there. I felt like an exhibit in a freak show, and thought that Clare turned away because she couldn't bear to look at my deformity. I wanted to be out of the house, to feel again the breeze on my face and to be aware that the world really existed. I kissed Clare's hair, smelling its healthy freshness, overwhelmed by a disharmony of emotions all at once. 'Daddy loves you,' I said. 'You will never know how much.' I turned and left her, going out into the evening. As I got into my car I saw Nuala watching from an upstairs window, and even through the glass I could feel her hostility towards me.

'You look like someone who has forgotten to post their winning pools coupon,' Barbara said when she let me into the flat. 'Who has been mistreating you?'

'Nobody loves me,' I said, half jokingly.

'Poor Peter.' She put her arms about my neck and pulled my head down on to her breasts as if I was a baby. She had a wonderful elusive smell, the natural odour of a woman's body complemented with the best perfume. I could hear her heart beating a lullaby for me, transporting me from the land of the living to a land of fantasy.

My lips were pressed against her cream silk blouse, the soft white skin of her breasts separated from me only by the material. I wanted to take all her comfort, to let it flow into me as if the supply was endless. She held me tighter still, and my lips left a wet ellipse on the silk. She said something, but I didn't properly hear or care. I felt safe for a moment and that was all that mattered.

'Do you want a drink?' she asked, louder this time and I nodded my head as best I could, and pulled my arms tighter about her in case she should try to move away. But in fact she tried to come closer, as if she wanted to share my skin. We shared the moment and then she pushed me away. 'Come on,' she said, 'and I'll get you that drink.'

In the lounge I sat in one of the armchairs and she brought me a whisky. She knelt beside the chair and put an arm about my shoulders, and began to caress the back of my neck with her fingers. It was simple and close and I felt content. The whisky warmed me, and the glow spread to all parts of my body as if little rivers of warmth were running through me.

I told Barbara about my day and about the meeting at the hospital the previous evening, and how I had drunk myself insensible. 'She's threatening to kill herself if I don't become the dutiful husband once more,' I said. 'What do you think of that?'

'We all have a right to our own life,' she said, 'to live or to die as we wish.'

'To kill yourself?'

'Sometimes there's no other alternative.'

'You think Margaret has no other alternative?'

'That's for her to answer. But it might be for the best.'

'For the best! You call killing herself something for the best?'

'You wanted your son to die,' she said. 'What's the difference?'

I thought I detected a note of harshness in her voice and I thought that she wanted to hurt me. I found my good feelings of a short time before evaporating into the air, and my old bitterness and cynicism rushed in to take their place. 'I loved my son,' I said. 'I didn't want him to suffer, and he had no life anyway. He was going to die . . . there seemed no point in keeping him alive. I would gladly have given my own life for him, but for the first time ever I was totally helpless.'

'Your son suffered,' she said. 'Don't you think that Margaret suffers too? And much more than the physical pain?'

'Maybe,' I said, 'but it doesn't give us the right to decide whether it would be better for her to live or to die. We have no right to another person's death.'

'But we have a right to their life? Is that it? We who are animals but who have got intelligence by some freak of nature. In the wild it's only the fittest who survive. But we have to be samaritans – we have to interfere. We do it for our own benefit, or worse still, in the belief of some benevolent god. We want to help these people, but on our terms not theirs. If someone wants to die and we genuinely want to help them, then it should be in helping them to die, and not in trying to prevent them.'

'So if I were to leave you and you were unhappy, you'd kill yourself?'

'No,' she said. 'I would simply look elsewhere. But if I failed I might want to die. Life is for living, Peter. If you no longer live then you have no life. Margaret doesn't live. She exists, just like a tree or a flower exists. If the tree is diseased you cut it down.'

I felt cold now, as if my earlier rivers of warmth had turned to ice, and the feelings I'd had belonged to someone else. 'I would look elsewhere,' Barbara had said, a mere statement of fact. I realized that beneath the shell she knew nothing about life or love, and that she would never know. She only wanted for herself, and I stopped short, seeing in that but a reflection of my own wants. It was only for ourselves that any of us wanted. The only difference between us was that Barbara would not allow anything to stand in her way.

'You sound so cold,' I said. 'I can't imagine why you need someone.'

'I've been alone too long,' she said, 'and I want children. Maybe that doesn't fit in with your idea of me, but there's little I can do about my instinct. It's your nature in the raw again.'

'Nature in the raw has no favourites,' I said. 'A child of ours could just as easily be handicapped. What do you do then?'

'Whatever is necessary for the child, not for you or me.' She stared at me, nothing decipherable in her eyes unless it were that they had no more feeling than if they had been made from glass. 'I know what you're thinking,' she went on, 'but you don't know me, Peter. Twenty years ago when I was a schoolgirl I watched someone close to me die. It wasn't a pretty death, no painful one ever is.'

'Your mother,' I hinted.

'Everyone assumes that children only love their mother,' she said, 'but some of us love our fathers too. He was the kindest man I've ever known. He was as big as a mountain and yet his hands were gentler than my mother's. He would pick me up with one of those hands and throw me above his head. Later I watched him toss up my brother and sister but I knew he liked me the best. He was a fireman and his picture was in the paper once – he'd rescued some woman from a burning house. I remember saying to him to be careful. "Don't you worry about your dad," he said. "He's too careful." Until one day he wasn't. A wall collapsed and he was trapped. His lower body was crushed and he was badly burnt . . . you wouldn't recognize his face. I saw him once in the hospital with my mother. I was so upset she wouldn't let me visit him again. But I would sneak off from school and the sister at the hospital would let me in to see him for five minutes. He lived for seven weeks and I watched him die little by little each day. I knew he had drugs for the pain, but they couldn't take it all away. And he knew he was going to die anyway . . . in fact he didn't want to live. In the end he brought about his own death by his sheer will to die. It's why I felt as I did about your son, Peter. No one had the right to keep him alive.'

'I didn't know,' I said. 'You've never said anything before.'

'I shouldn't have said anything now either. I've never told anyone else. But my father in his living and his dying made me what I am. If you understood that you might understand me.'

'Do we ever understand anyone?'

'No,' she said, 'least of all ourselves. We pretend to understand, but that's only because we're frightened of not knowing.'

'And if we did understand?'

'God help us if we ever did.'

'God,' I said lightly. 'You're not getting religious in your old age?'

'Man wouldn't be able to help us,' she said. 'We would have to turn to God. Even then *I* might need to believe in Him; I might need something for the dark night.'

'You mean you don't need something now?'

'We all need something, but I prefer the warmth of a man to the coldness of a mystery. That happens to be your good luck.' She cuffed me playfully, the old Barbara back with me again. 'We're all giving you a tough time,' she went on. 'Shall I be the obedient woman and get you another drink? And then you can be the big strong man and carry me off to the bedroom and make mad, passionate love to me. And we'll forget about Margaret, and our problems and people wanting to die; and we can even forget about tomorrow.'

I had another drink, and then we went to her bedroom and in the soft evening gloom we made love, and we did forget for a little while. But the sex drained away my resistance and ghosts came to taunt me, materializing from the furthest corners of the room, taking shape from the darkness.

They lined up before me like some sort of jury and every face said 'guilty'. Margaret and the girls and Sarah – then Father Mason and Barbara and my friend John, and Margaret again, and then all the faces in one, no expression now, the faces made up of bits of photo-fit pictures. Their accusation reached out to me, and then hands started to reach out, thousands of hands that might have had a place in some horror movie. They all wanted something – they all wanted a part of me but I had nothing to give. I tried to back away, but the hands only reached with more urgency, touching me, and I tried to push them away.

'Peter! Peter!' There was a hand on my shoulder, shaking me, and I woke to the soft glow of the teamaker. 'You were trying to push me away from you,' Barbara was saying.

'Just a dream,' I said. 'A bad dream.' I was struggling to climb up from the depths of my fear, struggling to be free of the weight of flesh – dead, lifeless flesh that had tried to hold me down.

'It's OK now,' Barbara said soothingly. 'It's OK now.' She put her arms about me and pulled me down on to her breasts, naked breasts now; and again as earlier I could hear her heart beat. But this time it was beating no lullaby for me, and the regular thump thump was like the sound of the executioner's drum.

'I have to go,' I mumbled. 'It's getting late.'

'No.' She still held me close and I could feel the stubble on my cheek like sandpaper against her skin. 'Don't go tonight,' she said. 'Stay with me instead.'

'You're not afraid of the dark?' I said lightly, still trying to ease the fear within me. I disentangled myself so that I could raise my head to look at her. 'And I always thought that you were the big, brave woman and would protect me.'

'No one is really brave,' she said seriously. 'But I like having a man in my bed . . . to wake up in the morning and see him there beside me. A double bed can be very empty and lonely on your own.'

'You've had experience of waking up with a man in your bed then?'

'Jealous?'

'No. Should I be?'

'We'll never have a life together,' she said suddenly. 'Do you know that?'

'Of course we will. It's only a matter of time really. Margaret'll be out of hospital soon.'

'You'll never escape her,' she said, 'not until one of you dies. Isn't that what you promised each other . . . until death do you part?'

'I'd better go,' I said, and she obediently released me. I got out of the warmth and disentangled my clothes from the heap on the floor and dressed. Years ago, I would have been about eighteen at the time, a friend and I had picked up two prostitutes and gone back with them to a flat somewhere near King's Cross. I had to pay first – with two crisp one-pound notes from my paypacket, a high price for a few moments of pleasure.

I'd taken off my trousers and underpants – had in fact struggled to get them off over my shoes. I was wearing a shirt with a tail, and afterwards I caught a glimpse of myself in the cracked dressing-table mirror. With the shirt tail hanging down I looked stupid and vulnerable. I dressed hurriedly, the shabby room with its smell of purchased sex oppressing me. And the thought of untold diseases rotting my genitals until they should drop off suddenly awakened in me nameless terrors.

It also awakened guilt in me – the deep-rooted guilt sown in childhood like a seed, which sprouted suddenly as if it had received a shower of nitrogen-enriched rain. It was a terrible feeling and the guilt seemed to settle in my bowels like a heavy weight.

Now I was touched by that same guilt, maybe induced in me by the gloom, or by shades of what was yet to come, though at that time I could have had no inkling of their full horror. Maybe it was generated by a left-over residue of the child's fear of hell, and the horror of the child's imagination of burning bodies. Or else it was the guilt of betrayal, for every human act is a betrayal of someone.

I looked at Barbara, alone in the big bed with its white semi-circular headboard, one half of her face in deep shadow, a hint of breast above the quilt. There was an indentation mark on the pillow beside her where my head had rested, and I knew that my place in the bed would still be warm. It was my place but I had to reach out and grasp it – take it now while it was still mine, before someone else claimed it for their own.

In the gloomy room I had a glimpse of the future, a continuation of my dream with all the hands reaching for me, but it would be no dream from which I would awaken. I felt vulnerable, as I had done in that shabby room twenty years before, besieged now by ghosts on all sides, ghosts I could neither identify or fight.

Earlier that evening for a brief few moments I had been happy. There was still hope for me then, nothing certain, for in this world there is no certainty, but the hope was there. Only I had to reach out and claim it for my own, even as the hands were reaching for me.

'It's difficult for everyone,' Barbara said, as if reading my thoughts.

'What is?'

'Making a new start . . . reaching out for a new future.'

'I'm nearly forty,' I said. 'I think I might have left it too late to begin again.'

'We begin every day,' she said. 'We begin and we end . . . The only difference is that some of us begin the same life every time.' She stared up at me, but the gloom hid her eyes and I couldn't see what was in them. She waited for me to speak, but I had nothing to say.

'You never find happy people afraid of dying,' she went on. 'Frightened of the diseases that cause death . . . of being crippled and ending up a vegetable, but of actually dying . . . They know they have to die . . . they've come to accept it. And at least they've had something out of life. It's the unhappy people who cannot face death. They feel that life has cheated them . . . they want another chance. You have the chance, Peter, but it won't wait for ever. One day you'll wake up to find it has gone. All you'll have then is regret, and no one should have regret because they're only regretting that which was theirs and which they didn't take when it was offered.'

I said nothing, and she pulled back the quilt cover so that her breasts were in view. Now that she was lying on her back they were flat topped mounds of flesh from the centre of which dark brown nipples stood erect. It seemed as if at some time pigment had seeped from the nipples and stained the surrounding skin. She patted the bed invitingly, and held out her hand to me. 'Come back,' she said. 'Come in here beside me. We've both been alone for too long.'

I should have taken off my clothes and got back into the bed beside her – I should have, but I didn't. And I knew that she was right about many things. She was even right about the regrets, but she'd got it wrong when she said that unhappy people didn't want to die.

I saw now that she had always taken what she wanted from life, like one might pluck an apple from a tree. If the apple was rotten she cast it from her, and if like me it refused to be plucked, she just left it and moved on to the next one. Then the birds came and picked at the stubborn apple, and left it to rot so that no one would ever want it again. But if she really had wanted the apple she wouldn't have allowed anything to stand in her way. It was what I thought now as I hesitated, and then she was pulling up the quilt and I knew that the world was full of others and that she didn't want me badly enough. Not then she didn't, but later she was to need me as neither of us could ever have imagined.

I should have stayed, but instead I kissed her goodnight and promised to call her the next day. When I was outside I looked up at the flat, and through the branches of the cedar tree I could see a light in her kitchen and I caught a glimpse of her as she drew the window blind. I knew that she would make herself some coffee and sit in the kitchen and weigh things up in her mind, wanting to run her private life as she ran her business. I could see the scale with my side unbalanced, Margaret holding all the weights and winning in the end.

I was going home now, but what was home? Home is where the heart lies it is said, trite words, but are they still not the truth? Did my heart belong up there where the light seemed to flicker as the breeze shook the branches of the tree? Or did it really belong to the little girl who earlier that evening had been frightened of me?

I had but one heart, and at the end of the day only one person could have it. I couldn't take it out and say 'half for you and half for you'. I had to give it all, and I had to give it now. For as Barbara had said, tomorrow no one might want it.

12

It seemed as if the chaos caused by the builders would never end, but one day they were gone and I would never have known that they'd been if it had not been for the work they had done. Mr Harris called on the last day and took me on an inspection of the house. He found a few things which required attention – a bit of painting missed here, a screw not properly countersunk somewhere else. 'Little things, Mr Ferson,' he said, 'but it's important to get every detail right. People who become handicapped develop a highly critical faculty. So I don't intend to leave anything for complaint. And by the way, when will the good lady be home?'

'Any day now. She's very depressed at the hospital. The doctors think that coming home might be the best thing for her.'

'Best thing in the world. But you'll have to help her to fight the depression. Don't let it get out of hand. You take my advice, Mr Ferson, firmness at all times. But with kindness . . . more kindness than anything else.'

But the only kindness I had for her was that I wouldn't leave home the minute she was discharged. 'She will need you in the beginning,' the doctor at the hospital said, 'even from a practical point of view.'

Faced with his accusing eyes I agreed to stay for a little while. Barbara was upset, but I promised to come and live with her when she returned from her holiday, and eventually she settled for that. Sarah saw my decision as a small victory, and I knew that she thought if I stayed for a little while I might stay for good. So for the most part she left me alone.

Margaret was discharged one July day, warm even by the standards of that summer. Sarah went to the hospital so that she could travel with Margaret in the ambulance, while at the house I waited with Martin and the girls. They talk about cutting the tension with a knife, but that day it would have required a chain saw and even then you would not be certain to succeed. The ambulance was late too, and that didn't do our nerves any good.

They arrived eventually, and two young ambulance men effortlessly lifted Margaret down from the vehicle and installed her in her chair. Sarah had a travelling rug which she tucked in around Margaret's waist, not for warmth, I knew, but to hide the truth. One of the ambulance men wheeled the chair into the hall, and smiled at me.

'We'll manage now,' I said. 'Thanks . . .'

Margaret didn't look at me but stared at the lift on the stairs, her face like that of a puppet, having but one expression. She opened her mouth to speak, but just then the girls, who were waiting in the kitchen with Martin, could contain themselves no longer and came rushing out to us. They kissed their mother, but her expression never altered and I thought that the puppet would have more response.

'We had the house done specially for you,' Clare said, 'and we've got a lift on the stairs. Look, I can work it myself.' She pressed the button and the seat began to glide upwards, and we all watched as if it was the most amazing thing we had ever seen.

'Stop it,' Margaret suddenly said. 'Stop it . . . stop it . . .'

'Stop it, daddy,' Clare pleaded in her frightened child's voice. 'Please stop it.'

I pressed the stop button and brought the seat back down, and as the motor stopped it seemed to break the tension which had built up.

'Go through to the kitchen,' Sarah said angrily to the girls. 'How can we get past if you're standing there in the way?' The girls retreated quickly and Sarah pushed the chair into the kitchen. And I followed like a man under sentence of death.

The wheelchair was in the centre of the room, with Sarah beside it pointing out the alterations to the kitchen. 'See the new work places,' she said, 'and the new sink unit; you can get a chair right underneath them. We had the new units made up to match the old ones, and you could never tell that anything had been touched.'

I looked around the kitchen at the white units with the blue mouldings and at the white wall tiles and the twin fluorescent tubes hanging from the stark-white ceiling, and I saw it as Margaret's prison, as cold and as alien as if it was a dungeon with dripping walls and huge cockroaches and sleek wet rats scurrying across the stone floor.

How often had she bustled about this room? Not the methodical housewife portrayed in television cookery programmes, but rather one who was in a perpetual hurry. As a child I had taken great pleasure in watching my mother cook, waiting patiently for the mixing spoon so that I could lick it clean. I would watch my father, still dressed in trousers and waistcoat from his best suit, carve the Sunday joint. He would slip me a piece, usually a crisp bit with an onion ring added, his wink to tell me that it was a secret and that I mustn't let my mother know. I was much older before I realized that it was no secret and that my mother had known all the time. But I in my turn had never slipped my daughters a tit-bit because Margaret's fury would have tainted any pleasure that I or indeed the girls might have had.

The kitchen of my youth had been the centre of the house, the heart from which all life radiated. It was a room of warmth and homely smells and security, with its dark red wallpaper and matching linoleum. With its pine dresser, butter-yellow from years of sunlight, the lower shelves bustling with cups and saucers and plates we used every day, the top shelf reserved for my mother's best china, used only on an occasion and taken down and washed once a month. There was an oak table, its polished surface reflecting warmth and cheery faces, and high-backed chairs with padded seats that were never cold to sit on, even in the depths of winter.

My kitchen would have comforted Margaret, wrapped her in its warm shadows, lulled her with the smell of baking bread, and of onions and bacon frying, and the sweet smell of melting butter on feathery potatoes. There were no cooking smells in this kitchen, the extractor fan ensuring that they were given out to the birds. Now there would be other smells to extract – the smell of sickness and suffering and the fermented smell of human fear.

The smell was here now and we were all aware of it. But we could do nothing to banish it, and what did it matter if the new units matched the old – they would never fulfil the use for which they were intended. I saw the future there before me for a moment, trailed out in a series of images like different coloured streamers on the tail of a child's kite. And then I was back to the present and Margaret's reaction to the alterations.

'I want none of it,' she said, 'none of it . . . And that . . . that thing on the stairs, who put it there?'

'It's your lift,' Sarah said, 'so that you can get up and down.'

'I don't want it,' she said. 'I . . . I don't want it.' She must have sensed my presence, for she swung round in the chair towards me. I could see only half of her face, but there was no mistaking the wildness and the fear. The last time she had been in this house she had been a full woman, and had laughed at me and damned me. She had walked out rather than face the truth, but the truth would be with her from now on and she would never again escape from it. 'I want it taken away,' she said to me. 'Just take it away . . .'

'You can't get up or down the stairs without it,' I said patiently.

'Upstairs! What's upstairs for me?'

'Your room . . . you have to sleep there.'

'Your room,' she said, 'your bed . . . I want no part of it.' She manoeuvred the chair with her pale, nervous hands, turning about to face me. Her eyes were empty, devoid of all expression, and it was only her voice that gave an indication of her feelings. The face was still that of a puppet, but I was wrong about the expression. The face was as dead as the eyes, and surely neither could reflect any genuine emotion ever again. The woman in the chair before me who had once been capable of so much would never hate or love anyone again. And I realized that Barbara, who had never met her, knew her better than I did. Barbara had been right when she said Margaret would be better off dead.

Her dark hair no longer shone but lay limp and lifeless like the wet fur of an animal. The task of actually living was taking up more calories than she consumed, and her face and shoulders reflected this. Her green floral-patterned dress hung on her and her breasts barely made a curve in the bodice. The woollen travelling rug trailed from her lap to the floor, but it was no more successful in hiding her tragedy than the blanket had been.

She saw me watching her, staring at the rug, and suddenly she reached down with her hand and threw the rug to the floor. She plucked nervously at the dress as if trying to pick one of the flowers. 'It's empty,' she said. 'It's all your fault that it's empty.' Her voice didn't accuse me, nor did her eyes. She was merely stating a fact.

Sarah picked up the rug and put it back in place, tucking it in round the edges of the seat. 'I'll make us a cup of tea,' she said soothingly, as if speaking to a baby. 'And don't be getting yourself all worked up. We'll have plenty of time to talk about things.'

'He hates me,' Margaret said. 'I'm the mother of his children . . . his wife and he hates me.'

'I don't hate you,' I said. 'You hate yourself.'

'Leave her alone,' Sarah said. 'Can't you see she's upset?'

'She has to face reality some time,' I said. 'Now might be the best time there is.'

'Maybe you should leave her alone,' Martin said, finding the courage to speak from some place. I stared at him and he looked away, all his courage in the words.

'You hate me,' Margaret said, staring at me. 'You've always hated me.'

'I can't stop you from believing what you want,' I said, 'but meanwhile you have to live.'

'You call this living!'

'It's all you've got,' I said. 'You'll have to learn to make the most of it.'

'You're glad I'm like this,' she said. 'It's as if you wanted me to have the accident . . . you wanted me to be crippled.' She had a burst of crying but there were no tears, and I knew that she would never have tears again – not real tears, anyway.

We stood and stared at her, we who had once loved her. Maybe Martin and the girls still loved her, I did not know, but had they loved her surely they could have helped her. We had compassion for her but we would have had compassion for a stranger, and that, I realized, was the most damning of all. We couldn't love her because we knew Margaret and we knew her sins. It is only God who can know everything about us and still love us all the same.

Margaret cried now, a dry caustic crying that did nothing to help her. She was crying for the things which had once been hers, and crying because of the things which had replaced them – like the empty dress and the wheelchair and the lift on the stairs and the special kitchen. She had given everything in the hospital and now had nothing left. And even if she had she would never give again. It was Margaret who was sitting in the chair in the kitchen, but a Margaret who had lost everything, even the malevolence that might have made her human.

Sarah tried to comfort her daughter, but had long ago forgotten how. Martin, not knowing how to react, and hurt by us all, escaped into the garden. Nuala stood in the corner behind the door, wearing a pair of tight jeans and a sweater, the ends of the jeans tucked into a pair of short boots. She looked like a young woman in the clothes, but her face was as much that of a child as Clare's. She stood by the table and watched me suspiciously, equating crying with pain, unaware that the ones who don't cry usually suffer the most.

There was nothing I could do, so I went out of the kitchen and down the hall, intently aware of the house as if it was the last time I should see it. The last time I would walk on the parquet floor, or hear the steady tick of the grandfather clock, or see the telephone with the automatic directory and the leather-bound message book, and the telephone lock lying discarded beside it. The lock had been Margaret's idea, to stop Nuala and Clare from using the phone without permission. But what did it matter now? I opened the door to go out and I heard Clare call my name, and she came running down the hall towards me.

'You're not going away, daddy?' she asked, her eyes uncertain.

'Just going to work,' I said.

'Gran said that you would leave us when mom came home. You're not leaving now?'

'No, I'm not leaving now.' I hesitated for a moment, not sure how much her child's mind could accept. 'But daddy has to leave some time,' I said quietly. 'Maybe soon . . .'

She stared at me, not fully understanding my words. I tried to imagine what was going through her mind, but I'd never had to suffer anything like the uncertainty that Clare was now facing. I knew that she wanted to be reassured that Sarah's story wasn't true, but all I had for her was the fact that it was true.

'Can I come with you when you go away?' she asked.

'Your mom will need you,' I said. 'You'll have to help take care of her.'

'Why?'

'Because you love her, don't you?'

'You don't love her,' she said. 'Why don't you love her, daddy?'

But I had no answer for her except maybe the truth, but the truth was too harsh and brutal.

'Can I come with you?' she asked again. 'When you go.' She was small for her age, and her long dark hair reached to her waist. She was wearing a candy-striped dress and ankle socks, and a pair of Clark's sandals, brown and strong and sensible. They gave her the appearance of maturity, and I realized with a shock that she wasn't really a child. Eight years old her last birthday, and already she had been through more than any child had the right to endure.

'I'll still see you,' I said, hurt by what I'd seen. 'And you'll be able to come and see me too.'

'I don't want to come,' she said. 'I don't want you to go away. My friend Julie – her dad went away and she cried in our kitchen one day and her mom said that her dad was no good. An' he was good. He used to buy me and Julie chocolate, an' he took us to the pictures once.'

'I'll buy you chocolate,' I said, 'and take you to the pictures. I'll come every week and take you wherever you want to go.'

'To McDonald's?'

'If you like. And you can have anything you want, and it'll be our secret. You can keep a secret, can't you?'

'Yes,' she said, nodding her head vigorously. 'And I'll tell everyone that you are the best daddy.'

'You tell them,' I said, aware that she was the only one who would believe it. I felt like a cheat, like the man who would rob his child's piggy-bank, and shamed by this, I had to get away. 'I have to go to work,' I said. 'I've got lots of work to do.'

'Goodbye, daddy,' she said, and her trust made me feel like Judas.

'Be good,' I said, and I went out, pulling the door shut behind me.

I had made arrangements to visit our North London service department that afternoon, and I went there now and took over the manager's office and spent the time going over the dated stock registers. A girl brought me a coffee and while I was drinking it I rang Barbara.

'I can't see you tonight,' she said. 'I'm having dinner with Ray. He's in London and we need to discuss some business.'

'What time will you be finished?' I asked. 'I could call then.'

'I don't know, Peter. You know what business is.'

'I know,' I said, thinking her answer somewhat evasive.

'Well I'm a little busy,' she said, 'so if you don't mind I'll let you go.'

Inwardly I did mind, but I kept my thoughts to myself and we said our goodbyes. I immersed myself again in the old registers, using the figures as a form of balm. They helped but they weren't enough, and by six o'clock I needed something stronger. The manager accepted my invitation to have a drink and we went along to the local, a drab pub that reflected the dying industrial estate.

We talked about work mostly, and we drank some beer and I didn't want to leave. But after a while I saw the manager glance at his watch, and I knew he wanted to go home. We shook hands and I assured him that he was doing a good job, and he went off, satisfied I supposed.

I couldn't face going home and yet I didn't want to spend the evening drinking alone. I was aware of what too much alcohol could do, and hoped yet that I might have some form of life to live. It wasn't a thought I had great confidence in, but I didn't want to be half-way towards an alcoholic if the opportunity for life should be presented to me.

I hadn't eaten since morning so I stopped at a Wimpy and ordered a mixed grill. I felt out of place there, my grey tailor-made suit with collar and tie and my expensive leather shoes contrasting sharply with the jeans and T-shirts and sneakers. They were for the most part young, couples for whom love was as untarnished as a new piece of silver, certain and content in their own world. There were the ones alone like myself, young and old, taking ages over a cup of coffee, trying to pass a few hours in a life where one minute could stretch out like a piece of elastic and yet never break.

I eked out over an hour myself and then drove to Barbara's. There was a light in her kitchen like a welcoming beacon, and I felt my spirits rise. Suddenly I knew that I wanted to spend the night with her, to wake in the morning with her naked body beside me in the big bed.

She answered the door and I saw the shock register on her face. 'You,' she said, blocking the door.

'Aren't you going to ask me in?'

'You shouldn't have called; I told you I was having dinner with Ray.'

'You told me. But you're finished now and here I am.'

'We haven't finished . . . exactly.' She was hesitant, watching me closely. 'We didn't get it all sorted out at the restaurant so we came back here. Ray's here now . . .'

'You want me to go then?' I felt all my pleasure draining

away, as if a leech that specialized in sucking out our gladness had attached itself to my body. I had been able to accept meetings in busy restaurants, but here . . .

'I suppose you'd better come in,' she said. She let me in to the hall and closed the door and I followed her, watching her bottom moving suggestively in the tight, white jeans. Normally it would have aroused me, but now I felt nothing but uncertainty about the future.

He was seated on the couch under the window, two glasses on the occasional table before him. The curtains were partly drawn and the room was gloomy. There were no papers on the table and the gloom wouldn't have helped one to see them properly, so now I had more reason to feel uncertain. The music centre was giving off a soft glow and I knew that they had been listening to records. Or maybe to one of the concerts on Radio Three, or wherever, a concert that a Philistine like myself wouldn't understand.

They had been having a nice cosy evening such as Barbara and myself had shared on many occasions, those now forgotten evenings before any question of permanency to our relationship had been raised.

Barbara introduced us and he stood up to shake my hand. He was forty, I would have guessed, big and heavy and with a thick, black beard which gave him a piratical appearance. He had that self-assurance that comes from money and power, and I didn't like him. 'You two get to know each other,' Barbara said, 'and I'll make some coffee.' She was calm now, and I knew she wouldn't care what I thought. 'My life is my own,' she had once said. 'Don't ever forget that.'

I didn't want a drink but I poured myself a small whisky, wanting to show him that I knew my way around. I even offered to refill his glass but he declined. I sat in one of the armchairs and stretched out my legs, the man of the house taking his ease.

'You're in the television trade,' he said. 'I'm sure Barbara mentioned it.'

'I work for a rental company.'

'Oh.' He paused as if trying to collect his thoughts. 'I'd imagined that you'd worked on the broadcasting side. Rental, eh . . . A business that's on the way out I should think . . . bit of a dead end now.'

I wanted to punch his stupid face for him, not because I felt insulted but because I considered him a rival. What I didn't know was whether Barbara considered him a rival too. She had never mentioned him in any other capacity except as her business lawyer, but then it probably was not something she would have talked about anyway.

We made desultory conversation, the only thing we had in common being our desire for Barbara. She brought in the coffee and poured it for us, and then sat on the other armchair. But I had a picture of them earlier in the evening, of Barbara sitting beside him on the couch, the music playing softly in the background. Easy enough for lips to meet, for hands to explore. Imagination, I wanted to pretend, but I couldn't dispel the doubts that easily.

We were a strange trio, sitting there in an atmosphere of almost total silence, a silence that was all but tangible. The loneliness I'd experienced earlier returned, and it swept over me like the fiery breath of a dragon might. And yet here in this room I shouldn't feel lonely; here my future lay, whatever it might be.

'I don't like to do it,' Barbara eventually said, stretching herself so that her small breasts pushed against her blouse, 'but I've had a long day. So I'm going to throw you two out.'

'Sorry,' Ray said, all contrite. 'I hadn't realized that it was this late.' He put the coffee cup on the table and rose to his feet, only then becoming aware that I hadn't got up. It was too late and he had already committed himself. Barbara got up too and was dwarfed beside him. 'Come on then,' he said, 'and she can chuck us both out at once.'

I waited for Barbara to tell me to stay, but she didn't say anything and I got to my feet. We said our goodbyes at the door and then she closed it on us. Out on the pavement Ray shook my hand before roaring away in his Porsche, and I was aware that he was more confident than I was.

For a moment I was tempted to go back up to the flat, remembering my earlier resolve to stay the night. But I knew that Ray would be there between us and that we would fight over him. Instead I got into my car and drove away, and I wondered if soon I might be driving away from here for the last time.

13

The experts said it was the best summer we had had in years, and as August drew to a close I couldn't believe that the sunshine had almost gone. I hated the winter, with its fogs and snow and ice, and opaque windscreens, and the coughing of sick cars.

Barbara was flying off on her holiday on the bank holiday Saturday, and I knew that I would miss her more than I would miss the summer. 'You could come with me,' she said. 'It could be our honeymoon.'

'I couldn't have four weeks from work,' I said, 'and anyway I just couldn't afford it. All our money has gone on converting the house.'

'And for what?'

'It had to be done. We can all know better with hindsight.'

'You'll have to put her away,' she said. 'It'll be the only solution.'

'Maybe.' It seemed more and more like the only choice, but I didn't want it. There was no love in me, but I knew that I couldn't live with myself if Margaret had to go into a home. And yet what was I to do with her? Her visits to the rehabilitation centre were a waste of time, and she refused to co-operate with the staff. With a daily visit from a nurse Sarah just about coped, and the cleaning lady I had employed, who came in five days a week, was in contention for a sainthood. But she couldn't do it for ever, and when her children returned to school she would have to limit her visits to two or maybe three a week.

We all tried to talk to Margaret but she just sat like a

zombie in the chair, most times pushing the chair to the back door and sitting there for hours staring out into the garden. She had become obsessed about many things – always wanting the windows open and no noise and eating the little she did eat by herself in the dining-room. And she had put the locks back on the phones, and the keys were always missing. But the phone in my study was not locked, I supposed because she couldn't get the chair through the door, or else it was part of her effort to convince herself that I didn't exist.

She seemed to have lost her faith too, and I'd had to take down the few religious pictures we had upstairs, and the small water font by the front door, which had been dry for a long time. And when Father Boland called at Sarah's request, Margaret refused to see him.

'She thinks that God has deserted her,' he said to me. 'But she'll come back to God in her own time. We must all pray for her.' But the prayers went unanswered.

She wouldn't speak to me, even as she wouldn't speak to God, and whatever words were necessary to reach me always came through Sarah or the girls. But they were rare, and then they were mostly to ask me to leave her alone, to say that she wanted no more visitors, that she could never love me again, that I would never escape from her and that she wanted to die. Until in the end I gave up as God had, and to put her away in a home seemed the only answer.

'It would be best,' Barbara said now. 'At least she would get looked after properly in a home.'

'I know,' I said, 'but if she goes into a home now she will never recover. It will mean she has been rejected by everyone.'

'But she has been rejected,' she said quietly, 'by everyone.'

I knew that Barbara was right, but knowing didn't make it any easier. We had all rejected Margaret; even the girls had rejected her after the first week, children more aware than any of us how difficult it is to love a horrible person. Martin, I think, was the only one of us who still cared for her, but he stayed for most of the time in Cricklewood and could afford to make allowances on the occasions he saw his daughter.

I stared at Barbara, her legs curled up under her in the chair, her tennis skirt showing off her thighs. She had a fine down of white hair on her legs, soft like a kitten's fur, never having had razor or wax treatment. I wanted to touch the hair lightly with my finger-tips to see the goose-pimples emboss her skin. She saw me watching her and she touched the hair herself with her finger tips, as if she could read my mind, but there were no goose-pimples. 'It needs another's touch,' I said, wanting to steer our conversation away from Margaret. Lately it seemed as if we talked about nothing else.

'You want to do it?'

'All the time.'

'I'll let you do it if you come on holiday with me.'

'I can't afford to.'

'Someone else can,' she said. 'Maybe I'll take him.'

'A tall handsome stranger?'

'Ray has asked me to marry him,' she said, and though her voice was still light we weren't joking any longer. She was watching me carefully, watching for my reaction, ready to file it away as if at some future date it might be of use to her. 'You know that he's madly in love with me?'

'Maybe you should take it while it's being offered,' I said bitterly. 'He should be able to afford it anyway. And he could always sell the Porsche.'

'Poor Peter,' she said. 'I do believe you're jealous. Ray's a little boy. He would never give up his Porsche nor his nights at the club . . . nor his women. Children don't like to give up their toys. Not that I'd mind the toys . . . it's the women I wouldn't be able to tolerate. We may not know how to love but we know how to be jealous. Now you don't have any toys and you won't run off with any woman. In fact you still don't want to leave Margaret, do you?'

'If you say so.'

'I've upset you,' she said. 'I'm sorry. You have enough to contend with as it is.' She held out her hand to me and I got up and walked across to take it; I knelt by the side of the chair and put my arms about her. She lowered her head on to my shoulder and I nuzzled her hair, drinking in its smell, an aroma that seemed too natural to have come from a bottle. Her hair was bluey black, and now caught in the light from the window it had the sheen of wet slates.

It felt good to have my arms about her, feeling her warmth through the cotton top she was wearing. I thought of four weeks without her, and I felt certain that if she were to ask me now to go with her I would say yes and to hell with everything. But she didn't ask me, and in a way her silence, unknown to us, was deciding our future.

'So what are you going to do with Margaret?' she asked me. 'Remember you've promised to come and live with me when I return from holiday. You haven't forgotten, have you?'

'No, I haven't forgotten. As for Margaret . . . well I don't know. Sarah has asked Father Mason to call at the weekend. Maybe he can make Margaret see some sense. If not . . .'

'You think that the priest might be able to do something?' Her voice was low and I couldn't tell if there was a note of sarcasm there or not.

'I don't know,' I said, 'but he's our last hope.'

It was a poor hope, and I knew when Father Mason called on Sunday and I saw Margaret's reaction that he could do nothing. We were to have had dinner together, but Margaret refused to sit in the dining-room with us. And sitting around the table I saw it as a very sad occasion.

When we bought the house Father Mason had called to

bless it the weekend we moved in. We had dinner in the dining-room that day too, but seated around the formica-topped table we had brought from our flat, not the beautiful oak one we bought later which was so rarely used now. That had been the first time Father Mason had seen the house and he had been enthralled with it. 'You'll have half a dozen children here,' he'd said. 'You're a lucky man, Peter. It's when I see people like your good selves, starting out, the whole of your lives before you . . . well I sometimes wonder if I've got the right profession. I'd make a fine grandfather you know.'

We'd all laughed at that, even Nuala joining in, her child's joy touching us all. 'You'll have grandchildren,' I said to him, 'all the ones we'll have to fill up the house. Even a grandson of your own one day.'

The dream had died even as his grandson had died, and now I remembered the time Father Mason had come to the hospital to see the baby, and how he'd cried in the corridor afterwards, torn by grief; not for the baby I knew but for all of us. 'You have to love your son,' he said to me, 'more than you have ever loved before. Because he's only going to be left to you for a very short time.' Four months to him was but a moment, but for my son and I . . .

It was a sad meal, and even Martin's home-grown strawberries with Sarah's home-made cream – twenty minutes of pumping in the kitchen, disdaining the use of our Kenwood Chef with its cream-making attachment – couldn't cheer us up. And I knew that Sarah had tried to put all her tensions into the pumping, but it was like the magic bottle and the more she pumped her tensions away the more they increased.

It was a silent meal too, and only the necessary words were spoken. As I looked around the table I was aware that it was to be the last time we would all be together. But I felt no regret, because we were together only in the physical sense. There was not one ounce of spirit between us, if one could have weighed that elusive quality. We might have been close once but we would never be close again.

After dinner Father Mason took Margaret into the garden and they sat in the shade of one of the apple trees. I think we all knew that it was the last chance for Margaret and if all failed now she was lost. It seemed to me as if Sarah thought the priest would be able to work a miracle, but I had no such hope. In thirty-eight years I had seen no miracles and had come to doubt in the existence of God. Not the God of the Catholic church, the wafer-thin piece of bread in the tabernacle, but of any God in any guise, even the God made up from the total goodness of mankind. Though I had doubts about God I had no doubts about the devil. In fact the devil was within ourselves and we had banished God to make way for him.

I went into my study to sort out some papers, Margaret and Father Mason not visible unless I stood at the side of the window and looked across the garden. But they were in my mind and they interfered with my concentration, making the figures at times into nonsensical blurs.

I was at my desk but minutes when Nuala tapped on the door. I looked up to see her framed in the doorway, her white shorts and T-shirt just coming down on the right side of decency by the very fact of her childish innocence, more noticeable today than it had been for a long time. She too was suffering the tension that was our lot this afternoon, and with that to combat she had forgotten to be a sex symbol.

'Can I use your phone?' she asked.

'Use the one in the sitting-room.'

'It's locked . . . they all are.'

'Unlock it then. I've given you permission.'

'I can't,' she said, her voice becoming irritated. 'The keys are missing. And she won't tell us where they are.'

'She!' I said. 'Who's she?'

'Mom,' she said, having to drag the word out.

'That's better. And I don't want to hear you refer to your mother as she again.' I stared at her but she just stared back, and now the clothes looked cheap and vulgar and she wasn't a child any longer. 'Now use the phone if you want to.'

'I don't want to now,' she said, and she turned and walked away.

'Nuala,' I called, 'Nuala . . . ,' but she ignored me and didn't reply. I made to get up to follow her, but sank back into the chair. There was nothing to be gained by chasing her, by trying to plead or threaten.

I stared out of the window to where the apples were heavy on the tree before me. Nuala had helped pick the apples that year we moved in, riding high on my shoulders, grabbing the fruit with both hands and squealing with pleasure when it broke away, heavy in the tiny grasp, most dropping on the ground where Margaret picked them up, laughing too, infected by her daughter. Some of the apples dropped on my head, but I ignored the hurt and shouted 'ouch' at every one.

The figures could never make sense and I pushed them away. Like an old man I heaved myself upright and went into the kitchen. 'The phones are locked,' I said to Sarah. 'Do you know where the keys are?'

'Margaret doesn't know where she put them,' Sarah said, 'but they'll turn up. They have done before.'

I nodded and went out in search of Nuala. I found her in her room, sitting in front of the dressing-table before the window. 'I'm sorry for being upset with you,' I said. 'You can use the phone if you want.'

'It doesn't matter,' she said.

Margaret's reflection stared back at me from the mirror, cold as the glass. My daughter, flesh of my flesh, closer to me than anyone on earth, whose love I had lost before she could have known the meaning of the word. Around and about me was her life – the pop posters on the wall, faces from the television but to which I could put no name; all having more relevance in her life than I did. There were cosmetics on the dressing-table – the first time I had seen any there. They had obviously been bought since the accident, with no one to check on her or to refuse her permission to have them. Margaret probably hadn't been in the room since her return from hospital, or worse still had been here but didn't care any more. And I hadn't been close enough to come in here to see. I knew nothing about my daughter's life. It was but one other failure.

I thought of my own upbringing in that little terraced house where there was always the warmth of genuine human feeling. And if in a way my parents had been strangers to me in later life, it was only because of shyness and awkwardness, and I'd known deep down in what some people would call the soul that they had really loved me. It was that which mattered, not the fact that they might have bought me a new bike, or anything else for that matter.

Around me in this room were thirteen years of false love, of love bought in any high-street store. The row of dolls on top of the wardrobe, some of them china and never played with because Margaret thought they might get broken. The black teddy-bear sitting in the child's rocking chair, too big to be of any use as a plaything, bought only because it was big and expensive and it had a lot of love to make up for. Recent presents like the clock radio on the bedside table, and the music centre with its pile of records, and the personal stereo bought for her last birthday. A mockery of things bought for money and given for love.

'If the phones are locked again,' I said, 'you can use the one in my study,' and I was aware that I was only giving another substitute for love. I waited for her to say something but she remained silent, and her green eyes watched me in the mirror.

I left her to her room and her possessions, given so easily. They only cost money after all. I couldn't put all the blame on Margaret but I couldn't carry it all myself either. Share it out, but it didn't ease the burden. It belonged to each of us, all of it, mirror reflections of our failure.

Sarah had made some tea and we sat in the kitchen to drink it, silent people, all of us failures. Father Mason brought the wheelchair and its pathetic burden back in, and at Margaret's request pushed the chair into the sitting-room. A moment later Clare came running in upset and angry.

'She switched the television off,' she complained. 'You tell her that I want to watch it.'

She. Not a human being any more . . . reduced now to a pronoun. 'You can watch the one upstairs,' I said.

'It's only black and white,' she said angrily. 'I want to watch the colour one.'

'You shouldn't be watching any,' I said. 'You either do what you're told or there won't be any television for a week.'

Hurt replaced the anger – a child's uncomprehending hurt. I thought that Sarah might intervene but she said nothing, silenced at last, maybe seeing the futility of words. She poured Father Mason a cup of tea, the cup and saucer shaking in her hand.

'Too nice a day to be inside,' Father Mason said. 'I think I'll sit in the garden. Peter?'

I went with him, taking a chair to the apple tree, a black shadow on the ground. There were children playing in a garden a few houses away, their voices carrying clearly on the still air.

'What's happened to us?' Father Mason asked, posing a question that needed no answer. He held the cup before him with both hands, but some of the tea had already spilt in the saucer and the rest sploshed around in the cup as if moved by some great turbulence.

A child began to cry in that other garden, the cries rising above the other sounds . . . the cries of an animal's fear. It lasted for a few moments, the fear lessening then disappearing altogether. All our primeval fear in the child's fear, but no one to hush us, no arms, no comfort, no love . . . I looked at Father Mason and I could tell that he had been listening and that he too did not understand.

'She's beyond hope,' I said. 'You must realize that.'

'We must never give up hope,' he said. 'After all, despair is one of the worst sins.'

'God has let her down,' I said, 'and you talk about sin.'

'God,' he said, looking at me, finding in himself the man who had once damned a bishop, digging him out from depths that he must have thought were too deep ever to be reached. 'Why are you so ready to blame God for everything?' he asked. 'All God's work – all the evil in the world down to Him. God hasn't let her down . . . He never lets us down. It's her own who have let her down.'

I watched as he tried to drink the tea, his hand as unsteady as Sarah's. Tea was of little use to him, and I knew that the only thing that might steady him was a whisky. 'I'll get you a drink,' I said.

'I don't want your damn drink,' he said. 'All I need is you. You!' He stared at me, the hands beginning to steady now. 'You have to give,' he went on, 'it's the only hope for Margaret. You have to be a family again here in this house which both of you have damned. You have to undamn it now or one day you'll regret it. You'll remember this afternoon under the apple tree and you'll wish that you had it all again. Come into the house with me, Peter, and I'll bless you all as a family. God will give the strength you need. You need Him now like you have never needed Him before.'

'I don't need Him,' I said. 'He's taken everything I've ever had.'

'It may be your last chance. God might not give you another.'

'There's nothing God can give me,' I said. 'From now on I take what I want.'

'We sat in this garden a long time ago,' he said. 'What has happened to us since? Sarah asked me here today to help . . . to see if I could do something. What can I do? You tell me, Peter.'

He didn't want an answer, and maybe knowing that there wasn't one he got to his feet and went back into the house. I was glad to see him go because his presence made me uneasy, could still touch something within me. He had wanted to reason with me as a man, but the man had nothing to offer him and he had fallen back on the arguments of the priest. I don't know what he had expected, but certainly not the Margaret or the Peter he had encountered.

Margaret's loss of faith was more than just superficial. The faith had gone from deep within her, just as mine had gone. She had lost the faith at the very moment she had needed it most, the very moment when it might have saved her. I supposed her faith was not so much a belief in God, as a fear of hell. Now that she had found herself in hell, there was no reason to fear any more.

Father Mason didn't stay much longer, making the excuse of the long drive, but I knew that it was the house and its occupants that sent him away. He shook hands with us all, but I was the one he had advice for.

'Don't forget what I told you,' he said. 'Put it into effect before it's too late. And whatever happens I hope you'll be happy. What else can I wish you? And maybe one day we can all forgive you.'

'Don't worry about forgiveness,' I said. 'I should manage without.'

'You'll manage,' he said, 'for now anyway. But you'll need forgiveness one day . . . only don't leave that day until it's too late.'

It was to be his last advice to me – maybe the best advice I ever had. But I wanted none of the implications of it or the price I would have to pay to implement it. I didn't think that I needed forgiveness, or that I needed to forgive anyone either. But soon I was to need both, only to find that I had left it too late, and there was no one to forgive me or for me to forgive. And I could never forgive myself.

14

The week till Barbara's holiday passed quickly and, more important still, quietly. The only slight hitch was on the Thursday when Sarah didn't feel well and I took her home to Cricklewood. On the Friday evening the girls went to see their friend Aine Butler to make arrangements for the weekend, promising me that they would be home by eight. But eight came and went and they hadn't returned. I had a dinner appointment with Barbara at eight thirty, and I waited another ten minutes but there was no sign of them. 'Damn,' I thought, aware that I would have to leave now if I wanted to be on time; and I wanted to be on time tonight of all nights.

Margaret was in the kitchen, sitting as usual by the door to the garden. It was a warm evening but she had a heavy cardigan about her shoulders and the usual rug on her lap, tucked in tightly at the sides of the chair. 'I have to go out,' I said to her back. 'Is there anything you need?'

'You can't leave me alone,' she said.

'The girls will be back soon.'

'You can't leave me!' She didn't turn her head to look at me, but spoke to the grass and the trees and the flowers.

'I have to go,' I said, 'I have an appointment . . .'

'No,' she said, 'no . . . no . . .', and her 'nos' followed me out into the hall; I felt certain they would have come out into the drive with me if I hadn't hurriedly closed the door.

I collected Barbara at her flat and we drove to our Indian restaurant. 'Maybe we should have gone somewhere else,' I said when we were seated at our table. 'Remember what happened last time.'

'It doesn't bother me now,' Barbara said. 'I know you'll come to live with me when I return from holiday. You can't live with her any more. In fact you're beginning to go grey already.' She pulled playfully at my locks and stared at an imaginary hair between her fingers. 'There,' she said, 'so white you can't see it.'

'No more,' I said. 'I can't afford to lose them. My father went bald at fifty. Not that it mattered much to my mother; she still loved him.'

'I'd still love you,' she said, stroking my hair with her fingertips, 'even if you were bald and fat and . . . and just ugly . . .'

'You don't believe in love,' I said, 'so I'd better stay thin and hairy and pretty just in case.'

'I do love you,' she said. 'I'll always love you.' She stared at me across the small table, suddenly taking my hand in hers, squeezing it until it might hurt. The waiter brought our starters and I tried to take my hand away, but Barbara held on to it. But the waiter paid no heed to our intimacy, and he gave us his best smile. Maybe he was in love himself.

'What's got into you?' I said to Barbara. 'Since when has this love taken you over?'

'Since today.'

'Today? What's so important about today?'

'We have to fall in love some day. Today's the day for me. It's up to you now to keep me loving you.'

'How do I manage that?'

'Come and live with me,' she said, 'and be nice to me . . . and to our children.'

'Oh my goodness,' I said. 'I knew I shouldn't have had that vasectomy.' I winked at her in my best lecherous style. 'I might have . . .'

'You haven't,' she said. She stared at me for a long

moment, and then laughed, taking the serious look from her face. 'I checked one night when you nodded off. Mind you, it wasn't easy . . . under the blankets with a torch and a magnifying glass.'

'And a deerstalker.'

'A what?'

'Elementary, my dear Watson.'

'Oh.' She laughed and I laughed with her and we were both happy.

It was an excellent meal and our conversation was the sauce, our plans for the future, our hopes, our dreams. And maybe one day I would come to love her . . . maybe it *was* possible to learn to love someone.

I paid for the meal in cash and Barbara laughed at me. 'It wouldn't matter,' she said, 'because I am your wife. I'll be your wife until death us do part. Isn't that what I'm supposed to promise?' She hit me playfully. 'Come on, let's go home.

Outside the evening had become chilly, and I shivered. Barbara put her arms about my waist and held me tight. 'Are you all right?' she asked.

'I'm fine,' I said. 'It's just that a man doesn't find out everyday that someone loves him. You get frightened that you'll lose it.'

'We won't lose it,' she said. 'We won't ever lose it.' We stopped by the car and she came close to me and we kissed, and her nails hurt my back through my jacket. I heard her moan and she physically went weak, and her passion was almost frightening. She was clinging like a child might cling, threatening never to let go. A car passed at that moment and its horn sounded and there were shouts and cheers. We came apart to look; the car had stopped at the junction, and two young male faces leered at us and then burst into laughter. They shouted encouragement, and suddenly Barbara was kissing me again, and then we came apart for the second time, doubling up with laughter. The car horn blew a fanfare for us, and as it pulled away it left the youth of its occupants behind with us.

'Let's go home,' I said to Barbara, 'before we're arrested.'

Her passion in bed that night was something I had never before experienced; it was as if I was making love to a totally different woman; as if for the moments of love she was the embodiment of passion. It was an experience that might have frightened me if the passion had not been infectious. 'You should go away more often,' I said, when we lay close together afterwards, 'if this is the result of it.'

'We won't ever be alone again,' she said. 'When I come back from holiday we won't ever again be parted. Promise me that, Peter.'

'I promise,' I said.

'Cross your heart.'

'You got religion, too?' I laughed.

'Cross your heart!' She pulled away from me and lifted herself up on her elbow, her breasts enlarging to small handfuls of flesh. She gripped my shoulder with her right hand, her nails digging into me until I felt certain she would draw blood. The teamaker light was on and I could see her eyes; there was something in them that was frightening, almost primeval.

'You're killing me,' I said. 'You've got long nails, you know.'

'Promise first.'

'I promise . . . cross my heart and hope to die.'

'I'm . . . I'm sorry,' she said. 'I've . . . I've hurt you.' Her lips were gentle on the marks left by her nails, and I could feel her nipples hard against my chest, and the softer warmth of the breasts around them. She just lay there, the weight of her body a comfort across my chest. I wanted to stay there for ever but it was time for me to go.

'It's late,' I said. 'I'd better be off.'

'No!' Her arms gripped me tightly and I could feel her trembling.

'I have to,' I said. 'I've got to be up early to take you to the airport.'

'Not tonight . . . stay with me tonight.' She raised herself up again and I could see the pleading in her eyes. 'It's our last night for four weeks.'

'I know. But the girls are on their own.'

'They'll be on their own soon enough,' she said. 'You can't be running home then, you know.' She looked at me long and hard. 'I won't share you, Peter; I want you all for myself. I don't want her to have any part of you.' She was a different woman in every way tonight: sometimes happy, sometimes like a frightened child.

I lay for a while still undecided, and then a car horn sounded outside and there was the squeal of brakes and tyres. A man's angry shout carried into the room through the partly open window, bringing in with it the harsh reality of the world outside. It was warm in the bed, Barbara's head on my shoulder and her easy rhythmic breathing beside my ear. My world was here if I wanted it. Stay now, or else venture out into the world of angry people and car horns and screeching car tyres. My choice – my life – no one else could live it for me.

I tightened my arms about Barbara and she tried to snuggle closer to me. Outside the other world went by, cars racing past us, the powerful roar of a motorcycle accelerating up the hill, disappearing into the night. I listened to the sounds, thinking that sleep would never come, and what seemed but a moment later there was the harsh note of the teamaker alarm and the light of the dawn through the window.

We made love but now there was only tenderness and closeness, and it was as if I had imagined the wild passion of the previous night. Afterwards I watched Barbara take a shower, her body reflecting the care she'd taken of it.

She laughed at me as I tried to get rid of my stubble with her Philips 'Ladyshave', and she rubbed her cheek against mine. I took a shower and the cold water stunned me for a moment as it always did, and then came the pleasure that was but a shower curtain thickness from being pain. There was a heated towel rail, and I wrapped the warmth around me and vigorously towelled my skin until I felt certain that it must glow.

Barbara made coffee and we had toast and marmalade, and I could taste the sun in the oranges, just as in the winter you can taste snow long before the first flakes begin to fall. The kitchen didn't feel cold this morning, although outside the weather had changed to typical bank holiday fare and I knew it wouldn't be long until it rained. 'You're lucky to be getting away to the sunshine,' I said. 'I only wish now that I was coming with you. Four weeks is a long time.'

'Four weeks. And then this for the rest of your life.'

'Don't,' I said, 'or I won't be able to wait.'

'I think,' she said, 'that you realize at last where your future lies.'

'I've known for a long time.'

'No.' She shook her head. 'You haven't known, Peter, but you know now, don't you?'

'We won't fight about it now,' I laughed. 'We'll have the rest of our lives for that.'

'I won't ever want to fight you,' she said seriously. 'I only want to love you . . . to make you happy. You will let me do that?'

'You think I'm daft?'

'It's your conscience,' she said. 'It's the one thing I have no control over.' She stared at me and again I was surprised by her uncertainty. She tried to blink it away but I'd seen enough to know, before she filled her eyes with a smile, too full, and it spilled over on to her face and rippled down her cheeks to her mouth. 'Come on,' she added, 'help me to get the bits and pieces sorted out. And you won't forget my plants. Twice a week, remember, and not too much water.'

'Don't worry,' I said, 'they'll be like triffids when you come back.' We had got to our feet and I walked towards her, my hands outstretched, my fingers curling and uncurling. 'They'll eat you up,' I said, growling like some animal, 'eat you up.' She giggled and backed away from me but I followed her, taking slow, heavy footsteps, and eventually she came up against the sink unit under the window. I held her tight and pushed her against the unit and she went weak in my arms. Then she was pushing me away, protesting that time was getting on.

But we had plenty of time to spare at the airport and we had a coffee. I always liked airports, the magic gateways to other worlds. Buy a ticket and I could be away from the rain which was now beginning to fall, from the problems of home and work, taking the happiness I now had with me. It was only a dream, and I knew that the problems would follow me like a piece of luggage.

The flight was called and we went to the gate, and in the moment of parting we became formal and awkward. We kissed without passion and she clung to me. 'Have a good time,' I said. 'Take care, and don't forget to send me a card and to bring me back a nice present.' And all the time she looked at me and held me. 'And I won't forget your plants.'

'I love you,' she said. 'I'll always love you.' She waited for my assurance that I loved her too – waited . . . waited . . . Another call was made for her flight and she pulled away from me. 'I must go,' she said. She turned away from me and passed through showing her papers. I waited but she did not look back, and now I wanted to shout, to run after her, to tell her that . . . maybe one day I would love her. But even if I never did I would always need her. But then she was gone from sight and I was alone.

I made my way out to the car park in a steady downpour, but the rain for once didn't depress me. Even the fact that Barbara had gone, that I wouldn't see her again for four weeks, that I wouldn't relive last night again until then, none of these could depress me. For she had left her love with me, and I knew that she really did love me, and that I would never again be jealous of Ray. Never again jealous of anyone.

I had felt guilty last night about staying with Barbara but she had banished the guilt from me. And I knew now that I could come and live with her and not feel guilt. Even the girls would accept it if I behaved as if it was the most natural thing in the world. And Margaret could do nothing even if she wanted to. It would be no more difficult to part from her than it had been yesterday evening. There would be an endless supply of nights like last night when I would awake to Barbara's naked body and make love to her. Four weeks and the world would be mine.

I arrived home to a house that appeared lifeless, and it reinforced my determination to get away. The sitting-room curtains were drawn, a sure sign that the girls were watching television, watching the Saturday morning fare of pop stars and glitter, and unmelodious music, and the television illusion that all's well with the world. For once it seemed they'd got it right.

It was quiet in the hall, no sound but that of the clock. I poked my head into the gloom of the sitting-room, but it was deserted, and a giant, blank, one-eyed television screen stared back at me. Puzzled, I came out and Martin was coming down the hall towards me, Atlas with the weight of the world on his shoulders. 'Peter,' he said, 'thank God it's you.'

'Something's wrong,' I said, knowing immediately that

there was, fingers of fear beginning to press against the walls of my stomach. I saw that Martin's face was tired and that there was evidence of sleeplessness about his eyes. 'Sarah?' I said, hoping against hope, relief just waiting to flow.

'She's all right,' he said. 'She's . . . she's at the hospital. You see, Margaret had a fall.'

The relief flowed, but the fingers began to press even tighter, no longer of fear but of tension, showing what it would have been like if it had been serious, had the fall been to Clare or Nuala. 'What happened?' I asked, not able to keep the relief from my voice.

'She . . . she fell in the bathroom – knocked herself out. Clare found her. They . . . they kept her in the hospital overnight.'

'Well, that's OK then. You gave me a fright. I thought for a minute it was serious.'

'It is serious,' he said, avoiding my eyes. 'You see . . . well, Clare . . . she's disappeared. No one has seen her since last night. We didn't know where you were.' He shook his head and ran his fingers through his sparse hair. 'We had to go to the police last night . . . there was nothing else we could do. But they haven't found her.'

15

The demons possessed me now but they were not the demons of nightmare. They had shape and form and were within me, and they taunted me with images of Clare – brutal images that at this very moment might be reality.

While I had taken my pleasure last night Clare had been suffering, terrified . . . in pain. I saw her child's body in a wood somewhere, her naked child's flesh, a leering face above her, lust-crazed. Animal moans of pain and pleasure, and the smell of fear. Afterwards blows, angry shameful blows, blows to ease a conscience, to take away the guilt, heavy blows, not aware of strength. Pain at first . . . then no pain . . . nothing . . . death. Scrabbling in the undergrowth now, trying to conceal, then out into the world again, creator of my horrors.

I saw her naked body being pulled from black, stagnant water by a frogman, her hair and skin covered in slime; or being unearthed by a sniffer dog, policemen now scrabbling with feverish but gentle fingers in the shallow grave; I saw her laid out in the cold mortuary, the sheet pulled back, formal identification, words at an inquest. My pleasure of last night with its reciprocal pain. 'We have to pay for everything, if not in this world then in the next.' Father Mason's words, to be laughed at – scorned. No price ever to be paid – not here, not in that other world which belongs to us all.

I must have asked Martin what had happened but I wasn't aware of having done so. And I was only half aware of what he was saying. 'I'm . . . I'm sorry,' I said. 'What were you saying?'

'Clare found Margaret in the bathroom – she'd fallen over and hit her head. Clare went next door and the Morgans called an ambulance. Then they called us at Cricklewood and we took a taxi to the hospital. The Morgans were going out and didn't want to leave Clare in the house on her own, so they took her back to the Butlers. They dropped her at the gate but the Butlers had gone out. We . . . We found that out later. It was the last anyone saw of Clare. She might have come back to the house, but she had left her keys behind the first time so she wouldn't have been able to get in. When we came from the hospital Nuala was here but no Clare. We tried everywhere for her but . . . in the end we had to get the police.'

'But she was with Nuala,' I said. 'They were together.'

'Nuala went off to the fair with Aine Butler. She sent Clare home on her own.'

'No,' I said. 'No . . .' I looked at Martin but he had nothing for me. 'I told her she wasn't to go to the fair. I told her . . .'

'Children . . .' Martin said.

'But I told her . . .' I clenched and unclenched my fingers and some instrument of torture had my chest in a vice and was tightening . . . tightening . . . And then there were more images of Clare crowding in upon me.

I saw her rejected by Nuala, coming back to her home, a mockery of everything the world stood for. Finding the wheelchair at the foot of the stairs, climbing up to the landing; the bathroom door ajar, walking towards it, peering in. The still body on the floor and the blood.

Her mother dead in the empty house; no one to turn to. Maybe the dress had ridden up and the stumps were visible, no sight for a child. Running down the stairs out into the evening banging on the Morgans' door. And I was laughing with Barbara, happy, carefree, thinking of no one but myself.

'She must be somewhere,' I said to Martin. 'She's got to be out there somewhere. Someone must know – must have seen her.'

'She's out there all right,' Martin said, 'but is she alive or dead?'

He had voiced my doubts aloud and for a moment I hated him – his long sallow face, and thinning hair, and stooped shoulders. 'She's alive,' I said, 'she's got to be alive. Maybe . . . maybe she went to Cricklewood?'

'It was the first place we thought of,' Martin said. 'I went to check myself last night. I knew she couldn't have been there but I had to do something . . .'

Another door closed and there was no place to turn to. 'She's got to be alive,' I repeated, and I walked past Martin and went through to the kitchen. Nuala sat by the table and she looked up at me and then quickly looked away.

I stared at her and she was a child now and was very aware of my anger; anger which should not be directed at her. But I had to blame someone, otherwise I would collapse under the weight of my guilt. 'How could you,' I shouted at her, 'how could you go off to the fair and let Clare come home on her own?'

'It was Aine Butler . . .'

'You went to the Butlers to make arrangements to go to the fair today, not to go sneaking off last night.'

'Aine's dad couldn't take us today.'

'So you decided to sneak off, is that it? You . . . you realize that all this is your fault. If anything has happened to Clare . . .'

She looked up at me and I was struck once again by her resemblance to Margaret. Now she had her mother's fear and desperation in her eyes, the only difference being that Nuala would lose hers. But if anything happened to Clare none of us would remain untouched. I wanted Nuala to fight back as I had once wanted Father Mason to fight, but now as then there was to be no help for me in that way.

'So now Clare is out there,' I said, sweeping the air with my hand as if to demolish the city that hid her. 'She . . . she might be murdered by now.'

'I don't want anything to happen to her,' Nuala said in a pleading voice. 'It wasn't my fault that mom fell over in the bathroom.'

'That's not your fault,' I said, 'but sending Clare home on her own is.'

'I said I'm sorry,' she said, near to tears.

'I think you should leave her alone,' Martin said. 'After all, it's not her fault.' He stared at me, and for the first time with Martin I had to look away. He knew, as I knew, whose fault it really was.

'I can't just hang around,' I said. 'I've got to do something. I'll have a drive around . . . see if I can see anything.'

They had nothing for me at the local police station except that they were doing everything in their power, and I had to be satisfied with that. Out in the car I felt helpless, not knowing where to start; aware only of what little I could do. The city I loved was sprawled out round me, and Clare was out there, small, lovable Clare who had never hurt anyone, who had only ever wanted to love and be loved in return. Out there now, certainly frightened; maybe dying . . . maybe already dead. And I could do nothing to help her.

I drove to Alexandra Palace and parked at the entrance to the funfair. I could hear the loud music as it blared out above the shouts and the noise of generators and motors. The fair was in full swing and lights winked and whirled through the rain, paint strokes of colour, the rain seeming to wipe them away, but not before the next stroke had almost completed another colour.

'No, mate,' to the photograph, smiling innocent picture,

rain splattered on the shiny face, corners smudged from the money-tarnished finger marks. 'Can't say I've seen her; fair's full of children,' both of us only too aware of that fact. 'We told the other bloke everything; we ain't seen no kid. You're not the police?' A shake of my head and then intuition telling them the truth. Sympathy or indifference in the looks, here and there an attempt at understanding, the reaction of us all to the newspaper headline, to the thirty seconds of air time on the radio, to the pictures of the roped-off area in the trees, the policemen on their hands and knees; pictures and words of someone else's tragedy.

I saw Clare in every dark head of hair, children staring at my stares. I saw her in every blue anorak worn against the rain, only too aware that her anorak hung in the wardrobe in her room, hung with her other clothes lifeless on the hangers. I saw her in every child, sometimes in ones who were smaller or bigger, younger or older. Like God she was everywhere, but I couldn't find her.

I reached the end of the fair and now there was only the Palace grounds sweeping away to the reservoirs, and the houses of Wood Green beyond. On my left on the hill the Palace stood, a wet skeleton staring out over London, seeing everything. 'Tell me,' I said, 'tell me . . .'; the building as cold and as empty as myself, its destruction behind it, the flames but a memory . . .

I returned to my car, and, cocooned from the world by misted windows, I felt fear and terror. It gripped my stomach, not the one hand of earlier but a thousand hands, long, bony fingers twisting and kneading. My heart stumbled in its beat like a dancer losing his rhythm, losing it, finding it.

I drove back to the house expecting everything to be different, to find it invaded by big, dependable policemen, red-faced, oozing assurance, saying 'Don't worry, Sir; everything will be all right.' But there were no policemen, just a wet street and two boys at the bottom of the hill chasing each other on bicycles. As I got out of the car I held a hope that Clare might have been found, but held it gingerly like I might hold a lighted candle in the wind. But as I opened the door Nuala came running from the kitchen and stopped short when she saw me alone, and the hope died.

'No news?' I said, wanting to see Clare come running towards me as she used to when a little girl, podgy little hands upraised towards me, then a tiny bundle in my own hands raised high, held for a moment at the reach of my arms, then suddenly dropped in a huge arc to the floor, a long squeal of fear and joy echoing in the hall. 'Again, daddy . . . again . . .' until my arms ached and she didn't have the breath to scream any more.

Nuala shook her head but I already knew. 'Mom's home,' she said, 'but we haven't told her.'

'I won't say anything,' I said, going past her.

Margaret was in the kitchen, her face a deathly white, a whiter dressing above her right ear. Martin was there, Sarah too, tense as startled deer ready for flight. Margaret stared at me with her lifeless eyes, staring through me to focus on something beyond. Abruptly she pushed the chair from the room, having some difficulty at the door, but none of us moved to help her.

'You didn't find Clare?' Martin said, aware that I hadn't, speaking only because he had to.

I shook my head more from helplessness than in answer to his question, noting as if for the first time the mosaic pattern of the floor tiles, and the plain narrow strip of border tile. 'I didn't find her,' I said.

'You should be ashamed of yourself,' Sarah said, her eyes telling their own story of worry and exhaustion. 'Your daughter's out there – maybe murdered for all we know.' Her voice began to break and she started to cry, not a cry that needed sympathy or pity, but the cry of an old woman who can no longer endure. The tears flowed on the wrinkled skin, finding the path of least resistance, rivers of pain, only the wetness capable of being dabbed away with the tissue. 'We have to pray that she's alive,' she went on when the tissue had done its work. 'God is the only one who can help us now. I haven't stopped praying since last night.'

Once I would have laughed, but now I would have prayed if I'd known how, gone down on my knees on the cold tiles and prayed. Yet but one week ago I had sat in the garden and scoffed at the idea that I might have need of God.

'It's all your fault,' Sarah said, 'going out and leaving Margaret on her own. Lucky for us all she did fall and didn't get her tablets.'

'Tablets? What tablets?'

'She was trying to get her sleeping tablets . . . she was going to take an overdose . . . Only she fell over and hit her head. It's a miracle it wasn't a corpse Clare found.'

'Surely you don't believe that.'

'It's true,' she said, 'and you know only too well that it's true. This whole sad affair is your fault, but you cannot bring yourself to take the blame. You can only pray that the blame is no worse than it is now, that God has some pity for you . . . that He has a hand on your daughter's arm.'

She stared at me, her blame too heavy for my shoulders, the guilt I carried already heavy enough for two. I saw the events of last night again, but this time as if through stereoscopic glasses, a different view in each glass. My pleasure in one glass – eating at the restaurant, the kiss on the pavement, making love in Barbara's bed, her breasts like warm water-melons in my hands. Staying the night for the warmth, from a fear of the world outside, of screeching car tyres and angry shouts. But the latter was the world depicted in the other glass: and Clare was out in it, no warmth or comfort for her. Out there while I lay in a warm bed, the silk sheets like a film of lubricating oil against my skin.

It increased my guilt even more and I wanted to explain, to find some relief for my conscience. I wanted confession and absolution, but this was not the place, and these were not the people who would, or could, forgive.

'I'll go out again,' I said, 'drive around and see . . .'

'I'll come with you,' Martin said, and I offered no protest. After all, we didn't even have a mechanical lawnmower.

To the tourist, London is the city of Buckingham Palace and the Houses of Parliament and Trafalgar Square; and the lights of Piccadilly and young people around the steps of the statue of Eros; and the narrow streets of Soho with the window displays of erotica. But I know another London. The London of suburban streets and roads and squares, of drab council estates and graffiti; of parks and woods and waste ground, and vast areas of abandoned houses ready for demolition – a thousand, a million places where a child could die.

It was hopeless, but I drove around the streets and the roads and the squares, into the council estates with the wet clothes hanging slack on the washing lines and the graffiti of bigotry and racialism and the sad pourings of the sexually inadequate scrawled everywhere. I drove down streets which were now no more than alleys of galvanized iron. Behind each and every corrugated sheet Clare lay dead; a million places to search. Not even a small army could hope to search them all. She could be anywhere . . . anywhere . . .

I drove back to where there were people and more certainty of life, and I parked the car. My mind was numb, my stomach the abode not of butterflies but of frightened, radarless bats. I couldn't accept that Clare might be dead, for even to think of that was to open the door to even worse horrors. To have them rush towards me like the spectres in the ghost train, and to know that there was no end to the ride, no swing doors through which I would burst into the world of living and of sunshine, and of the man who collected the money.

'It's hopeless,' I said to Martin, 'utterly hopeless.'

'There's a church on the corner,' he said. 'I'll . . . ah, say a prayer. Sarah was right . . . God is the only one who can help us now.'

I watched him cross the road and go into the church, the door swinging shut behind him. In there God waited, ready to give me what He would never give to Martin. For Martin was not the sinner I was, and it was the sinner that God loved most; that He was most willing to give to.

Pride might have prevented me from getting out of the car, but I would never be proud again. For Clare I would be willing to do anything, too well aware that there might no longer be a Clare to do anything for. Sarah was right; it was a miracle we needed.

I crossed the road to the church and went straight in, aware that to hesitate might be fatal. Immediately there was the silence that belongs to all churches, the feeling that in here life has slowed down. I sat in the last seat, the tax collector from the parable, but the tax collector had had faith. I looked up to the altar, raised higher than the rest of the church, looked to the Tabernacle, God's house, God there now looking down on me, waiting for me to ask. God crucified on the cross which stood above the Tabernacle, the red light of the sacristy lamp before Him, a light to keep God from being lonely, to protect Him from the dark, to comfort Him when we had gone, saints and sinners alike. Both of us needing comfort, and had we but known each other we could have found comfort in our mutual loneliness.

Ask, I had been told; ask and you shall be given. I stared at Martin, who was half-way up the aisle in front of me, kneeling, head bowed. He was asking too.

'Adulterer,' I heard a voice within me say. 'What's happened to Clare is a punishment for your adultery. She has died to punish you, died with the knowledge that you betrayed her.'

It was all my fault, and if there was to be a judgement day then the blame would be laid at my feet; all mine – all stemming from my selfishness. Let me have Clare back now and I would give her anything, do anything for her. I would give up Barbara, never get into her bed again; I would go home and be Margaret's slave.

'You hear me?' I said, speaking silently to the altar. 'What more can I do? Maybe you don't exist but for the moment I have to believe in you, because you're the only one who can help me. Give Clare back to me and you can have anything – my body . . . my soul . . . anything . . . But let her be alive. She doesn't deserve to die for me to be punished. I will punish myself. I will deny myself the only happiness which might have been mine. Isn't that enough for you? What more can you want?'

No answer, only the silence; no miracle; no Clare suddenly walking down the aisle towards me, smiling . . . happy . . . no Clare. Just the huge building around me, the rows of seats, the confessional boxes, the plaster statues – Joseph and his Son, the Blessed Virgin, Christ Himself – but they could not help me.

I got up and made my way outside, out from the silence to a world where there was no mystery except that which could hurt, a world I felt I understood. What could the church offer me? What could God offer me? I looked upwards, the grey beginning to break up, patches of blue here and there, but the sun still hidden.

I felt now that Clare was dead, raped and murdered in some dark corner of this city I professed to love. Giving pleasure while I took mine, dying for the pleasure she'd given, for the pleasure we all want. I felt cold and alone, wanting somewhere to hide, some place where the pain could be locked out, the memories of Clare locked out, the little girl with the long hair, the brown, child's eyes, the ability to laugh and to cry too, to be sad and lonely and afraid. What thoughts in those minutes of her child's fear? What feelings of betrayal?

Martin came out and stood beside me; he too had been granted no miracle. We watched a bus pull in at the stop across the road – a red double decker – faces peering from the windows. On the top deck a child's face was pressed close to the glass, the nose squashed flat. Looking down at us, seeing us distorted; looking funny, as Clare had put it. 'I want to ride on the top deck,' she'd said, 'because the people look so funny.'

'It's got to be,' I said to Martin, as if a fog had lifted from my mind. 'It's the only answer. Clare went to Cricklewood last night. It was the only place she would go to.'

'But I checked. And she didn't know the way.'

'She did know the way . . . she said she did. Remember that night at the hospital?'

'What night?'

'The time she was going to the zoo. She said she knew all the buses.'

'But if she did go where is she now?'

'I . . . I don't know. But someone must have seen her. We can ask . . .' The hope was dying even as it had been born, but I couldn't stand still and I led the way across to the car.

I drove across Hampstead and thought about stopping at the funfair on the Heath, but I was aware of the futility of doing so. I was aware now too of the futility of going to Cricklewood; as Martin had said, where was she now?

I stopped outside the house, wondering if Clare had come here, had walked down the path to the door, heard the bell ring in the empty hall, no light or voice or sound to answer her.

Martin hadn't brought his keys and the house was locked to us too. I went down the path and stared through the window into the front room, but there were only the new cheap armchairs and the pack-flat furniture and the green wallpaper – all a reflection of Sarah. I rang the bell a few times and called 'Clare' through the letter-box, and tried to force open the door.

'She couldn't have got in,' Martin said, and I nodded and we went back down the path to the gate.

We knocked at the houses on either side but there was no reply. 'They'll be shopping,' Martin said, 'although Pat – he's at number six – doesn't usually go. He might be in his garage.'

We went down the rutted track which gave access to the garages, and Martin banged on the door of one of them, but there was no reply. 'He must be out shopping all right,' he said. He stared at me, wanting to give me something, but wanting it just as badly himself.

'It was just a chance,' I said, aware of how poor the chance had been. I turned to go and Martin's call stilled me. I didn't catch what he said, and I swung back to face him.

'The key,' he said, 'the key from the door to the garden . . . It's gone. There . . . where the brick is missing.'

The garage was built of red bricks and one was missing from the column to the right-hand side of the up and over door. 'You kept a key there?' I said to Martin. 'Did . . . did Clare know?'

'I showed her it once . . . a sort of secret . . .'

I tried the wooden door to the garden but it was firmly shut. Held taut by tension I pushed against it, but it wouldn't budge. The wooden fence into which the door was fitted was about seven feet high, but I hauled myself to the top almost without effort and dropped on the other side. The side door to the garage was on my right, and I walked towards it and pushed it open. There were only a couple of small windows and the interior was gloomy. But even in the gloom there was no mistaking the old settee Sarah had recently thrown out, on which Clare was asleep. Even in the gloom I could see the movement of her body as she breathed.

Time seemed to slow to the rhythm of her breathing, and for a moment I was seeing things in a state of heightened awareness I had not known before. I saw her blue cotton dress with the yellow flowers, her long hair rich and dark even in the gloom, one white ear lobe peeping at me. Her white ankle socks were stained on the soles and her sandals were on the floor beside her. As the gloom dissipated I could see a graze on her left knee, and I had the sudden urge to kneel before her and kiss the hurt away.

Clare was alive. She was alive! I began to laugh, a sobbing shaking laugh which drew my navel back tight against my spine and held it there until it hurt. I screwed up my face in an effort to stop the shaking, but it was as if I was tied to a tree in a storm. I had to wait until the storm blew out. And all the time I watched Clare, and all the time she never faltered in her breathing. I had my miracle.

I knew that life would never be the same again. My future for whatever it meant was no longer my own. It now belonged to the little girl before me, who was not even aware of the gift I was giving her. Barbara had always thought that Margaret was her rival, but it wasn't so. In fact she didn't now have a rival. Barbara didn't exist any more.

16

'It's a miracle,' Sarah said. 'God be praised, but it's a miracle.' She held Clare to her, large arms enfolding the thin body, discovering that she could be human if she wanted to, that there was love and comfort to be earned just by giving. As I myself had discovered in the gloomy garage in Cricklewood, where I had knelt on the floor and stroked my daughter's dark hair, slowly bringing her out of her sleep, touching her cheek with my finger-tips, whispering assurances. And then she was in my arms, pressed tight against me, sobbing from relief and threatening by her grip never to let go. It was the worst moment of all because now, with her living closeness pressed to me, I could better imagine her dead, imagine that it was a cold lifeless body I held, and that the dampness seeping through the knees of my trousers was Clare's blood.

I had no blame for her, no admonishing word. 'I thought mom was dead,' she said, 'and I didn't want another mom. You weren't there, daddy, so I got the bus to gran's. But I had no money for the bus home. I stayed awake all night and I was very frightened, but I never cried.'

'You were very brave,' I said, and tears pricked the back of my eyes.

Once home I watched the scene of welcome and was glad. Even Nuala was glad, the old childish jealousies forgotten for the moment. But in our joy we thought of the figure in the sitting-room, watching a film on BBC2 with the sound turned down.

'She's sick,' Sarah said to me later. 'Otherwise she

wouldn't have done what she did. I haven't told anyone about the tablets, but it worries me. It can happen again.' She looked at me with her tired eyes, all the fight gone. The events had quietened her and she had forgotten that she thought me to blame. But I hadn't forgotten . . . I would never forget.

'I'll attend to the tablets now,' I said, and went up to the bathroom. There was no evidence of what had happened, but I shuddered to think of what evidence there might have been. I found Margaret's pills in the medicine cabinet and slipped them into my pocket. I checked the remaining medicines but they were the usual accumulation . . . throat lozenges, aspirins, cough mixture, some creams and plasters, and a couple of thermometers.

Downstairs in the sitting-room I showed the pills to Margaret, holding them between finger and thumb as if their container was a live creature. 'Your pills,' I said, 'I've taken them from the bathroom. If you should need one you are just to ask. We can't have you trying to commit suicide again. Clare found you last night and she got such a shock that she ran away. She could have been murdered because of you.'

I hadn't wanted to tell her, but it had no effect anyway; she continued to watch the black and white images on the screen, and I realized that I made no more sense to her than the images did. Up till then I had doubted that she had intended to commit suicide, but now I couldn't be sure any more. I put the pills back in my pocket, and then on second thoughts I went out to my car and put them in the glove compartment.

'They'll be safer there,' Sarah said. 'That's all we want – a suicide on our hands.'

After some tea I went out into the garden; the rain had brought out the smell of the roses. Along the fence were Penelope and Will Scarlett, the latter so richly red that I felt that I should see drops of colour on the ground. There were bushes on either side of the path, Fragrant Cloud and Peace and Whisky Mac, reds and yellows and golds. And entwined round the Cox's Orange Pippin, the copper-pink Albertine, set by Martin the year we moved in. He had read somewhere that the Cox would thrive if it had a rambler set with it, but the Cox had never responded.

The garden hadn't changed since I had sat here with Father Mason, just as I hadn't changed if I was to look in the mirror. And yet we had changed. We were one week older, the grass had grown in those days, the apples on the trees had got bigger and riper, the branches had bowed a little more under the weight. The roses too had changed and were one week closer to the end of life. Even as I was. But the change in the garden was nothing compared with the change in myself. Even to the change that had taken place in the last twenty-four hours, which had devastated me inside like an earthquake might devastate a landscape.

I was stuck here from now on, stuck here with this garden, this house, this life. There could be no escape. My former dreams were diamonds turned to paste in my hands, though the price I would have to pay would be for the diamonds, not what they'd become. 'Fool,' Barbara would say, 'fool . . .' She would laugh at and scorn me, and maybe she would have Ray round to see her more often, pirate Ray laughing at my foolishness.

The grass needed cutting; it had held the rain and little drops of water clung to my shoes, reflecting the sky if I could but see it. Just as it might have reflected my future, but I wouldn't have been able to see that either. All I knew was that I would never share my life with Barbara, never share her bed, never wake in the morning with her beside me. Or even better, in the middle of the night, to hear her breathing beside me in the darkness, to feel her warmth, to reach out and touch the warmth with my fingers, to feel the down on her body like a film of dust on a warm surface. To turn to her and put my arms about her, and feel her snuggle to me in her sleep, shaping her body into mine. Never . . . never . . .

The fence at the bottom of the garden was in need of repair, had been for a long time. Next week I would get some wood and repair it. Or I could pull it all down and put up a new fence. And then later I would decorate the house. And hate every minute of it – hate every blow of the hammer and every stroke of the brush. And each day Clare would grow older, one day older, one day farther away from me. Only so many days and then she would be gone, returning one day with a boyfriend, later with a husband, later still with a family. I would play with her children in this garden, lift them on my shoulders, and they would pluck the apples from the trees and bounce them on my head and Clare would watch and laugh and never know the promise I made for her or the sacrifice it demanded of me.

Margaret would sit in her chair by the back door and watch, her body thin and wasted and dead like mine. When Clare had gone the house and garden would be silent once more and the apples would litter the ground beneath the tree, not the Bramleys or the Cox's or the James Grieves, but crab apples, for even the trees would grow wild and then wither and take on the characteristics of the people in the house.

'Wait,' I would say to Barbara when she returned. 'Wait until Clare is older and can understand. Wait . . .' I kicked at the fence and the rotten timber broke away, soft and yellow like sponge, the seemingly solid outside just a deceptive skin. Hiding what was inside as we all hid, always wanting to pretend. Barbara wouldn't wait. Fool to even think that she might.

Martin came out to join me and he was tired and beaten, the events having killed whatever little resistance he'd had. Martin my living reflection, what I'd sentenced myself to become. 'Poor Clare,' he said. 'I can't help thinking about her.'

'She'll get over it,' I said. 'Youth can survive anything.'

'We were lucky,' he said. 'We may not be so lucky again.'

'There won't be a next time,' I said. 'I won't be leaving.'

'You . . . you won't be leaving?'

'No.' I kicked again at the fence and more wood crumbled away. 'I'm going to get some timber one weekend,' I said, 'and build a new fence. I might take a week off from work to do it. I hate doing bits and pieces.'

We both stared at the fence, thinking I supposed of how it would look when it was all new again, and painted with creosote, the end of the garden sick with the aroma. We weren't to know that the fence was never to be built, that the apples were to fall and rot on the ground; that the house was to be locked up and one day sold to strangers, and that they would come to look at the fence and see the life that had made a home for itself out of the broken wood, the only life they would find among the sad failure of a house and garden. And they might congratulate themselves at having got such a place so cheaply, sold at well below market value because of the tragedy. They wouldn't think of ghosts walking here, for someone of that disposition wouldn't have bought the place in the first instance.

But there would be no ghosts here, only whatever ghosts they themselves brought with them, just like the ghosts we ourselves had brought. Ghosts which could frighten no one but ourselves, and which we would take with us when we went.

Yet that Saturday afternoon I knew nothing about the future except that I had marked it out. Or I thought I had. But in a matter of weeks it was to be my future no longer.

The next afternoon I took the girls to the funfair and spent twice as much money as I would normally have done, trying to buy something which doesn't exist if it isn't already within you. The girls enjoyed themselves and I was happy in their enjoyment, but inside I felt lonely, like someone at a party who doesn't speak the language of the other guests.

On the Monday evening I went to Barbara's flat, keeping my promise to water her plants. There were two letters inside the door, one in an official-looking brown envelope, the other in small scrawly handwriting. I stared at it, part of her private life, a life I knew nothing about, that I now would know nothing about ever. I would never see her in the morning opening the letters, laughing at something, saying 'It's from so and so.' All part of her other life, people she would still see when I had gone.

In the flat I felt as if I had no right to be there. That the right I'd felt on Saturday morning was now no more; could never be again. I watered the plants, aware that they had more of a right to the place than I had, and that they would still be here when I was gone, maybe even when I was forgotten.

In the bedroom I stared at the empty bed; no sign now that I had ever occupied it. Here I had crossed my heart and promised, promised as I had promised in the church only hours later. Two masters, both loving me if I believed the truth. A man could serve but one master, and maybe he could love but one too.

I opened one of the wardrobes and stared at the rail of clothes. I put my hand in to touch the silk and cotton and wool, feeling the textures between my fingers, aware of the scent of the wearer, perfume and a woman's sweat held in the pores of the garments, not totally capable of being removed by cleaning. The intimate smell of a person, Barbara's smell; even to that I had no right any more.

My task complete I left, locking the door behind me. Out on the road I stared up at the flat, the windows like great, black eyes staring out across the city, indifferent eyes reflecting what the future held for me. Frightened, I got in my car and drove away.

I stopped at my local for a pint and Terry came to me immediately. 'Glad your little girl's OK,' he said. 'It must have been a worry.'

'It was,' I said, aware of how quickly news travels, of the whispered gossip and innuendo. I took my pint to a small table in the corner, usually left vacant by the regulars because directly above it was one of the speakers from the juke-box. There to the music of the latest hits I drank my pint. I was probably making the corner my own, I realized; one day it would become mine and people would point me out, the grey-haired old man with the crippled wife. 'Stuck by her,' they would say. 'Must have loved her a lot. Comes for a pint every evening and sits there. She never comes out but some kids climbed the fence at the bottom of the garden and saw her sitting in the wheelchair by the back door. One of them went into the garden to get some apples but they were all small and sour.'

My corner in the pub, part of the scenery like the oak panelling and the framed black and white prints and the copper kitchen ware hanging from the ceiling; and the gas log fire which was the prized position in winter. My place; I was already making it my own. I drank my beer and went out waving goodnight to Terry, thinking of how many times a man might say goodnight in a lifetime, unaware that I was to say goodnight only twice more to Terry. And that the corner under the speaker was never to be mine.

17

The day of Barbara's return crept near, and then it was the Saturday and I knew she would soon phone to tell me that she was back and was looking forward to the beginning of the rest of her life. I remembered my promise, made so easily in the warmth of the bed and cast away in the quiet church to a God I now knew existed and who wanted everything from me, even eventually my soul. What plans had Barbara made during those four weeks, unaware that the promise was no more? The card she'd sent me didn't hint at anything, and I remembered how I'd held it in my hand and thought how easy it would be to break my promise to God.

I dreaded the phone call but it came on the Saturday afternoon, her voice cheerful over the line. 'I'm back,' she said, 'brown as a berry. I'm at the airport – I met some people on the plane and we decided to go for a meal together. They know a little restaurant at Chiswick. I thought maybe you could pick me up there if it's not too much trouble.'

'It's no trouble,' I said.

'I'm going to be nice to you,' she said, 'and I've brought you a present. But I can't tell you what it is now.'

'It doesn't matter,' I said.

'You don't sound very pleased to hear from me,' she said, her voice no longer gay. 'Is anything the matter?'

'Something's come up.'

'What's come up?' She had become uncertain, and I imagined her frowning, gripping the receiver tightly, tapping on some surface with her fingers, one of her habits when she was troubled. Waiting now for my response, trying to work out in her mind what might have gone wrong. I remained silent and her voice came back down the line. 'What has happened? Is . . . is Margaret OK?'

'She's all right. Look, I'll tell you everything later.'

'It'll have to do, I suppose,' she said, and after giving me the address she hung up.

I thought I had given myself plenty of time on leaving for Chiswick, but there were roadworks at Hanger Lane and when I got to the restaurant Barbara's new-found friends had gone; she was alone at a table, spinning out the time with a cup of coffee.

She greeted me civilly enough, and we kissed as if we were old friends meeting after a long separation. And for a moment I wished we could have been nothing more than good friends. She was wearing Levis and a T-shirt, her figure for a moment making me doubt my promise, making me aware of how thin the ground was on which I stood. One word – one gesture and everything might be lost.

'Shall we go?' she said.

'Finish the coffee first, and I'll have one myself.' I sat at the table and gave the waiter my order. I didn't want the coffee but it gave me the opportunity to break the news here – here where convention would tie her reaction, where she could but imagine her fists beating me.

'Did you have a nice holiday?' I asked, the words mocking and belittling us and whatever relationship we once had.

'It had been nice until I phoned you.'

'I'm sorry.'

'Are you going to make it better?'

'No,' I said, going straight for the truth. 'It can never be better again.' I looked at her but she was staring into her coffee, watching a collection of bubbles. She put a finger into the cup to touch them, the gesture like that of a child, concentrating on the bubbles, knowing that while she did so she could keep her emotions in check, keep them in one place though they might swirl wildly within the confines she had made for them. And I couldn't help but think that wherever I went, whatever I touched turned to dust as if I was some form of inferior Midas.

The waiter brought my coffee and I sipped some of it, groping for words to say to Barbara, searching for words like the torture victim, anything that could be spoken instead of the truth. But the electrodes were set and there were no words.

I stared at Barbara and saw a reflection of her I hadn't really seen before. The Barbara sitting before me now could be hurt; she was the businesswoman no longer. It was the Barbara that I could love, that I would do almost anything for; who could make me feel guilty, make me deviate from the path I had chosen. I had to banish her now before she could make me change my mind.

'I won't be coming to live with you,' I said. 'Something's happened since you went away.' I waited for her response but she just went on staring into her coffee, the swirl of bubbles gradually disappearing, her finger no longer trying to keep them intact. Quickly I told her everything, the telling making it all sound petty, four weeks a long time and already I was forgetting the pain I'd endured, the horrors that had gripped me. Now I wished that it could have been more dramatic, that someone had actually kidnapped Clare, and that she had almost been murdered. That I had not found her sleeping in Martin's garage.

'So,' I said, having expected anger, having wanted anger.

She looked at me with something in her eyes that resembled fear but which I felt certain could not be fear. But it was fear – I could almost smell it. It made her look unnatural, and it made me uneasy, and I could have sworn that her face had paled even with the suntan. 'So it's over,' she said, 'just . . . just like that. All wiped clean as if it had never been . . . I . . . I knew . . . I always knew that it would end like this. You . . . you . . .'

'I didn't want it like this,' I said, not knowing what to say. 'It hurts me too, you know.'

'It hurts you,' she said, finding some anger, some scorn. 'It . . . it hurts you! Don't you ever think of anyone but yourself? You made me a promise . . . you promised me. Cross your heart you said . . . I was happy that night. Don't you understand that? For the first time in years I was happy . . .'

'I'm sorry . . .'

'Don't!' She gripped the cup with both hands and I thought she would crush it, and that her blood would drip on to the tablecloth. But the cup held, though her knuckles showed white, and then the blood returned as she released her grip, and she eased herself back to the world of normality, whatever normality might mean now. 'Sorrow,' she said, placing the cup carefully on the table, but not releasing it, aware that she might need to squash it again, 'is that all you have for me? Sorrow?' She looked at me, forcing me to look down, to examine the tiny red rose on the outside of my cup, so real that I felt I could have plucked a petal and squeezed the sap out between my fingers.

'No,' I said, 'I don't have sorrow for you. The sorrow is for myself . . . I need it. I have to live with the fact that I can change everything right now if I want to; but I can't. That's my punishment.'

'Punishment? Why does there have to be punishment? What do you want, Peter? You wanted Margaret to die – you actually wished that she should die when she had the accident – and straight away you set about saving her life. But to save her for what?' She stared at me, and again I found the rose of interest – one two three petals, thorns that would draw blood, and I would feel it too between my fingers, warm and wet like the sap. 'You say you care about me . . . you want to live with me . . . to be happy. I picked you up when you were down, when your son lay dying and no one else understood. Whose breasts did you lie on? Whose comfort did you take? I believed you . . . I really believed you . . .' She began to caress the cup with the tip of her finger, watching herself do it as if it was some feat of amazing dexterity.

I had nothing to say, and I listened to the traffic outside as I had listened to it on that Saturday night, but now it was welcome, a sign that there was another world out there, that I could enter it, forget this scene – not forget exactly – but out there it would look different, it would lose its tension, make me wonder how I could feel like this. It would pale even as the memory of Clare being missing had paled, as the memory of my son had paled until now I could but wonder why it was that I had ever hated my wife. I looked at Barbara, aware that I didn't love her, that I could never love her; that it was a barrier against loneliness I had wanted, a barrier against myself, to my own knowledge of myself. I'm sacrificing myself for Clare I would claim; I'm doing all this for her. Poor Clare! It wasn't for her at all but for myself. All we ever did was for ourselves.

'Can we go?' Barbara said, and I nodded. I paid for the coffee and took her cases and put them in the car. 'I . . . I need a drink,' she said. 'Can we go somewhere?'

There was a pub nearby, one neither of us could have been in before and where therefore the past had no claim on us. But the past was there like a ghost at our table, like the persistent beggar who will not give up. It was a part of us, and it raised its spectral glass to drink with us, and we couldn't have banished it even if we'd wanted to.

Barbara had a whisky and I brought it to our table along with a beer for myself. 'I need the whisky,' she said as if by way of explanation. 'It will be the first hard drink I've had in four weeks.'

'No late night boozing,' I said, my voice light, wanting to keep our conversation easy. 'I thought that was the idea of a holiday – four weeks of not having to worry about early mornings.'

'Maybe it is, but I didn't need any late night boozing. Maybe I was happy.' She didn't look at me or accuse me but the accusation was more than if she had. I watched her gulp down a third of the whisky and not move a muscle, apart from the ones which were necessary to carry out the action. 'I was happy,' she went on. 'Until today I was happy. Maybe four weeks is too long for anyone to be happy. What do you say, Peter?'

'It's a long time if you're unhappy. I wouldn't know about the happiness bit.'

'No,' she said, 'I suppose you wouldn't.' There was no sarcasm in her words and I searched her face for it but there wasn't any. 'So it's over, one word and it's over. What'll you do if she tries to kill herself again? You must have few options left. Self-flagellation, or would that be too much fun?' There was still no sarcasm, and I realized that she wasn't trying to be sarcastic. She was just uttering thoughts as they came to her . . . putting them into any old words. The real words were going on elsewhere in her mind; in there the reality of what was happening was being enacted.

'There won't be another time,' I said. 'I've taken away her pills.'

'Poor woman,' she said. 'I never thought that I might pity her. Who do you think you are, Peter? God . . .' She was agitated for a moment like someone who has mislaid a valuable, a diamond maybe. She found it very quickly though and the agitation died, killed by another mouthful of whisky. 'So it's all over . . . that's what you're saying.'

'I have no choice. But if you could wait . . . five or six years . . . until Clare is older . . .'

'We don't have five or six years; all we have is now. You promised to come to me . . .'

'I would come if I was free.'

'Free? But you are free. Only you want to give your freedom to some God. Because you saw a bus – a double decker bus . . .' She began to laugh and the laughter took hold of her and shook her like a child might shake a rag doll. And I couldn't believe she was capable of such anguish, or that a person could tear inside with such evidence of merriment on their face.

The laughter ceased as abruptly as it began, and she finished off the whisky and got to her feet. I watched her walk to the 'Ladies' and I couldn't believe that I could see her so beaten and so lost.

She emerged after a few minutes and I wondered what thoughts had crossed her mind, had shaken her as the laughter had shaken her; but there wasn't any hint of them on her face. 'We'll go,' she said, and I followed her to the car.

'Your keys are in the glove compartment,' I said, wanting her to have them now, to have it all over and done with at once.

She opened the lid and stared inside for a moment, then removed the keys and dangled them in mid-air. She snapped the lid shut and turned to me. 'I have another set,' she said. 'These can be yours.' She held them out to me and for a long time I stared at them, but I had no control over my hands. And then she took back the keys and put them in her handbag.

We were the worst kind of strangers and our silence was oppressive. I hated every turn and twist of the North Circular Road, every traffic light and hold up. I was low on petrol and felt relieved to pull into a service station and get out of the car.

The evening had got chilly and there was a hint of approaching winter in the air. A long winter to face alone, the central heating not sufficient to warm my small room, the duvet on the bed inadequate. I thought of Barbara's bed and the warmth and the feel of clean sheets and the closeness of her body. And I remembered the long cotton nightie I had found her in one night last winter, buttoned up to her neck. And how sexy I had found it, having to ease it up from her ankles, and thinking as my finger trailed along that her legs went on for ever. All over now, and I shook my head as if to clear away the memories.

A young girl who was standing beside a car at one of the other pumps gave me a long, hard look; the eyes of a woman and the body of a child. Clare in six years' time, and I would have given my life for her. Too late then for love or to make another start, the passion dying if not already dead.

There might be sexual encounters like that one in the dingy room in King's Cross all those years ago, the crinkle of money trying to buy love and pleasure and something for the dark night. Later trying to buy a look or a feel, ten pounds for the glimpse of a pair of panties, twenty for the feel of a memory, lonesome and lost, one day a statistic in a newspaper report – a dirty old man. People would point to me, but only the ones who weren't lonely themselves, who were unaware that one day we can all be statistics, that fate, as uncaring of human pain as the money lender, might tomorrow turn us into something we could not dream of becoming. It was all there for me to see, to cast it from me if I so desired. I had but to get back into the car and ask Barbara for the keys. But I didn't ask her when I got back in, and we finished our journey in the same oppressive silence.

At the flat I got her cases out of the boot and made to carry them in for her. 'I can manage,' she said. 'I don't want your help.'

'But they're heavy, and . . .'

'Heavy! You say they're heavy. Why the hell should you care whether they're heavy or not? You don't care a damn about anyone but yourself.' I thought for a moment she was going to strike me with her fists, and then she picked up the cases and struggled towards the door with them. As she went through the entrance her shape was outlined in the doorway and I could have sworn that her shoulders were shaking. Then the door was closed and she had gone and I felt certain that my eyes must have been playing tricks with me.

It was all over and my future wasn't something I wanted to contemplate. It lay before me like a road through a desert, monotony all round me, the sky itself a monotonous blue; and here and there the skeleton of some animal, an omen of what lay in store for all of us at the end.

Sunday was a taste of the future, the day wet and miserable, and I couldn't get out even for a walk. It was a long day in the house, and I played two games of Monopoly with the girls and lost both to Nuala. 'You made lots of mistakes, daddy,' Clare said, but I could have told her that I'd made nothing but mistakes in my life. My mistakes all round me, reflected for me here in this kitchen, in the fact that it was my home and I didn't feel at home here. Another mistake of mine in the sitting-room watching the silent images on the television. Barbara my final mistake in her own flat, maybe staring at the rain, listening to it splattering against the window like fistfuls of thrown sand.

I thought I wouldn't hear from her again, but she phoned me at work on Monday afternoon when I was out. Carol took the message and said I would call back but I didn't. I went to the pub that evening to get away from another call, and Nuala told me that a woman had called and I was to call her back as it was very urgent.

But I didn't call her back, thinking that there was nothing of any importance between us any more. There couldn't be anything between us because the tenor of my life depended on it. The decision I'd made hadn't been easy, and to keep to it would be even more difficult. I didn't need any contact with Barbara even over the phone because her voice might weaken my resolve. So I didn't ring her but took some aspirins and went to bed and slept before the pills could take effect. What I didn't know was that from the next day on I would have a headache that no pills or sleep could remove. That the future I thought was settled would never be settled again.

18

I was visiting our shops in East London the next day when I got the telephone message. 'I've been trying to contact you,' Carol said. 'There's been an accident, Peter; you're needed at home immediately.'

'An accident . . . ? Who to? What's . . . what's happened?'

'I'm sorry but I don't know. A Mr Morgan rang, but he wouldn't give any details.'

'Thanks, Carol,' I said; and all I could see in my mind was Clare's broken body.

It was a wet, cold afternoon and I could see her hurrying from school. Running along the pavement, reaching the corner of the road, not stopping, rushing blindly across; the car tyres finding no grip, not even screeching. Only the sound of the sickening thud, life stopped for a moment, everything so still that you could hear a million heart beats and the drip . . . drip . . . drip of warm blood on to the wet road – Clare's blood. Or maybe Nuala's, and I knew that I would cry for her too.

There was only one image now, that of a crumpled body on the road, and a stain like spilled red wine; and the eyes staring sightlessly, and crying with the rain. And a huddle of women clutching their own children to them.

I sat for a few seconds, the receiver in my hand. Then I dialled my home number, letting it ring and ring, but there was no answer. And I envisaged Margaret in the sitting-room, watching the silent television, the phone ringing beside her. Answer it, damn you, I willed, but I knew that she wouldn't.

The Morgans' number was ex-directory, so I had no means of contacting them. 'I'll have to go home immediately,' I said to the manager of the East London Service who had accompanied me on the visits. 'I won't have time to go back to your department now and get my car. So I'll get a taxi and collect the car later.'

He offered to take me but I declined, and I left by taxi with his optimistic comments ringing in my ears, and the undoubted relief in his voice that the bad news hadn't been for him. The traffic was heavy, and we inched our way through Hackney and Stamford Hill, and Haringey and Wood Green, seeing schoolchildren everywhere behaving in the manner I'd imagined. At last we made it home, turning in at the top of the road, the normality frightening. The world hadn't stopped – hadn't even hesitated – and I thought myself a fool for thinking that it might.

The house was the same as ever, no hint of any tragedy to be seen. For a moment I could have believed that there hadn't been a phone call, that I was merely returning from work as I normally did. I asked the taxi-driver to wait, and as I got out Bill Morgan came hurrying from his house, a black umbrella above his head. This was the moment I had waited for – the moment I now didn't want to face. Bill held the umbrella for me, ignoring the rain which in moments would wet his black hair and his wool suit; he felt the need to give me something, even if only the cover of his umbrella.

'Has . . . has something happened to the girls . . . to Clare?' I asked, wishing that I didn't have to know.

'No . . . they're fine . . . they're inside now. I'm afraid it's Margaret . . . she took some pills.' He stared at me, he the man who's never welcome, the harbinger of bad news; and I understood now why he held the umbrella above my head. He was the director of his own company, a man who'd always exuded confidence; yet now the news he had for me had reduced him to the level of all men. In happiness or tragedy we are all equal, just as we are all equal in death.

'We'd better go in,' I said, 'or you'll get soaked.' We turned and went in, and his news now had had time to register; and I felt the relief flood my body. I was physically weak but I could have grabbed the umbrella from him and done a singing-in-the-rain act. The girls were OK. That was all that mattered. It was only later that my callousness towards Margaret shamed me.

Bill's wife Madeline greeted me at the drawing-room door, a tall elegant woman whose loose dress seemed to flaunt her body rather than conceal it; yet she was a woman I'd always instinctively felt would be cold. 'I'm sorry, Peter,' she said, as if in some way she was to blame. She hesitated a moment, not sure of what to say. 'I'll make you a cup of tea,' she continued. 'The . . . ah . . . girls are in there . . .'

'Can I get you a drink?' Bill asked. 'A whisky . . . ?'

'No . . . no, ah . . . tea will be fine.'

'I'll, ah . . . see how it's coming along,' he said, as if it already had been ages, and he ducked out of the room, leaving me alone with the girls both sitting side by side on the reproduction sofa.

'Are you two all right?' I asked, but they didn't answer. Clare was examining the parquet floor, or else the edge of the Indian carpet, taking care to avoid looking at me. But Nuala was able to stare at me, aware that the blame was mine, and that it made me inferior. 'Was your mother here when you got home from school?' I went on.

'No,' Nuala said, 'the ambulance had taken her away by then. But we don't know what's happened.'

'She must have fallen over,' I said, not wanting to tell them the truth now.

Clare now raised her head to look at me, and she was crying. Since I'd received the phone call I'd hardly stopped thinking about her. My earlier image of her dead had changed during the journey home, and I'd hoped that she might be only injured. Not too seriously, and I would put my arms about her and comfort her, and love her. But now I had no comfort for her . . . no words . . . no arms . . . Useless man who had nothing for anyone, unless it be pain or deceit. Unable to offer her anything but my deceit, I went along to the kitchen.

'I can't tell you very much really,' Bill said, avoiding my eyes, uncertain, as he had been on the pavement. An accident he could have coped with, but suicide was a very different matter. 'About three I think I heard some sirens and I went out to see what was happening. There were some policemen banging on your front door . . . peering through the windows . . . you know, generally causing a commotion. They said that a woman had dialled 999 but had been incoherent and the call had been traced to your number. I told them about Margaret and they decided to force entry. Margaret was in your study . . . on the floor by the desk. The chair was outside . . . it was obvious that it wouldn't go in the door. She must have crawled in and pulled the phone off the desk . . . it was beside her on the floor, you see . . .'

There was the chink of china and the sound of water being poured, and the splat as the water was thrown in the sink; and Madeline was spooning tea into a pot from a tea caddy with the word 'Jackson's' on the outside; and then she was pouring the boiling water into the pot, the steam rising in puffs like the breath of the postman as he comes to the door on a winter's morning.

'Margaret was unconscious,' Bill was saying, 'and the ambulance men took over and I went outside out of the way. At that time I'd assumed that she'd been taken ill, but the police found an empty pill-box in the kitchen, and a glass that smelled of whisky. They . . . they assumed that she'd taken an overdose. They asked about you and . . . and I said I would try to contact you. Then they . . . they took Margaret off to the hospital . . .'

'You . . . you said there were pills . . . ?'

'I didn't see any . . . it was just what the police said.'

'Thanks . . . ah, Bill,' I said, 'and for taking the girls in.'

'Oh, don't be silly, Peter,' Madeline said. 'What are neighbours for after all.' She smiled her cold smile for me, and I knew that though she might want to be the good neighbour, she would have preferred to show her goodness in different circumstances.

'Were there pills in the house?' Bill asked. 'I mean dangerous pills?' making them sound as if they were something that might go off with a bang when you least expected it.

'No,' I said. 'There were only the usual medicines – aspirins and that . . .'

'They wouldn't do any harm to anyone,' he said. 'Margaret may have just been drinking . . . I'm sorry, Peter, but you know what I mean. She may have taken a few aspirins for a headache. A drop of whisky with them . . . well, you know what it's like for someone who isn't used to it.'

'You're probably right,' I said. 'Margaret wasn't a great one for drinking. Why, I remember . . .' but I stopped, not wanting to tell him about that night the first year we'd been married. When we'd drunk a bottle of wine I'd won in a raffle. It had made us both tipsy and I had helped Margaret to bed and had undressed her, and all the time she had giggled like a schoolgirl. I'd made love to her and her nails had scratched my back, and she'd moaned as if in pain, and we didn't care if the people downstairs heard us or not. The next weekend I'd bought a bottle myself, but Margaret refused to drink any of it, and I put it away and never touched it again. When we moved we found it, and

Margaret had poured it down the sink and put the bottle out with the rubbish. But it wasn't only the wine or the bottle she'd disposed of.

'There you are,' Bill said. 'A couple of aspirins and a drop of whisky would knock Margaret for six . . .'

I nodded, certain in my own mind that it had to be aspirins; but not just one or two taken for a headache – the bottle had been half full last night. Margaret had been trying to cure her headache for good, or else had intended to stage another suicide attempt. Whatever, she had taken too many and must have realized that she could die before anyone found her. Well, maybe she would have learned her lesson by now and we would have no more nonsense. Unless the pills and the whisky had done serious damage and she was already dead.

I thought of her as she must have felt when the cold, clammy hands of death reached for her. It would have been instinct to run, but you cannot run without legs. I saw her push the wheelchair to the wall-phone in the kitchen, her fingers scrabbling at the dial, trying to open the lock, not knowing where the keys were. I saw her fear beside her, her mind beginning to fog. She would be aware that she would have to face God's judgement, and that the fires would show no mercy.

Out to the hall, but the phone there locked too, the one in the sitting-room also locked. Only one available now – the one in my study; but the chair wouldn't go in the door. I saw her getting out of the chair, crawling across the floor, pulling the phone off my desk, scrabbling again with jelly fingers, the voice answering, but already a long way off; trying to speak . . . words slurred . . . drifting . . . aware maybe for one horrible moment of the reality of death. Not beautiful and pleasant with hosts of angels and trumpeters, but rather with the touch of decay – the smell of putrefying flesh – the sight of worms crawling out of empty eye-sockets. And the voice growing further and further away, the receiver dropping from gripless fingers . . . then nothing.

I felt pity for her like a sickness invading my body and I had the desire to vomit, to feel my stomach lighten and relax. But there was to be no voiding of what gripped me, what I knew to be a premonition of my own death.

I thought of Margaret dead and God's judgement, but surely God would feel pity for her just as I did, and I didn't love her. In the garden of Gethsemane God had sweated blood, and surely in the final moments Margaret too had sweated. Who needed the fires of hell when they had already been there?

Madeline gave me a cup of tea, bringing me back to the present. Back to the world where Margaret could still be alive, maybe sitting up in bed, drinking in the sympathy, making me out to be an ogre. I drank the tea quickly, wanting to get along to the hospital, wanting to know the truth.

The girls didn't ask to accompany me, maybe frightened of what might be there to greet them. They knew about death, as if the clock ticking away on the mantelshelf had a special significance only for them. As if they knew it was ticking away their lives, that one day they too would die. I wanted to protect them from that day, but what could I do?

It took half an hour to the hospital, enough time for me to imagine a thousand possibilities. On my walk to the casualty department a million ants crawled in my brain, and some of them escaped from my skull into my body. A million tiny stings, as if I was naked and the drops of falling rain were red hot.

A nurse in casualty directed me to the intensive care unit on the first floor, and I knew then that it had been more than a couple of aspirins. In the unit another young nurse came to help me. 'Oh, yes,' she said when I told her who I was, and she gave me a strange look. 'If you'll just wait a minute I'll get the sister.'

The sister was a middle-aged woman who seemed possessed of enormous energy and who found standing still a strain. 'Mr Ferson?' she said, and I nodded, feeling the uncertainty tighten its grip on me. 'Your wife was brought in a few hours ago . . . she's still unconscious; the doctors are with her now. It would appear that she has taken an overdose.'

'Will she be OK?'

'It's too early to say, Mr Ferson. There's a rest room across the corridor. If you'd care to wait there the doctor will be with you shortly.'

'The pills . . . they were aspirins, I suppose?'

She looked at me for a long moment, maybe wondering why someone should want to die, maybe looking for the reason on my face. 'They weren't aspirins,' she said. 'Now if you'll excuse me.'

It was a small room with a couch and a matching armchair and a coffee table with the rings of tea and coffee cups. The one window looked out on to a drab building with an iron fire escape crawling down the side, and with lighted windows opaque blurs in the rain. And I thought of another time and another wait. Could that have been but so few months ago?

I sat in the armchair, my existence heightened, somehow on a plane far above the normal one I resided on. Margaret was alive, but what did alive mean? Had she in fact been alive since the accident? And the sister had said that the pills weren't aspirins. But then to me all pills kept for 'flu and headaches were aspirins, though I was aware that they might not contain aspirin at all. Was that what the sister meant? And if not, where had Margaret got the pills?

I nursed these thoughts for about fifteen minutes, coming to the conclusion that the sister had merely meant that the pills had not contained aspirin. But the doctor had a shock for me. 'It was what the layman would call a sleeping pill,' he said. 'Coupled with the whisky they are very dangerous. It was only the excellent skills of the ambulance crew that saved your wife's life.' He continued talking but the only words I could hear were sleeping pill. And then my mind plucked two more out of what he was saying. 'Brain damage . . . brain damage . . .' and they echoed on and on and on in my mind.

He'd stopped talking and I stared at him – his short blond hair, his hint of a moustache; the white coat and the stethoscope and the clip of the hospital paging system visible in his top pocket. I saw it all and yet I saw none of it. Instead I saw Margaret on the first day she had come from the hospital, lifting her dress with her fingers and letting it fall back like an empty paper bag that the wind would whirl through the gutters. Crippled then, but now no longer a member of the human race.

'Did she have sleeping pills?' the doctor was asking.

'Yes. She did. The . . . the brain damage – how serious is it?'

'It's really too early to say, Mr Ferson. Now if you will excuse me. I'll be available to talk to you later. The sister will come to tell you when you can see your wife.'

The impossible we can come to accept but not the inevitable. It was the impossible I accepted now, making my way out of the hospital and hailing the first taxi that came along. In the taxi I appeared to be cut off from the world behind misted windows, and the headlights of other cars only isolated me all the more. It was as if the whole world was in motion and I was standing still, watching it all go by. And yet it wasn't me who watched, but someone who now lived within me who was willing to believe anything but the truth.

During the drive all the ants in my skull escaped, and by the time I reached the deserted East London Service Department their stings had numbed both my body and my mind. It wasn't me who got into my car and opened the glove compartment and searched frantically, taking the contents out one by one. The A–Z of London, some pens, a half-eaten packet of Polo mints, my notebook, my A A member's book, a packet of tissues . . . But there were no pills. I saw them now as I had held them up to Margaret between finger and thumb – a small live creature. And I saw Barbara on Saturday stare into the glove compartment when she had taken her keys, and I remembered her moment's hesitation before she had snapped the lid shut.

I had to face the inevitable, but I could feel nothing now. It was as if my insides had been removed and my skin was kept in place by taut strings, stretched to breaking point, ready to snap and let me collapse into nothing. I thought of Margaret when I had loved her so long ago, when I had defied Sarah to marry her, when I had stood at the altar and promised so much. And I thought of the first time I'd betrayed her, a moment of weakness that first betrayal, an opportunity taken because I was lonely.

I sat in the gloom for a few minutes, no longer isolated from the world. I was now the centre and the cars outside were my satellites, dependent on me but unaware that I existed. No one was aware that I existed but myself . . . and God. Once I would have laid the blame on Him, but now the blame rested where it was due. It didn't matter whose hand had given the pills to Margaret; the blame was still mine.

But what did I mean by blame? At the hospital they had assumed that it was a suicide attempt. And I had thought no different. But the fact that the pills were missing from the car, and that I knew who had taken them, put a different light on the subject. We might not be talking about suicide any more. We might be talking about attempted murder.

19

'Peter,' she said, taking a step backwards into the dark hall, looking down so that I couldn't see her eyes, couldn't see her guilt, or worse still her lack of it.

I stepped into the hall and caught her chin in my hand and lifted her head so that I could see her face properly. She averted her eyes from mine, but not before I saw the guilt and something akin to fear. 'You're hurting,' she mumbled.

I released her and she backed away from me and gingerly touched her chin with her fingers. 'You hurt me,' she repeated, the hurt visible in her eyes.

'Hurt you! You say I hurt you when I should break your bloody neck.'

'Because I took the pills from the car,' she said, roused to anger. 'Because I called at your house today and left the pills with your wife. Is that it?'

'You didn't count them out for her, did you? Or pour her a whisky to wash them down?'

'She . . . she didn't take them? . . . She isn't dead, is she?'

'She isn't dead,' I said. 'Not what a doctor would call dead. Brain damage was how they described it at the hospital. Will that do for you?'

'No,' she said. 'Tell me it isn't true. I won't believe you. I . . . I never wanted this.'

'So what the hell did you want then?'

'You,' she said. 'Just you.'

'You love me that much,' I said bitterly, wishing I hadn't come, aware that there was nothing to be gained by having done so. The bitterness came rushing in like vinegar, pushing its sourness into every part of my body. The oak panelling seemed to close in about me, and I turned to the door to leave.

'No,' Barbara said, closing the door and grabbing my hand. 'What you said isn't true. Tell me it isn't true.'

'It's true all right,' I said, 'but it isn't the whole truth. You don't know yet what she went through this afternoon.'

'Please come in,' she said. 'I have to talk to you . . . please.' She still held my wrist and I followed her as she led the way to the lounge. 'Sit down,' she went on, 'and I'll get you a drink.' She poured two generous whiskies and I sat in one of the armchairs, and she sat on the couch, the window dark and wet behind her.

'What did happen?' she asked.

'I thought that you could tell me.'

'I took the pills on Saturday,' she said, 'when you stopped for petrol. I . . . I don't know why. Maybe to scare you, I suppose. I rang twice to tell you but you wouldn't talk to me. I was desperate, Peter – you chucked me aside and you promised that you wouldn't ever. I . . . I didn't know what to do.'

'You knew what to do all right,' I said.

'No. I didn't know. I . . . I called at the house today – I was going to ask Margaret to give you a divorce. She didn't answer the bell so I went round the back. The kitchen door was open so . . . well, I just walked in. Margaret was in the sitting-room watching the television. The test card was on – she was just sitting there watching it. They weren't even playing music, or else the sound was turned down. She was beyond talking to . . . I could see that.' She tried some of the whisky, shivering as it hit her, unable to control the tremors as they rippled through her one by one like a chain reaction. 'I talked to her, Peter – I told her everything, but I was certain she didn't hear a single word. I had the pills in my pocket – I had intended to give them to her to scare you. But I saw that it was pointless – it was pointless even talking to her. But I left the pills on the television . . . I hoped she might have understood – that she might show them to you. When . . . when I saw her as she was I couldn't have done anything to hurt her. I . . . I just left her then – I couldn't bear to watch her. If she took the pills it was because she wanted to die.'

'She didn't want to die – she phoned for an ambulance.'

She tried some of the whisky but it didn't help her, and the horror that now possessed her reached me across the room. 'It's not true,' she said, not wanting to believe. 'Someone found her . . . Clare found her when she came home from school. That's why you're upset.'

'No one found her. You see, she had all the phones locked except the one in my study. She crawled in there somehow but she could only dial 999. The post office traced the call. Only the skill of the ambulance crew saved her life – that's what they told me at the hospital. Saved her for what . . . ? You can't even try to imagine those moments when she realized she was dying. For any Catholic suicide is the unforgivable sin. You wouldn't understand, but Margaret believed. She had wanted nothing more to do with God, but she believed . . . Remember what you said about the grain in the timber. It wasn't so that she could live that she called the ambulance – it was to save her soul. In those moments she must have felt the fires of hell. That's something you can never forget – that you brought someone to the point of eternal damnation.'

'You believe all that?'

'What I believe doesn't matter a damn. It's what Margaret believed . . . She must have believed strongly to have phoned for help.'

'I'm sorry,' she said, staring across the room at me, wanting even one kind word.

'There's no point apologizing to me,' I said. 'I can't forgive you.'

'I need your forgiveness,' she said. 'I need you . . . you have to help me.'

'I can't help you.'

'You have to!'

I shook my head. 'I have to go,' I said. 'I . . . I won't say anything to anyone about what you've done. Just . . . just hope that you don't get charged with murder. You realize that it could come to that. Or at worst charged with helping someone to commit suicide. They don't take very kindly to that kind of thing now.'

'Don't go, Peter. You . . . you don't understand.'

'There's nothing to understand.'

'Oh, but there is. You talk about what I've done to Margaret, but I've done nothing to her compared to what you've done yourself over the years. Do you understand how she suffered? How could you? You could only understand if you actually suffered yourself. Unless you've endured the pain how can you hope to understand?'

I looked out of the window, the night closing in about us, darker than it should have been because of the rain. The holm-oak tree in the garden was a black bulk against the skyline, a black evil presence that might envelop me at any moment; and I turned away so that I would not see its approach.

'Pain,' I said. 'You can't know Margaret's pain; no one can.'

'No one can know another person's pain. We can only measure it against our own.'

'You told me about your father,' I said brutally. 'It must have broken your heart.'

'Shut up,' she said, 'shut up . . . You talk about pain but what have you ever suffered? What . . . ?'

'And you have suffered. I've heard it all before.'

'No,' she said, 'you haven't heard it. But you're going to hear it now.'

'I don't know that I want to hear it.'

'You're going to hear it all right – every little detail. You see it's really your story – only the name is different. His was David. But apart from that it is your story – every word.' She looked hard at me, something in her eyes I hadn't seen before, visible in the gloom that seemed to move if I took my eyes from it. Outside the rain splattered against the window, but gently, like a child playing who's been told to shush.

'He wasn't like you, Peter,' she said, 'except in one respect – he too made me a promise . . . he promised to take care of me, and like you he didn't keep it. One day he didn't turn up and I went round to his bedsitter to see what had happened. But all I got was abuse from his landlord. David hadn't paid the few days' rent he owed. The landlord acted as if it was my fault – claimed that I should pay as I had used the room too.' She stopped for a moment, clearly agitated. 'He didn't want money though – he wanted payment in kind. I ran out of the house and he stood in the doorway swearing at me. Then he laughed and it frightened me even more . . . I just ran until I reached the High Road and I could see people and lights . . . I went home then and I cried and thought I would die.'

'So what?' I said. 'You don't think you were the first or only lovesick woman ever?'

'We were to be married,' she said. 'He promised to marry me.'

'You talk about promises as if they were the centre of the universe.'

'It wasn't just his promise to me he broke . . . You see I was three months pregnant when he ran out on me. He broke the promise to the baby too. I was eighteen at the time – pregnant and alone. You talk about pain, Peter, but you don't know the meaning of the word.'

'I didn't know,' I said. I took some of the whisky, needing something, but the whisky wasn't what I wanted. 'And the baby? You had it adopted, I suppose.'

'Abortion was legal then – it was no more difficult to obtain than it is now if you knew how to go about it. But I lost more than the baby . . . It hardened me – made me realize that no one would give you anything; you had to take for yourself. I became determined that I would never depend on anyone again. I never did – not until you came along.'

'Me!'

'Yes, you, Peter. I relied on you – I wanted you to give me back the baby I'd lost. I trusted you and you promised never to let me down.'

'We're not children,' I said. 'We can't just go on talking about promises. Anyway, you can't take seriously a promise made in passion.'

'But it wasn't made in passion; you have to admit to that at least.'

'So there was no passion; but we're still not children. Lots of women make mistakes . . . everyone makes mistakes – we just have to learn to live with them. It doesn't excuse what you did today. You . . . you may end up with more than an aborted baby on your conscience.'

'And you?' she said bitterly. 'What will you have on your conscience?'

'Enough. Now I'd better go.'

'Not yet.' She sat forward on the couch, ready to stay me with her hand. 'You haven't anything on your conscience – or you think you haven't. You're just going to go now, the slate wiped clean . . . everything neatly sorted out. But you haven't even had your present yet . . . the one I brought you back from holiday.'

'I don't want it . . . I have no use for it.'

'You have to want it,' she said. 'You just have to want it.

Remember what I said – your story too . . . every word of it. But you're not going to run out on me – you wouldn't want me to have an abortion, now would you?'

'No,' I said, 'no . . ,' and the holm-oak loomed at the window, toppling towards me, ready to crush me, to engulf me in eternal darkness. But there was one moment before the darkness when all the images of horror I kept stored in my mind came out to haunt me. Images from childhood, fears of the dark and the bogey man, the memory of my father dead in his coffin, his forehead cold and hard when I kissed it; seeing him in the mortuary, and although I wasn't a child I feared him dead as I had never feared him alive. Images that might have been better left buried, that had no place in this dark room where once I had known happiness. Images that marched across me like one day the legions of the living might march across my grave, the heavy tread of their boots pushing the soil down my throat – into my eyes . . . my ears . . . my nostrils – smothering me. My hands and feet immobilized, the soil trickling down into my lungs like the trickle of sand through an hourglass; the wriggle of a worm on its way down into my guts to eat from the insides out. And as I opened my mouth wider to scream there was more soil and then the blackness, not just darkness like the night, but the utter blackness of a mine deep in the bowels of the earth; so deep down that no man had ever returned alive from there. All the images – too many for one man to endure in those fleeting moments when what he doesn't want to believe becomes more certain than his own death.

'Peter,' she said, and she came to me and knelt before me and put her arms about me. I began to tremble as she had trembled earlier, and the more she tightened her arms about me the more I shook, until I felt that the shudders could start an earthquake. 'Peter,' she was saying, repeating my name over and over again, her arms like the tentacles of some powerful animal, intent on squeezing what life I had out of me. And then the images left me, and the legions stopped their marching, and the worm in my stomach died. Only the soil remained in my throat, not soil but gritty sand.

Now that the images had gone I returned to normality, whatever normality might mean; if I should ever be actually normal again. I saw that night at the restaurant, how we'd kissed outside and didn't care. 'Cross your heart,' she'd said later in bed, 'and I will love you always.' Cross my heart and hope to die.

'You see,' she was saying. 'Tell me you understand.'

'Why didn't you tell me?' I asked.

'I wanted to keep it until I came back from holiday – a sort of present for you – a moving-in present. But you didn't make it easy for me, did you? There was no place to turn to. What I did today wasn't for us – it was for our son. He needs us . . . he needs you to love him. Tell me that you'll love him.'

'Him?' I said, fighting for time.

'It's going to be a boy – I just know it is. I knew today when I told Margaret. Peter's son, I said to her.'

'You told her that?'

'I told her, but you wouldn't understand the reasons why.'

I looked at her, aware that I would never understand. I saw her as a young girl, the beginnings of another life within her, suddenly finding herself alone, the dream shattered and the hope gone. Turning to abortion because it offered the easy way out, but carrying the scars around with her since, as if the surgeon had actually cut her open and had failed to stitch the wound. Now it had burst open and the horrors of long ago were being enacted once again.

My son, as she had said, growing within her; my son. With as much claim to me as anyone else, maybe with more claim because he would have no one else. But what to do? Where to go now? I voiced the questions aloud, but as much for my own benefit to know what was needed of me as for Barbara to give me answers.

'Only the baby matters,' she said. 'No one is going to take him from me this time. But you don't want him. Is that what you're saying?'

'I don't know. I need time to think – to get my thoughts together.'

'If she dies you'll be free.'

'Whether she dies or not I will never be free. It was a foolish thought to think that I might. None of us are free.'

'It shouldn't have been like this,' she said. 'It's like children whispering the facts of life to you in a smelly school toilet and the shame you feel afterwards.'

The dark had seeped into the room now, enveloping everything, and it would never dissipate again . . . never. 'I have to go,' I said. 'I have to tell my daughters the truth. Or half the truth. Just deceit everywhere.'

'I need you,' she said, 'and your son needs you. You don't love me, Peter . . . you won't ever love me, but you have to love the baby.' She gripped my hands tightly and waited for my assurances, but I had none for her. 'You won't desert me,' she went on. 'Promise me that.'

'Promises,' I said. 'I have no more promises for anyone.' I got up abruptly and her hands fell away, and I walked out of the room into the dark hall; and more than ever before I had the feeling of secret passages on either side, and cobwebs and giant rats, and knots in the wood which weren't knots at all but holes; and there were eyes squinted against the holes watching me – a thousand, a million eyes . . .

Barbara switched the light on and there were no passages or eyes, just the grain of the oak and the darker knots that were knots and not peepholes. I walked the length of the hall and opened the front door. I turned back to look, and Barbara had made it half-way and had stopped opposite the door to the bedroom in which we had created life.

'Will you call tomorrow?' she said. 'We . . . we have to talk . . . about your son.'

'I haven't a son,' I said. 'All I have is hell.' I turned and closed the door and I heard her call my name. I heard the door open as I went below the level of the landing, and then the door closed and I went on down the stairs and out into the rain. I drove off, not looking up to see the light in the flat where one day my son would cry and I wouldn't know. Barbara would grow to hate him and he would grow up to hate in his turn, as I had grown to hate. And in my childhood I had known only love. Love!

What we all needed now was a surfeit of love, but I thought there was no more love left. There wasn't, I discovered, but I was to find a little from somewhere, and mixed with a touch of compassion, and all the virtues and vices of humanity, it was to make a man out of me for just one moment. The man I should have been long before that – the man I had been too frightened to be.

20

I came back to the empty house – to its ghosts and bad memories and seemingly inevitable unhappiness. The wheelchair stood opposite the door to my study, Margaret's rug thrown across the arm. I picked up the rug and it hung heavy in my hands, and I felt the warmth and texture of the wool, overwhelmed for a moment by a maelstrom of emotion. I threw the rug back on the chair where it fell to the floor; but I left it.

I went into the kitchen, the modifications a symbol of my care for Margaret. But they had been unable to compensate her – to give her the confidence to no longer need the cover for her non-existent legs. Here she had found herself a prisoner; not just in the house but a prisoner within herself. Death in the end had been the only way out; but death had a price and she couldn't be certain that she wouldn't have to pay.

The kitchen itself may have been a symbol of my uncaring, but the cardboard covering the broken glass in the door was a reminder of what had gone on here today. I wondered why Margaret had bothered to lock the door when it had been open when Barbara called. Had she not wanted to be interrupted? Did she in fact want to die? If she had, then the fear had come later when she had crawled along the floor of my study.

I let these thoughts filter through my brain because it was easier to think about them than to think of Barbara and *that* problem. My son or daughter, unborn yet and already a problem. 'Damned,' a voice seemed to whisper. 'Everything you touch is damned.' And I knew I had to get out of the house to escape it.

I went next door and faced the curiosity of the Morgans and of the girls, my daughters, real, present, not a foetus that threatened. I faced the curiosity and lied and pretended, and was glad to get back to the house. It was easier to lie to the children, though they too were learning not to trust me.

We were three strangers thrown together by chance, but strangers who needed each other; but in our mutual need we had nothing for each other. We were the worst kind of stranger because once we had been close. A long time ago, but time could not erase the fact, nor do anything now to help.

'What happened to mom?' Nuala asked.

'She took some pills.'

'You said she fell.'

'I didn't know then.'

'Will she die, daddy?' Clare asked.

'She won't die,' I said, giving her hope, aware that tomorrow she would have to face a more harsh reality than even death itself.

'Have you told gran?' Nuala asked, reminding me that others had a claim on Margaret too.

'It's too late to tell her tonight. She's not well and would want to go to the hospital. She wouldn't be let in this late and it would only upset her even more. We'll tell her tomorrow.'

'I'm hungry,' Clare said. 'Can I have something to eat?'

'Of course,' I said, glad of mundane things like hunger. 'What would you like?'

'McDonald's would still be open . . .'

'OK,' I said. 'Get your anoraks and we'll go and get something.'

We bought hamburgers and chips and hot apple pies and milk shakes, a normal family for a moment like the other families around us, children out even this late. I didn't want to sit among the reminders of what I had lost, so we returned with the food to the house and ate in the kitchen.

The girls enjoyed their treat, maybe only too aware that they had the rest of their lives in which to be unhappy. But I had no such time, and had to be unhappy at every given opportunity. I finished my food and watched the girls go sparingly with theirs, wanting the pleasure never to end. The simple faith of the child, and I envied them and pitied them. If I had a wish now it would be to go back to the time when Nuala was born and start again. But there were no wishes, and we'd already decided the rest of our lives by what had gone before.

'It's time for bed,' I said, and they went without protest. I said goodnight but only Clare responded, mumbling words that could have been anything. They were my daughters and surely I could have had their love. But one of the harsher lessons of life is that we learn too late. We discover that what we would pay anything for was once ours for free, and that like the picture of the 'Mona Lisa', refused by the very man who had commissioned it, yet now priceless so that he could not buy it even if he wished to, we too may not buy what we now want so desperately.

I was ready to go to bed when the doorbell rang, and I answered it to two policemen on the doorstep, the night wet behind them, the raindrops black and heavy caught in the hall light. And as if reflected in the shiny buttons of their uniforms, I saw Margaret dead; but with eyes open . . . staring . . . accusing . . .

'We've called a few times, sir,' the older of the two said, 'but you were out. Inspector Bowman would like you to call in at the station.'

'Now?'

'Oh, no, sir; in the morning will be fine.'

'It will be about my wife, I suppose?'

‘Yes, sir.’ From his tone I knew he would not want to say any more, and I didn’t press him. He bade me goodnight, and they turned on the doorstep and went out into the rain.

The fact that some inspector wanted to see me didn’t worry me too unduly. I’d already realized that there would be some sort of investigation. All I had to do was to keep Barbara out of it and there would be no problem. Satisfied as to that fact but to little else, I went upstairs. The door of Clare’s room stood open, and I peered into the darkness but could see that her bed was undisturbed. I went down the landing where Nuala’s door stood a little ajar, and I could hear them whispering but couldn’t make out what they were saying. I envied them their companionship, wishing I could have had it for myself. I knew that they were inseparable for the night, and I left them and went to my own room. Sleep was a long time in coming, and when it did come it was accompanied by dreams. But dreams that were without substance when I awoke the next morning, except for the one memory of a hand reaching towards me, a tiny hand that wasn’t a hand at all but a webbed limb which I knew would leave fingerprints on me as if it was somehow human and had been dipped in ink.

The memory of it stayed with me as I washed and dressed and went downstairs to my study. ‘Your wife’s had a comfortable night,’ they told me at the hospital when I rang, and I had to be content with that. I called the girls and prepared breakfast – cereals, toast and tea.

‘We’ll be late for school,’ Clare said when she came down.

‘You don’t have to go today,’ I said.

They said nothing but watched me suspiciously, and I thought I could do nothing any more without arousing someone’s suspicion. After breakfast I went along to the police station and saw Inspector Bowman. He asked after Margaret and apologized for any inconvenience to me. The only awkward moment came when he asked if there were pills in the house, and I just said yes and breathed a sigh of relief when I found myself outside once more. As I'd thought, there'd been nothing to worry about.

We went to Cricklewood, where Martin opened the door to us, tentatively, like a child might who is scared of the bogeyman. He'd nicked himself shaving, and the marks were like the result of torture. He was wearing a collar and tie even this early, and I supposed that he was on his way out shopping or else had just returned. 'Peter,' he said looking from me to the girls, knowing that something dreadful was wrong but hoping that it wasn't as bad as he imagined it to be.

'Margaret's in hospital,' I said. 'She took an overdose of pills.'

'Is . . . is she all right?'

'She's comfortable,' I said, the word covering a multitude of possibilities. I felt sorry I had to tell Martin, lost in his world he neither understood nor was capable of mastering.

'Sarah's lying down,' he said. 'She's not been . . . ah, too well . . . 'flu, I think. I'll . . . ah, go and tell her. You . . . you can wait in the kitchen.' He let us in and went up the stairs, slowly, putting off the telling for even a few seconds. He disappeared around the bend in the landing and we went through to the kitchen.

It was a sparse room lacking in comfort, the old Welsh dresser with the willow pattern tea service, and the gas fire – twenty years old at least – the only items in the room with the possibility of warmth. But I never remembered seeing the fire alight, even in the depths of winter when we sat shivering at the table for dinner on a Sunday afternoon, Sarah complaining about how warm it was while I hoped that she wouldn't open the window or we'd all catch pneumonia. Clare was the only one who had ever dared to mention the cold, but a smack from Margaret had taught her the importance of saying little when she visited her gran.

I hadn't been to dinner here since my son was born, and I knew now that I would never have dinner here again.

Sarah came down in a pink dressing-gown and matching slippers. She'd tidied her hair a little, though the grey showed through as if it had been badly camouflaged; but she couldn't camouflage her eyes. Her whole face sagged, as if she normally lifted the loose skin to the top of her head and tied it in a knot but this morning she had forgotten to do so.

'I . . . I knew this would happen,' she said, accusing me with eyes and voice. 'I just knew it would.' I didn't say anything, and Martin came in and pulled out a chair and Sarah sat on it, the legs seeming inadequate to hold her weight; but the chair stood firm. She was an old woman now, bitter at the way life had treated her. She had seen Margaret as a baby, had watched her grow up, and I supposed in her own way had been proud. What dreams had she had for her daughter? Dreams that we all nourished for our children. But whatever they might have been mattered little now.

'What happened?' she asked, and I told her. Half-way through she began to cry but I went on with the telling. I said that Margaret was unconscious, but nothing about the brain damage or the fact that she might never be normal again.

'She took aspirins and some whisky?' Martin asked when I'd finished.

'It would seem so,' I said.

'Does it matter what she took?' Sarah said. 'She's taken it and there isn't a lot we can do about it now. I . . . I must go to the hospital. She needs someone there that she knows . . . someone she can trust.' She got up, a purpose about her, and went out of the room, and we heard her weight on the stairs.

'I'll make some tea,' Martin said and in the silence he put the kettle on the gas and made the tea and handed it round. Sarah came back, the hair in place now, the face brighter, but she could still do nothing about the eyes. Martin offered her some tea but she refused.

'How can you be thinking of tea at a time like this?' she said, the rebuke meant for me more than for Martin. The tea didn't taste right any more and I put my unfinished cup on the table. We left then for the hospital, the girls coming with us, and none of us thought to tell them that they couldn't.

'Visiting times are at set hours,' the sister at the hospital told us, but seeing Sarah's distress she agreed to let us in. 'But only for a minute and the children must wait outside. And only two at the bedside.'

'I'll wait with the girls,' I said, not wanting to go into the ward and see the result of my carelessness and inhumanity. I waited with the girls in the room where I had waited the evening before, where the doctor had spoken two words that would haunt me for the rest of my life. Haunt me as Barbara's words would haunt me; both to be before me in the flesh one day, my wife and my child, two helpless human beings. I had travelled a long road to this room and to this day; and maybe yet the journey was but beginning.

Martin came back and the girls made room for him on the couch. 'Sarah is going to wait in the ward,' he said. 'They . . . they've sent for a priest; she . . . she doesn't look too well.' He looked at me but I had nothing for him, and in order to avoid his eyes and also my daughter's, I looked out of the window at the grey building and the fire escape still crawling down the side.

After he'd been in the ward the priest came to see us, bringing with him his smells of stale food and washed clothes. He had nothing for me and he was embarrassed by his poverty. He had no defence against what he had seen in the ward, the obscenity of sickness, his God's pornography for man. The priest and myself were failures – we had nothing for anyone but for ourselves. 'I'll pray for your wife,' he said, but not for me; I was beyond his prayers.

Sarah came out a few minutes later and we got up to go. I'd expected some sort of an attack but she hadn't so much as a glance for me. Down at the car she got into the front seat, a spot she'd never occupied before. But I didn't say anything, and I even ignored the seat-belt law, knowing that she just wanted to be left alone.

'You want to come back to the house?' I asked.

'I want to go home,' she said. 'I don't feel well.' She cried a little as we drove away, but she didn't have enough tears to make it worth while. She would never have enough tears again to wipe away what she'd seen.

I stopped outside the house at Cricklewood and only then she turned to me. 'Margaret is dying,' she said. 'What I saw on her face just now was death. You'll soon have what you wanted all along, won't you?'

'The children . . .' I said.

'The children have to know the truth – they have to know that you have killed their mother.'

'It wasn't my fault she took a box of aspirins,' I said, my voice implying that I was the injured party.

'It's all your fault,' she said, 'if it was aspirin.'

'What else could it be?'

She stared at me and I felt her eyes on my cheek almost burning me. She leaned forward suddenly and fiddled with the glove compartment catch, eventually getting the lid open. She searched as I had searched the previous evening, but she found no pills. Again I felt her eyes on me and this time they did burn. 'The pills,' she said. 'Where are the pills?'

'I threw them away.'

'No!' I could feel her certainty, and the stirrings of disbelief. 'No,' she said, 'you didn't throw them away. You . . . you gave them to Margaret . . . you gave them to her.'

'No,' I said, 'I didn't give them to her. I . . . I didn't give them.' I looked at her and I knew that she didn't believe me, and I felt the first fingers of fear. Something crawled on the back of my neck, and slithered down my spine. A long slimy snake, and I felt its tongue on my skin. And then Sarah's heavy hands were reaching for me, pounding me, and I was aware of her hysteria and Clare crying in the rear seat, and then Martin trying to intervene. And then Sarah was subsiding into the seat, and was trying to crush her large handbag, and there was only silence, punctuated by indrawn breaths that were half sobs, Clare's sobs regular as the tick of a clock, counting out the beginning of the end. For me at least – maybe for all of us.

21

Inspector Bowman called that afternoon and I took him into the sitting room. He sat on the couch, sinking into its softness and comfort, but like myself when I sat there he found the very comfort itself uncomfortable. His sergeant sat in one of the matching armchairs, and for a moment we were in suspended animation. Then Clare came running into the room, stopping short, looking from me to the two policemen, Nuala following on Clare's heels.

'Who are those men, daddy?' Clare asked in a whisper.

'They're policemen.'

'Has something happened to mom?' Nuala asked.

'No, nothing's happened to her.'

'Is it about the pills?' Clare asked, looking at me now with her hunted rabbit's face.

'You two run along; I'll tell you about it later.'

They went reluctantly, leaving silence behind – silence and tension and the world closing in about me. 'Would you like a drink?' I asked. 'A whisky . . . ?' wanting to put them in my debt, to have them owe me something. But also because I needed a drink myself.

'Not on duty, sir,' Bowman said. He watched me carefully with his grey eyes – sad dog eyes that could never belong to a policeman. He waited for me to pour the drink for myself, the drink he knew I'd wanted; but I didn't pour a drink, and as casually as was possible I sat in the other armchair.

'Now then, sir,' Bowman said, 'we have received certain information regarding your wife's alleged suicide attempt.'

'She didn't waste any time,' I said bitterly, eighteen years of Sarah becoming too much to bear any more. Eighteen years a long time to wait for her revenge, but what use that revenge now, tainted as it was by so much tragedy?

'Your wife attempted suicide before,' Bowman said, paying no heed to my outburst.

'So she said. She fell over and hit her head. Not a very effective method, would you say?'

Again he didn't comment, didn't move a muscle, so much experience hidden behind those eyes. He would have seen others attempt flippancy, and sarcasm, and a thousand other things because inside they were frightened, inside they felt insecure. 'At the time of the first attempt your wife had sleeping pills which you removed. I understand you put them in your car for safe keeping. Can you tell me where those pills are now?'

'I threw them away.'

'Could you be more specific – did you throw them out of the window as you drove along? Chuck them out with the rubbish? Or what?'

'I flushed them down the loo.' I looked at him, wanting to show him that I had nothing to hide, trying to behave in the manner I had been rehearsing since I left Cricklewood with Sarah's threats ringing in my ears.

'You didn't return them to your wife?'

'Look, I just told you . . . What's all this, anyhow?'

My outraged act didn't work with Bowman. He didn't even change the expression on his face – that look of non-expression. 'You had asked your wife for a divorce?' he said. 'Is that correct?'

'Yes, I'd asked.'

'That was so that you could marry Barbara?' He watched closely for some tell-tale sign, but I remained as calm as anyone could when the box is about to be opened – all the money or nothing. There were only first prizes here – no rewards for coming second, only the threat of a prison cell.

'It wasn't to marry anyone,' I said; 'after what I'd been through I couldn't contemplate marrying again.'

'This woman Barbara . . .' Bowman began.

'Barbara? Who's Barbara?'

'We hoped you might tell us that,' the sergeant said, speaking for the first time. He didn't have Bowman's patience or calmness, but he had the bulldog's tenacity – he would never let go. He watched me now, they both did, and I saw walls of blue uniforms push in towards me.

I felt sickened by it all – by the questions and lies and evasions; by the game that wasn't a game at all. As if any of it mattered now to Margaret – as if it mattered who had given her the pills. Nothing mattered but the baby growing in Barbara's womb – my son. Were they going to arrest him? Were they going to put him in prison? Would they stigmatize him for the rest of his life? Taint him even before he was born, taint him with what tainted each and every one of us?

They were closing in and there was no escape. They would find out who Barbara was and she would admit to everything. She had once been on the fringe of some group who had sought a change in the law on euthanasia a long time ago, but maybe there were still records. I saw it all coming together, nothing adding up to everything, and I remembered other cases and long prison sentences. My son to grow up without his mother, to learn to call someone else mamma, to be confronted one day by a stranger, to have a new mamma he'd never seen before.

'*I* gave my wife the pills,' I said, 'because I couldn't bear to see her suffer any more. Write it down – I'll tell you everything.' The words came from my mouth but it wasn't me who spoke them. It was the man they would try and sentence and lock away, the man I had to become if I didn't want to succumb to madness.

I looked at Bowman and then the sergeant, but they didn't react. Maybe they were used to hearing confessions.

Nothing there but the blank faces. I looked away from them and stared around the room. Here one summer evening Margaret and I had planned our future, sitting on two unopened tea chests; trying to see our future in the faded wallpaper and the bare floor and the peeling paint on the ceiling. We had hung new wallpaper and painted the ceiling and two men had come one afternoon and fitted the beige wool carpet; we painted the windows and sent the door along with the others in the house to my company's refurbishing department, where they were stripped and sanded and polished. One day the furniture came – the new suite, without the loose covers then, the teak wall units, the onyx coffee table. The two teak table lamps and the matching lamp standard – or had they come later? They had all come into this room, been arranged and admired, and even I myself had felt a little proud on seeing around me the best that money could buy. But even then I had the feeling that we were giving away that which money could never buy. We were paying for what Margaret wanted by instalments but not just in money. Now it looked as if I was about to begin paying for my own wants too; and the two men before me had come for the first instalment.

I called a cab to take the girls to Cricklewood and they went off reluctantly, Clare looking back until they were out of sight. I went with the two policemen to the station and there I told them the 'truth', and they wrote it all down.

They took it away to be typed and then brought it back to me to read, and I signed it with Bowman's cheap ballpoint. They charged me with aiding and abetting my wife's attempted suicide and sent for a solicitor for me, a Mr Brown, who shook my hand as if I was a business acquaintance and we'd made ourselves a lot of money.

'You'll be charged in the morning,' he told me, 'and then we'll be able to get you out on bail.'

'And if they don't grant me bail?'

'Don't worry, Mr Ferson; we'll have you out of here.' He smiled his assurance and went on to tell me about procedures, to rebuke me for having signed anything, to order me not to sign anything else. But I paid little heed to what he said, my mind already filled to overflowing with chaotic thoughts and fears and doubts, the fears rising above everything else.

He told me that I would plead not guilty, justice seeming to me a strange commodity when I'd already confessed. But I didn't argue with him; it was out of my hands now. He went off eventually, promising to phone Cricklewood and let them know what had happened, and I tried not to think of what their reaction would be.

Night came but it brought no sleep, just the full impact of what I had done. 'No choice,' I thought over and over again. 'I had no choice.' There had been too much selfishness already, too much wanting for myself. Sometimes we have to do for others, to want for others, to draw back the boot as it descends to crush the scurrying beetle. We have to if we do not want to become the man who is for ever passing on the other side.

It might all be so but it brought little consolation. It couldn't take the lock from the door, or level the walls or even let the night air into my cell. And when I thought there was to be no sleep for me it came like the thief in the night, silently, unnoticed, and I dreamed of my father.

I was a young boy and he carried me on his shoulders and I caught his dark hair in my fingers and pulled and it came away in my hands, great tufts of it, and blood seeped from his raw scalp. He was lying on a bed, the sheets wet from his blood, and my mother was moistening his lips with the wet corner of a handkerchief; only it wasn't my mother but Margaret, and there was blood on her fingers. 'The cancer,' I said, 'the cancer . . .' but it still ate him until the unsupported skin began to collapse into the empty spaces, only prevented from collapsing completely like a deflated toy by the bones. Now there were only hills of bone and empty hollows, the skin lying on the skeleton like snow on an undulating landscape. I awoke suddenly, the latter picture still clear in my mind, seeing my father as I had seen him only hours before he had died. For a moment I was disorientated, and then as reality returned I felt the salty tears prick my eyes, and I knew that the nightmare of blood and torn hair and cancer was the easiest to bear.

I appeared in court later that morning and was granted bail. It was wintry out, bitterly cold with driving rain, but it was like a breath of summer to me and I was glad to feel the rain on my face. The flash bulbs suddenly going off startled me, and instinctively I put up my hand to shield my face, frightened like a child. Mr Brown grabbed my arm and hurried me down the steps. I was conscious of a bearded face beside me and a mouth moving in the hair, and a microphone thrust at my own face. In our rush I could hear Mr Brown repeating, 'Mr Ferson has nothing to say,' and then he was pushing me into the front seat of a car and a moment later we were speeding away, the misted-up windows hiding me.

'A bit unfortunate, that,' Mr Brown said. 'Some builder is appearing this morning – the local paper had conducted a campaign against him so they were here to see justice done. You being local – well, they soon latched on to your case. Still, you'll get used to the publicity.'

'Publicity?' I was settled in the seat now, and though my heart still beat wildly it was no longer trying to smash through my ribs. I was beginning to see the road in front of me and the shops and the traffic and the people, a very normal scene far removed from the flash bulbs and the mouth moving in the hair.

'Can't be avoided.' Mr Brown swung into a roundabout on the inside of a lorry but somehow squeezed through, more by luck than by judgement. 'It's sort of in vogue at the moment – all this talk about euthanasia and suicide pacts and doctors allowing babies and chronically sick patients to die. It's the kind of thing that sells newspapers.'

'So there will be publicity?'

'I'm afraid so; but you'll get used to it. Now would you like me to drop you home?'

The house hadn't changed, but I knew that things would never be the same here again. I rang the hospital and they told me that Margaret had been conscious, but when I pressed for more information as to her condition they said I should I see the doctor.

I rang Cricklewood and Martin answered, and he lowered his voice and began to stutter and mumble. I told him what had happened, but he didn't make any comment and I didn't say whether it was true or not. 'I'll call for the girls in the evening,' I said and hung up.

I got Barbara at her office, and her agony came down the line to me like tiny electric shocks. 'Peter,' she said, 'what's been happening? I rang you but there was no reply and you weren't at work. I didn't know what to do.'

'It's a long story,' I said, and I told her as briefly as I could.

'You fool,' she said. 'Why did you do it?'

'I had no choice.'

'But they'll put you in prison.'

'I don't know what'll happen,' I said. 'All I know is that I had to do it for the baby.'

'I knew you would love the baby,' she said, and I thought she was crying. She was silent for a moment and I imagined her dabbing at her eyes. 'I'm going to go to the police,' she went on, as if having made up her mind.

'No . . . no . . . you mustn't. It wouldn't do any good. They would only make it attempted murder.'

'But I have to do something . . . Look Peter, I'll go and see Ray; he will know what to do. I'll . . . I'll ring him now. He'll help us.' She stopped a moment. 'I love you,' she said, and I saw her waiting for my reaction, but I didn't have any. The time for lies was over. 'I'm sorry, Peter. I've got you into an awful mess. But I won't let you go to prison, I could never let that happen. I'm . . . I'm sorry for everything, especially what happened to Margaret.'

'It's over and done with now,' I said. 'It can't be undone.'

'Is . . . is she very ill?'

'I don't know. I haven't been in to see her.'

'I didn't want anything to happen to her,' she said, a tremor in her voice. 'When . . . when I saw her that afternoon I knew I couldn't do anything to hurt her; I knew that I had been wrong all those years. We don't have a right to anyone's life – no one has. You know, I just ran out of the house; it was later I realized that I had left the pills. But I couldn't go back for them . . . I was too frightened. You . . . you believe me, don't you?' Again she waited for my response, but I had none for her. 'I have to talk to you,' she said, 'to . . . to explain everything.'

'There's nothing to explain . . .'

'You blame me,' she said, 'but I did it all for you – everything I did was for you. Even the baby was for you – I wanted to give you a son. You will love the baby and maybe one day you will care for me even if only a little. It's all I ask – that you care for both of us.'

For the third time I had nothing for her, not even a kind word. I searched for something – anything – but the humanity had been threshed out of me and all I'd been left with was the chaff.

'I'll call you,' she said, and she hurriedly hung up on me, frightened by my coldness, by the fact that I might say something that would leave her with no hope.

I went to work, and the backlog on my desk helped me through the rest of the day. But at six o'clock I had to go out into the evening and the inevitable rain. In the car I put on the radio to listen to the traffic reports – an accident on the M1, a jack-knifed lorry on the approach to the Blackwall Tunnel – and I drove out into the rush hour. The car warmed up and the warmth lulled me and I began to relax.

The newscaster spoke my name and gave details of my appearance at the court, and I listened, aware that he was talking about me; that my name was going out on the air-waves and people sitting in traffic jams, people I worked with, people at home in kitchens preparing or eating dinner, people half-listening in places of work, they were all hearing my name and the damning details at this very moment; hearing them exactly as I was hearing them.

The traffic moved on, and I turned down the next side street and parked; I made my way back to the main road and walked to the pub I'd passed a few minutes earlier. I ordered a whisky and took it to a table away from everyone. Here I was a stranger; there was no possibility of anyone associating me with a name on the radio; and yet I felt exposed and vulnerable and the whisky did little to help.

A man sat at the next table to me and began to read the evening paper. I happened to glance at it, and my frightened face stared back at me, my head tilted back and sideways as if I'd been attempting to avoid a blow.

It was the moment when nightmare ceased and reality took over. I was public property now, and people who never knew me, whom I would never meet, could never defend myself to, would condemn me. I gulped the whisky and stumbled outside, glad of the darkness that hid me. And yet I felt that every person I met recognized me and thought me a murderer, and moved away from me.

In the car I just drove, aware after a little while that I was heading in the direction of home. But I didn't want to go there, to face the emptiness of the house; to have the walls and ceilings and floors, and the dust on the shelves and the house mites in the carpets and the cobwebs in neglected corners, all accuse me. I couldn't face the hospital either, to feel the accusation of anyone I met there; to see Margaret – to see for the first time the reality of the words 'brain damaged'. Or to meet Sarah or Martin or my daughters, the last people now I wanted to face. So I just drove in the rain, and the tyres swished on the wet road and the wipers beat a monotonous rhythm. It became warm again in the car but it didn't relax me now, and I opened the window to let in the air. I smelt the rain and the petrol fumes and the misery of the commuter, and I drank it all in like an alcoholic at a river of whisky.

I came up Wood Green High Road and turned into Station Road and came round to the entrance to Alexandra Palace. At the top of the hill I looked out across the city and I could see the Post Office Tower, its lights winking in the rain. Above the embankment the burnt-out shell of the Palace stood, a giant reminder of the impermanence of everything. I remembered driving home on the evening of the fire and seeing the flames leap high in the air and the pall of smoke that lay over the hill like some great bird of prey. Now the shell stood as if to remind me that even the mighty can fall; that maybe one day the Post Office Tower would no longer stand; that even the great city spread out below me like a chaotic tangle of fairy lights thrown on the ground – the city that had survived the plague and the fire and the bombing of Hitler – might one day lie in ruins and return to the swamps that had existed before the Romans came. I felt that if I closed my eyes and my ears, if I shut out all existence, I might be able to stare into the blackness behind my closed eyelids and imagine what it looked like those long years ago.

Out there a small encampment and the flicker of torches and man with fear and loneliness and the inevitability of death. It had changed so much since then and yet it hadn't changed at all. It was the same fear and the same loneliness and I was certain the same hell. It was the same earth we were tied to, the same people we were trying to escape from, the same desire to be alone.

Tonight I was driving through the jungle of a modern city, trying to escape from myself, trying to be alone, but with the knowledge of the inevitability of my failure. God was the only one who was alone, the very reason He was God. It was that that the devil had tempted Eve with in the garden of Eden – the secret of complete aloneness, because our pain and suffering comes from the fact that we have contact with others. That we love and hate; that we give birth to and murder; that we live and die, and in the living and dying others live and die with us, and that we all suffer. But if you are totally alone, totally withdrawn from everyone and everything, you can never suffer again, you can look at all the horrors and be indifferent. That was God, the only entity in existence who could not be troubled. For even the torturer may be touched by the injured kitten and with one hand stroke the animal while with the other hand he attaches the electrode.

Maybe the indifference was God's real love for us; the fact that He leaves us alone to enact our gift of free will. What other answer was there for the pain and the indifference and the suffering? Except that there was no God and I had made a promise to nothing in the church that Saturday.

Suddenly I didn't want to be alone. I needed to talk to someone to be assured that I might still be human, that I hadn't turned everything to dust. I drove to Barbara's flat but her Metro wasn't parked in the slip road and the window-eyes of the flat were black and crying in the rain.

I just couldn't drive for ever, and there was no one else who would understand, so reluctantly I turned for home. There I made myself a coffee and a sandwich, surrounded in the kitchen by so much that was familiar, and yet feeling a stranger. Margaret had touched all the things here. They were hers, not mine.

I went into the sitting-room and was drawn to the framed photographs on the mantelpiece – Clare's and Nuala's first communions and the latter's confirmation. The three days depicted had belonged to the girls, not to Margaret or myself. Somehow we had been aware of this and had been able to forget ourselves; and in the very act of forgetting – caught for ever by the camera – we had been a family. It was there before me, but enshrined behind the glass so that I could never again touch it or have it – not with Margaret . . . not with Barbara . . . not with anyone.

I needed a drink and I got out the whisky. The first glass gulped quickly had little effect, but after two more I found some balm. Things began to drift away from me, and my sense of loss blurred and shrank to the very size of the pictures which depicted it. A few more glasses and maybe I would find some peace.

A bell rang somewhere a long way off, rang stridently again and again, closer now, and then it was inside my skull. 'Barbara,' my mind whispered, and I was certain that I repeated the name aloud. She'd come back from Milton Keynes – she was at the door now. In a moment she would put her arms about me and I wouldn't need the whisky any more.

I got up from the armchair, aware of nothing now but the comfort to come, and the words I would speak; kind words, loving words, words found discarded in the chaff; words I had to speak for my own benefit, words for the sake of words; words to make something as God had made everything from His Word.

'Peter,' she said when I opened the door, but it wasn't Barbara on the doorstep. 'I . . . I was going to phone you,' Mrs Parks said, 'but I couldn't . . .' She stared up at me, no longer the confident secretary, the matron who protected Barbara from the world.

I tried to adjust to the fact that it wasn't Barbara, that her secretary was here instead. But the whisky had fogged my brain and there were only bits of thoughts, scraps that would never make a whole. 'She went to the police?' I asked, that the most certain fact of all.

Mrs Parks was trembling slightly, like a well-tuned engine when it's cold. Trembling . . . trembling . . . 'What?' I said. 'What . . . ?' Urgent – harsh – frightened . . .

'She's dead,' she said. 'Barbara is dead. She was killed this evening – an accident on the M1 . . .'

22

Mrs Parks had gone and I was alone, and Barbara and her baby were dead; my baby too – my son or daughter. But I wouldn't weep, and even if I did it would only be for myself – for my own loss. But then who else should I weep for? Barbara was beyond my tears, beyond my touch; in some cold mortuary where nothing would bother her again. She was the lucky one.

'She must have panicked,' Mrs Parks had said. 'At least, that's what the police think. She just suddenly pulled out into the middle lane and another car hit her. She swerved back into the inside lane then, into the path of a juggernaut which had been following her.'

'She never went on motorways,' I said, 'because she was terrified of the juggernauts.'

'I begged her not to take the car,' Mrs Parks said, 'but she wouldn't listen. When you phoned her – well, she just couldn't let you take the blame. She was like that.'

'You knew?'

'She told me everything; she never had any secrets from me. She didn't really have anyone else to confide in – she had no family.'

'She has a . . . had a brother and sister.'

'They're in Canada. But they were never close. Barbara was a loner. She was the most insecure person I ever knew. She never trusted anyone.'

'Barbara insecure?'

'You never knew her,' she said. 'No one knew her. In fact, she didn't know herself.'

I stared at Mrs Parks, grey eyes, greying hair, a hint of make-up on the severe face – not severe now but lost. Aware of all my secrets, of the hurt I had caused Barbara; aware that in a way I was responsible for her death.

It was for me she had gone to Milton Keynes, for me she had braved the motorway, daring to take the car because she loved me. She could have married Ray, but me she'd loved. Coming back on the M1 the traffic moving fast, the juggernaut coming up behind her, lights on in the rain. Coming right up close, filling the rear window; nowhere to escape to, turning out in panic – out into death.

'I heard about it on the radio this evening,' I said, words to banish the image of those final few moments.

Mrs Parks said nothing; there was nothing to say. She declined a drink and left and I was alone. Barbara was dead. That's what Mrs Parks had said, just words, like 'It's raining outside.' Just words. As yet there was no reality; but there would be plenty of time for that. A whole lifetime, in fact, with the memories of Barbara crammed into a few still frames; like one coming away from the Chelsea Flower Show with just the memory of a single rose, the splendour of all the flowers and colours and scents embodied in the solitary image. With more power to move and gladden and hurt than all the roses in the world put together.

I wandered out into the kitchen, a lost spirit now, damned I thought to wander for ever. The wind had risen, and it pushed against the cardboard which covered the broken glass; and I heard the door of the garden shed rattle as if a ghost had put an invisible hand on it, trying to open the door to get into the shelter. But it wasn't Barbara's ghost I knew. She didn't need shelter any more. The ghost outside was my own ghost, not trying to escape the rain but trying to escape from me. And I knew how the ghost felt, for I wanted to escape myself.

On the day that my son had died, that damned December

day, I'd come out of the hospital into the sunshine which had had no warmth, needing to escape then too. That day I had walked and had found myself among the bustle of Christmas shoppers; and everywhere there was movement and people and excitement, and the hopes of children; and fairy lights and tinsel paper and a blind confidence in some mad future; all as false as the beard of Father Christmas himself – some out-of-work actor or some old pensioner trying to earn a few extra pounds to make his own Christmas bearable.

I had found no escape and no matter where I walked or how far, my son remained dead. Dead as I had left him, staying with him until the end, not wanting him to die as he had lived – alone.

There had been no escape, but hours later there had been some relief. Barbara had poured the whisky, never allowing my glass to go dry, and she had listened. Suddenly now the memory of her, not a specific memory but a memory of everything she had or ever could have been, washed over me in wave after wave like the ocean. And I caught the pine kitchen table in my hands and doubled up over it, the tearless sobs shaking my body, bouncing the end of my nose against the hard surface until I felt certain I would splatter the table top with my blood. Maybe then the pressure in my brain would drop as my blood pressure dropped, lower and lower until there was no blood left in my veins and my ghost could join Barbara's ghost; and they could keep each other warm and comfort each other and shake their skeletal heads at the stupidity of human beings.

I needed relief for myself now, relief from my stupidity and loss. But a walk was out of the question because the rain would soak me through in a few minutes, bringing but more misery. The only relief I might find was in the bottle, but when I went into the sitting-room I knew I could drink a distillery dry in this house and not find a crumb of comfort.

Here there were too many things to remind me of the reasons I needed comfort.

I had to get out of the house, and I did so quickly. Outside I couldn't face the car, so ignoring the rain I walked round to my local. I went into the public bar where Martin and myself had had a drink that summer evening, when the world had been mine and I was so certain that no one could take it from me; that summer evening that seemed so long ago now.

There were only two darts players tonight, neither of them from that evening. They nodded at me and went on with their game, and I realized that they either didn't know who I was or else didn't care. Whichever it happened to be, it suited me.

Terry knew, though, and so did most of the people who frequented the place – but would they care? It was too late to worry about that, and now I was here there was no turning back. 'How are you, Mr Ferson?' Terry asked, a barman too long to allow any visible feelings on his face.

'Damp,' I said, acutely aware that I shouldn't have come here. I had wanted to talk to someone, to hear voices, to see people, but I shouldn't have come here. Because here too there were reminders, like pictures engraved in the polished bar top or reflected from the mirrors behind the bar or trapped in the bottles of spirit like the model sailing ships one sees in seaside souvenir shops.

I had a double whisky and Terry went off to attend to someone else, or to attend to nothing, just wanting to be away from me. It was how it would be from now on – the furtive stares, the whispers come on unexpectedly; sometimes an open accusation, for after all there were people in the world who were better than me and who knew it. Later I was to see a jury composed of a dozen of them, each one a twelfth of God.

I drank the whisky, but it had no more effect on me than if it was water. I'd had my third double before it began to mix with the earlier lot I'd drunk at home, and by the fourth I had to face their combined potency and everything began to close in upon me; and the legions who had marched on the night Barbara had told me about the baby began to move again now.

But it wasn't the sound of legions of soldiers marching in jackboots I heard, but the patter of tiny feet, the stumble of the lame and crippled, the scrape of the protective leather of the legless as they swung themselves forward on their hands, the clanging of the chains of the fettered, and the swish of wheelchair tyres on wet pavements. All pouring towards me in waves, labelled like goods on a supermarket shelf. Unwanted baby, foetus, cripple, disabled person, pervert, murderer, prisoner – all names for what I could have been, for what we all could have been if chance had acted differently.

I needed another whisky before they came too close, before they took substance before my eyes. My dead son with a hole in his back that had seemed so big that I'd imagined I could put my fist into it. Margaret with the raw stumps of her legs, and Barbara with her body broken and her womb torn asunder; her son still alive, reaching for me as I had dreamed the other night – reaching with webbed hands.

Terry poured the whisky and looked at me strangely, but said nothing. Or maybe he did, because I couldn't be sure any more. I gulped the whisky and called again for Terry, but when he came he was no longer behind the bar but beside me, his hand on my arm. 'You've had enough, Mr Ferson,' he said. 'I think it's time you went home.'

'Home?'

'Come on,' he said. 'I'll walk with you.'

I was aware of the darts players watching me, of eyes and faces and cigarette smoke; of Terry's soft voice and his hand on my arm; of the pattern of the carpet, red diagonal stripes that wouldn't stay still, and the legs of stools and men's trousered legs, and shoes; and then I was at the door and felt the breeze on my face, cold and damp, and I began to shiver. I was out in the street now, Terry still beside me, still speaking, but in a foreign language. My eyes were hurting and I put my hand to my face, puzzled as to how my cheeks could be wet when it was raining no longer.

I stopped, and Terry and I looked at each other and I could see that his face was yellow in the light from the street lamp – death yellow. We stood there on the corner, two people who had known each other a long time but yet were not friends; and we would never be friends now.

I wiped my face with my hand, under one eye then the other, a grown man crying; crying here where once Martin had cried; the wheel now had turned full circle. 'The whisky,' I said to Terry, 'it's just the whisky,' both of us aware that whatever it was it most certainly wasn't the alcohol. 'Bad news,' I went on. 'I only heard it this evening. It's just the shock.'

'Has something happened to Mrs Ferson?'

'No,' I said. 'She was never Mrs Ferson. But we would have been married; one day we would have. My – my son too was killed.'

'I know,' he said. 'It was a terrible thing. Sure I still remember it.'

'No,' I said, 'my son was killed today – in the accident . . .'

'Your son? I didn't know you had another son. In an accident you say?'

'I didn't know myself until the other day. I'd only known a few days and then Barbara was killed this evening. I heard about it on the radio – on the traffic reports. An accident on the M1. You – you never met Barbara. I don't even have a picture to show you; I never had a picture of her. She never gave me a picture and I never asked her for one. I was going to marry her and I never bothered to get a picture. I killed her, you know; she wouldn't have died but for me; and I never had a picture.'

'It's all right, Mr Ferson,' Terry said. 'It doesn't matter.'

'I know,' I said. 'It doesn't matter now.'

'Come on, I'll walk with you. I have to get back before closing time.'

I didn't feel drunk, nor was I unsteady on my feet, and we reached the house in the five minutes or so it normally took me. I had problems getting my key in the lock, and Terry took them from me and unlocked the door. 'Come in,' I said. 'Come in and have a drink.'

'I have to get back,' Terry said.

'It's the house,' I said. 'It's not my house; it's never been mine. It – it frightens me.'

'You've had a drop too much,' Terry said. 'Get yourself a good night's sleep; you'll feel much better in the morning. Goodnight, Mr Ferson.' He nodded and turned on the doorstep, and I watched him go out of the gate and raise his hand to wave me goodnight.

'Terry,' I thought I heard myself saying; or maybe it was something else. Or maybe I didn't say anything at all. I closed the door and went into the sitting-room where the whisky bottle still stood on the table. I'd already had too much, according to Terry, but there was never enough to cure what ailed me. I left the bottle untouched and came back out and went upstairs.

The girls' rooms were dark and empty and I closed the doors of each one. I went into Margaret's bedroom, which had once been my bedroom too but where now I felt like an intruder. Someone who had no right to walk on the rust all-wool carpet or see the white wardrobes with the gold trim, or the kidney-shaped matching dressing table; or the double divan with the blue duvet cover cut into squares by faint white lines. Or the two pillows with matching covers, one piled on top of each other in the centre of the bed, a sign that the bed no longer slept a marriage.

In this room love had lived and died and been replaced by hatred. But hatred too had to be nurtured in order that it should thrive; and it was a sign of our damnation that neither of us had thought it worthwhile to nurture either the hatred or the love.

Margaret's nightie lay along the foot of the bed, a short cotton one, no legs now to keep warm. And I thought of Barbara's nightie, folded neatly and tucked under the pillow; all those nighties of hers, the cotton ones and the nylon ones and the solitary silk one I had bought her last Christmas, never to be worn again . . . never . . .

The shock had worn off now and even the whisky couldn't keep reality at bay. It boiled within me, and I threw myself on my knees by the side of the bed and gripped the duvet cover with my fingers. I buried my face in its softness, boring down through the softness to the firm mattress beneath, down . . . down, wanting to return to the womb, the frightened child that is in all of us unshackled at last.

I don't know how long I remained like that, but when my fingers released their grip I was sober and rational and cold. I was the human being who had caused all this, who had brought it all about. Not by inhumanity as I had thought, but by the very fact that I was human. And being human I had wanted for myself. Inhumanity was something different all together.

This house, this room, this bed, even the very fibres of the duvet cover, I had damned by my want. Now I could only undamn them by wanting too. By wanting my daughters back – by wanting Margaret back; back here in this house where I could carry out the other things that being human meant. Where I could remember Barbara too, who had died because I was human. Here where I would never love again, but that would be my punishment. For not to be loved was but a glimpse of hell; the real hell was not to be capable of love.

Tomorrow I had to begin the rest of my life, even if it should be the beginning of the end. I had to get my daughters back, to make a home for them here. To have Margaret back too, to be kind to her even if she didn't understand. I had to do it because without the doing I had no future, only days and weeks and months and years – just time with death at the end. I could say that time was all that I had anyway; but there are many extremes between a minute being a brief moment or a whole lifetime. Tomorrow I had to learn to want for others if I didn't want each and every minute to be a lifetime. There simply were no other choices left.

23

I faced the director across his polished desk, with its in and out trays and two telephones; and the marble pen holder with the gold Parker I had never seen him use; and the leather-framed photograph of two children and a small, dowdy woman. The preliminaries were over now and we were down to the real fighting.

'You're aware of the problem,' he said, watching me, a pained expression on his well-cared-for face, the skin shiny from shaving and soap and good living. 'We have discussed it – the other directors and myself – and we feel it might be best for everyone concerned if you took a break – say for a month – let the thing die a little.'

'No,' I said. 'It wouldn't achieve anything; I'd be just running away.'

'I hoped you wouldn't make it difficult,' he said. 'If you don't take the month voluntarily we will have no choice but to suspend you. It's your decision, Peter.'

'You just want to be rid of me,' I said bitterly. 'One month – enough time to get someone else to take my place – to say "Sorry, Peter, but it has to be this way and we do have a little job for you." You'll have a job all right – in one of the warehouses where the staff are too thick to be able even to read. Shunt me around and eventually I'll get the message and leave. It saves a nice little bit in redundancy money doing it that way. I don't quite believe you can sit there and try that little trick on me. How many times have you and I sat here and planned that very little scenario for someone else?' I shook my head in disbelief, unable to comprehend any more. 'If you had wanted me to leave you only had to ask,' I said, 'just ask. Well, I'll make it easy for you; I'll bring you my resignation; it'll be best for all of us.'

'It doesn't have to be like this, Peter. Go away – think about it.'

'I'll bring you the piece of paper,' I said, and went back to my office. I wrote out my resignation, just a few moments to destroy a lifetime that had been twenty-two years in the making. I tidied my desk and put the few things that belonged to me in my briefcase – so few things after all the years. An era was at an end and the world was closing in on me, and wherever I turned there was but accusation and blame; and the demand that I pay the price. There was little left me now – just my wife and my daughters; and when I thought about it what more could I want – what more could any man want? It was by wanting more that I had come to this. I could only hope now that I had not learned too late.

I took my piece of paper to the director and he again spoke of my haste and his regret, but in a way I knew he was relieved. 'I'll take it as if you are working your month's notice,' he said to me. 'You can keep the company car until then. And if there's ever anything I can do for you . . .' He looked at me, wanting to give me something, anything that might ease his own guilt. Now that his problem had been sorted out he could afford to be generous.

I thanked him and shook his hand and went back to my office for the last time. Carol was near to tears and we stood in silence – maybe in memory of old times, of the things we had laughed at, at the odd cross words we had had. I held out my hand to her, but she ignored it and came close to me and put her arms about me, holding me tight. She kissed me, letting her lips linger for a moment, and then she stepped back leaving me with so many memories. The first wet kisses and fumbles of the teenager, the love kisses of a new marriage, the Judas kisses of betrayal; and last of all the kisses of false promise, of disillusionment, of more betrayal – of death . . .

I left Carol in the office to await her new boss and I went out to my car. There were spots of rain falling and the sky was sullen like a child ready to cry, the falling drops the first trickle of tears. And I thought of John at Feltham and of that June day when I'd shown him no mercy. And my glib words to Father Mason that maybe Margaret was only reaping what she had sown. But who was reaping now?

I didn't want to return alone to the empty house, frightened by what I might find in the big, uncaring rooms, in the furniture and the carpets and the paint on the walls. I couldn't return and see the wheelchair, and the rug, and the cardboard over the glass in the kitchen door, and the locked telephones. When I returned my daughters would accompany me. The house was theirs too, theirs and mine, and we would make a home of it yet for Margaret. In fact they were the only ones who could. With what I knew to be a final hope, I started the engine and drove across London to Cricklewood.

Martin answered the door, the small knot in his tie visible above the round-necked pullover. He was lost for words for a moment, and I could see that he had aged in the few days since I had last seen him. 'Come in,' he managed eventually, backing ahead of me into the hall. 'Sarah's having a lie down – she's not been too well.'

'I don't want to see her,' I said. 'I've just come to collect the girls.'

'They're in the front room,' he said, 'watching television.'

They were sitting in front of the set, the sound on low so that it wouldn't disturb Sarah. 'Hello,' I greeted, my voice cheerful, and they turned to look at me. Nuala's eyes were blank but Clare's were alive with fear and uncertainty – the little animal caught in the trap again. 'I've come to take you home,' I said.

They said nothing, nor did they make any move; then Nuala turned back to the television and Clare took her cue from her sister, and I was left with their backs to gaze at. 'Come on,' I said, my voice brusque, 'you can watch the television when you get home.'

'We're staying here,' Nuala said. 'Gran says we can stay.'

'You can't stay,' I said. 'Gran can't look after you for ever.'

'She'll have to,' Nuala said, 'when you're in prison.'

There was only the sound from the television now, unmistakably the sound track of a cartoon. I could see the action on the big black and white screen, tiny cavorting figures, more real than we people in the room.

Clare turned to look at me, her eyes wide with fear. 'I don't want to go,' she said. 'I don't want to go home ever again.' She stared from me to Martin, seeking reassurance from him. 'I don't want to go,' she repeated. 'Please don't make me go, grandad.' She was clearly very frightened but it wasn't from fear of going home; she was frightened of me.

Instinctively I reached out to her, reached out with my comfort, but she shrank from me like proven dough left in the cold. She got to her feet and scampered to Martin for protection and clung to him; and her desperate sobbing was loud in the room.

'We saw your picture in the paper,' Nuala said, not turning to look at me. 'You tried to kill mom. Clare is frightened of you.'

'No,' I said, 'I didn't try to kill your mom – I . . . I would never hurt her.'

'You did . . . you did,' Clare said. 'You did . . . you did . . . you did . . .' rising until her child's voice filled the room and overflowed into the hall, desperate, it seemed, to escape from its source.

'Maybe you should go for now,' Martin said. 'You – you could call back later.'

I looked at him and saw myself, not as I would be in years to come but as I was at this very minute. We had both been defeated. 'Please go for now, Peter,' he said. 'I'll talk to them – they're just upset.' Clare still clung to him but he didn't know what to do with her, and his hands made crazy movements as if he was stricken with St Vitus's dance.

I could only do as he asked, and I turned and went out of the room. Sarah was purposefully striding down the stairs towards me, but stopped abruptly. 'You,' she said, staring at me with wild, old woman's eyes. 'You . . .'

I stared back at her, framing her in my eyes for the last time. She had her revenge now, more sweet than even she could have dreamed of. She'd lost her daughter to me but now she had taken my own two daughters in return. But I didn't hate her. In fact I felt nothing. She was just an old woman in a quilted dressing-gown that would last her until she died. The dressing-gown would be burnt one day and all her other clothes – the sensible skirts and the tweed coats and the heavy stockings she wore winter and summer. It would be a sour worm that crawled out of her, and sour weeds and grasses that flourished in the soil. She had won and she had lost and it was the loss she would have to bear.

'They're not going home,' she said. 'They couldn't go back to that house; they wouldn't be safe.'

'I never hurt anyone,' I said. 'I didn't give Margaret the pills.'

'You gave them,' she said. 'You wanted her dead so that you could marry your whore.'

'My whore, as you call her, was the only decent person I ever knew,' I said. 'She was worth every one of us. You can't touch her with your words – you can't touch anyone any more. You think you can hold on to the girls . . .' I shook my head, blinded by my own superiority. 'The girls will come home in their own good time; you can't keep them for ever.'

'Not to you,' she said. 'Not to you and *that* woman.'

'They'll come home,' I said. 'You can't stop them.' I hesitated, staring at her, trying to keep my face under control, to keep the tremor out of my voice, coming to the realization for what was really the first time of what Barbara's death actually meant. I would never go home to *that* woman again – to Sarah's whore – never, never . . .

'All you can do is pray,' Sarah was saying, 'pray for your own soul,' but I was already turning away from her, making my way to the front door – opening it . . . Martin was beside me now, holding the door open, and then I was out in the rain, Martin still with me. I heard her call his name but he acted as if he hadn't heard, and we walked the few steps to the gate. Again she called his name from the door, unable to come out because of the rain.

'The girls will get over it,' Martin said, looking at me. 'They just need a little time.'

I nodded and looked back at him, the rain splattering his hair and face, drops clinging to the fibres of his pullover, perfect drops of water. 'I had nothing to do with Margaret's attempted suicide,' I said. 'I could never want to do anything like that.'

'I know,' he said, and his eyes told me that he believed me. 'I said that very thing to Sarah but she wouldn't listen. She will only believe what she wants to.'

'Martin,' she shouted now, calling the dog in from the rain.

'I'd better go in,' he said. 'The girls will go home at the weekend; they'll be well over things by then.'

'I'm going to take Margaret home,' I said, 'when she's better. We'll all be a family again. What sort of family I don't know but at least we'll all be together.' I waited for his approval, but he said nothing. 'Go in,' I said, 'or you'll be soaked through,' and I turned away from him and went out to the car.

I turned the car in the narrow street and as I drove away I

realized that for the first time in my life I was totally alone. It is the moment we all face in death but I was facing it now, and I would take a long time dying.

There was but the one open door left now, not exactly open but slightly ajar; maybe just enough space to squeeze through; maybe just enough hope to prise the door open a little more. But if not? And all I could see in the 'if' was a grey future of memory, and regret for all the things which had been mine, and that I had so wantonly thrown away. 'Please God,' I found myself thinking, 'just a chink and maybe one day I would burst through into the light.'

Margaret had been moved from intensive care to another ward, and when I was told this my slim hopes were raised a little. I found the ward – a long cheerless room with two rows of beds and tall narrow windows along one wall; and I thought that they had sent me to the wrong place because there were only old women here.

'This is the right place,' the sister told me when I had voiced my doubts aloud. 'But your wife isn't in the ward itself; she has her own room.'

'But why here? Surely this place is for geriatrics.'

'We're best equipped to look after her,' the sister said. 'But it's only temporary, while arrangements are being made to transfer her to a place where the staff are specially trained to look after such cases.'

'She won't be coming home?' I asked, aware now that there was no light, not even a chink.

'I think you should speak to the doctor,' she said, trying to be kind. 'He's busy right now, but if you would like to wait.'

'Can I see my wife?' I asked, not wanting to accept the inevitable.

'Certainly. If you'd like to follow me.'

She took me to a small room with windows to match the ones in the main ward, but here a blind was drawn and the room was gloomy. There was a bed with cot-sides in the room and the sister went to the head of the bed and switched on the angle lamp which was attached to the wall. The shade was turned into the corner and the light made a distorted circle, and threw the rest of the room into deeper shadow.

'Your wife is sedated,' the sister said, turning towards me, a ghost in the gloom. 'She's been very agitated.'

'Is she aware of anything at all?'

'I think you should really speak to the doctor – he will be able to explain everything. You can wait in my office if you like.'

'Thanks,' I said, 'but I'll wait here.'

'I'll send the doctor to see you as soon as possible. Now if you'll excuse me.'

Left alone, I stood for a moment, and at first there was silence; and then I could hear Margaret's breathing. Taking in the air of life, breathing as I was breathing; heart beating as mine beat; blood coursing through her arteries, as red and as warm as mine would be; and no longer human as I was not human; but I had no excuses.

We had loved and we had laughed and we had cried; and now we had lost and come to this – alone in a darkened room, the strangers we had wanted to be. I had wanted a divorce – to be parted from Margaret – but could there be a more permanent parting than this; except maybe death.

Here before me was the result of my carelessness – of the fact that I had never given anything. I had wanted for myself but in the end hadn't been enough of a man – enough of a human being – to reach out and take. Ruthlessness would have been more acceptable; it might have left someone untouched. As it was, no one had been safe.

I walked over to the bed and stared down at Margaret, her face vague, outside the circle of light. The eyes were closed and the face itself seemed peaceful, but what could anyone know about what went on behind the closed eyes. Maybe peaceful now, not even the trauma of a dream; but what terrors roamed there in the hours of waking?

'A special place,' the sister had said, and now I saw straitjackets and padded cells and beds with cot-sides and leather straps; to lie in her own faeces and urine and not be aware even of the smell; and half of a whole lifetime still stretched out before her. Not just the months that had faced my son, but years and years . . . Locked away in a dark room, the shades for ever drawn. Cleaned up for my weekly visit, taken out like a piece of merchandise for my act of empty charity, and then put away again when I had gone. Maybe to die one night, choked by her own vomit, helpless and alone. But that only if she was lucky.

I felt grief swell up within me, grief such as I had never felt before, and there was the salt of tears in my eyes. But too late – too too late, and the tears couldn't move the guilt, big as a mountain; guilt I would never evade. There was to be no forgiveness and in the moment when I would have said sorry, in the moment when I needed to say sorry, there was no one to hear – no one to raise a hand in absolution.

I remembered that summer day now under the apple tree when Father Mason had warned me of a need for forgiveness. 'One day you will need forgiveness,' he'd said, 'but don't leave it until it's too late, Peter.' But I had left it too late and maybe the only valid advice I now had was Sarah's, she who had said that I should pray for my soul. But the time for praying was long past too; it was time now for doing but was there anything left to do? I didn't need any doctor to tell me the truth about Margaret – I knew the truth only too well, and that truth said there was nothing.

Maybe I'd known the truth all along – had known it even on that summer's day when I'd first come from the hospital, my dreams for the future clutched to me. In the depths of my mind had I known that the dream was but a dream after all?

That I would come to this time and this place – stripped of everything but my shame and my guilt.

'You've never given anything,' Barbara had said. 'Never thought of anyone but yourself. Pray,' Sarah had said, 'pray for your own soul.' Give – pray – ask forgiveness – it's sad for a man to have to search always – words and more words piling in upon me, a sea of faces and the events of the summer squeezed smaller and smaller, collapsing into each other like a black hole in space, sucking me with them into the darkness.

I gripped the rail of the cot-side and experienced what the emperor must have felt when the truth dawned on him that he was naked to the world. Naked and ashamed and maybe a little afraid. Pride after all can destroy a man – pride and envy and hatred; and jealousy and bitterness and despair; they can all destroy a man more surely than death itself.

And yet I was a man, and man wasn't born with hatred in his heart. Surely within me there had to be a little love – a little compassion – a little kindness. Didn't we all have some of each? Didn't we at least have the seed that needed but a word – a gesture – in order for it to flourish? Surely I had some, just enough to implement the prayer of Saint Francis, he who loved all living creatures as distinct from me who loved no one.

'Where there is hatred, let me show love; where there is injury, pardon, where there is despair, hope; where there is darkness, light; where there is turmoil let there be peace. Let me not seek so much to be consoled as to console; to be understood as to understand; to be loved as to love. And remember that only in death is there eternal life.'

If a man can love but the once he can always love; if he can have compassion but the once he can always have compassion. I knew now that everything was possible; that no greater love has any man than that he lay down his life for his friend; no even greater still that he lay down his life for his enemy. There was no problem about giving when one forgot the self.

I knew now what I had to do – what I had to give. There was no turmoil any more – no black hole sucking me in. I had reached the one time in my life when I was a man, when I was human. That I might not be human afterwards mattered little. Now I had reached the one moment that would condemn me for life; but the one moment that might save me when I came before the judgement of God.

I took the chair to the door and wedged it under the handle, and checked that it would hold. I came back to the bedside where the shell of a human being lay – the woman who had once loved me, who had married me, who had borne my children and who had eventually learned not to love me.

But who needed me to love her once more as I had not loved before or would ever love again.

I did not kiss the face or touch it; neither did I weep or feel sorrow. They were all the things that might have saved me in the court of man's justice. But of what matter is that justice when I have to one day face God?

It was a simple act to take the cot-side down and to take the pillow from under Margaret's head; to place it over her face and to push down on it with my two hands. Her hold on life was tentative, and she died like a snuffed candle. Even in the throes of dying that last involuntary act was denied her – she couldn't even beat her heels on the bed.

Afterwards I placed the pillow to one side and pulled the sheet up to cover her face. I removed the wedged chair and took it back to the bedside, and sat down to wait.